The Bump of 2019

Chris Cheek

2FM Limited

Consultancy and Analysis
Publishing & Communication

Rossholme, West End, Long Preston
Skipton, North Yorkshire, BD23 4QL

Tel: 01729 840756
e-mail: admin@two-fm.co.uk

Copyright © Chris Cheek 2018

The right of Chris Cheek to be identified as author of this work has been asserted by him in accordance with the Copyright, Designs and Patents Act 1988

All rights reserved. This book is sold subject to the condition that no part of this book is to be reproduced, in any shape or form. Or by way of trade, stored in a retrieval system or transmitted in any form or by any means, electronic, mechanical, photocopying, recording, be lent, re-sold, hired out or otherwise circulated in any form of binding or cover other than that in which it is published and without a similar condition, including this condition being imposed on the subsequent purchaser, without prior permission of the copyright holder.

Cover image: Shutterstock.com

A CIP catalogue record for this book is available
from the British Library

ISBN 978-1-9996479-0-2

Dedication

For RMA, who gave me my future back.

Acknowledgements

My grateful thanks to my editor Karen Holmes and the creative team at 2QT for their hard work in helping to deliver this book.

Thanks also to Olga and Tony Depledge for their support.

Book One

England. May 1968.

Chapter 1

PETER Harvey awoke with a start and looked at his clock. Half-past ten – another early lecture missed. Hardly surprising, since he had lain awake for hours during the night after a particularly nasty nightmare. It had been well after dawn before he eventually drifted off to sleep again.

He regarded the disordered bed with distaste and left it, hunting for a cigarette. The memory of the dream stayed with him like an undefined threat, leaving him drained before the day had even begun. He looked through the curtains and the day glowered back at him. The buildings of his Oxford college seemed grey and forbidding; it was obviously going to be another humid day, which would probably end in a thunderstorm.

He found a cigarette and, pausing to light it, caught sight of himself in the mirror. He grimaced at the sight of his sweat-tousled blond hair but could not help feeling vaguely pleased with what he saw. He had failed by two inches to reach his childhood ambition of being six feet tall; despite that, he thought he was rather good-looking. Sally certainly seemed to think so. Thinking of Sally brought back memories of this whole dreadful week, culminating in the dream. His smile disappeared as the details forced

The Stamp of Nature

their way back into his consciousness.

There had been a road, straight and wide, shimmering in the summer heat. The air had been heavy with the smell of melting tar and newly-mown grass. In the distance he had seen a house, a beautiful white detached house, which stood on a slight rise overlooking the surrounding countryside. The garden was well-kept, with large rhododendron bushes in full flower bordered by a neat beech hedge. Children were playing in the garden, splashing and laughing in a swimming pool. A woman emerged from the house, carrying a tray of drinks and calling to the children.

Peter stopped to survey the scene and smiled. The children and the house were his. The woman was his wife. He started towards them, expecting the children to run to meet him. He shouted but his words were carried away by a sudden gust of wind. He began to run but the wind grew stronger and held him back.

When he looked up again, the woman was hurrying the children inside, away from the sudden storm. The wind abated for a moment and Peter moved forward again as the rain started to fall. As he neared the hedge, it began to change – vicious thorns replacing the leaves, spreading quickly, growing thicker and taller. By the time he reached the gate, the hedge was dense, impregnable. He tore at the thorns, crying out in frustration as they threatened to engulf him.

He started to run again, following the line of the hedge to find a way through, but the thorns beat him back, forcing him to follow the line of the road. Then he had heard laughter, soft at first, but growing steadily louder. He looked round to see where it was coming from but he could not. He shouted, 'Let me go! I want to go home! Let me go!'

The laughter redoubled. It was all round him, and he realised that he was powerless to fight. The road had drawn him away. He started to walk but the road suddenly disappeared and he started to fall...

He had woken up, sweating and terrified.

It was a long time since Peter had dreamt so vividly and recalled the details of a dream with such clarity. He realised that the memory was making him sweat again. 'This is ridiculous,' he said out loud and shook his head to clear it. He stubbed out his cigarette and headed for the shower.

He felt better for the shower but desperately tired. He took ages to get dressed, taking long pauses between garments to recover from the effort. Eventually he heard the college servants approach. Unable to face an exchange of pleasantries, he decided to go for a walk.

Outside the heat was even greater. Walking into the quad was almost like opening an oven door. This was the fourth day of high temperatures and heavy cloud; surely it must break soon. He checked his pigeon-hole for his post and headed towards the junior common room and coffee. He sat down with his cup, lit another cigarette and turned to his mail: a reminder from the library, a returned essay and a note from the admissions tutor. This last was a weighty document, setting out in detail the arrangements for an open day for next term's freshers to be held the following week. In a rash moment, Peter had volunteered to be one of four second-year students who would act as guides; reading the instructions, he began to regret the offer.

Eventually he reached the last paragraph, from which it appeared that he and his colleagues would each act as host to about ten new students.

In general, your groups have been selected at random, with the one exception that anybody from your own old school has been allocated to you.

Peter glanced at the list of names, wondering idly whether there would be anybody from his own old school, Warton. There was.

TAYLOR, *John Christopher. Warton College, Lancashire.*

He spilled his coffee, swearing loudly, drawing much attention, blushing and brushing. Getting another cup: standing, queuing, putting sugar in, stirring, sitting down. The name was still there.

TAYLOR, *John Christopher. Warton College, Lancashire.*

No mistake. There was definitely only one minor public school called Warton. There may even have been more than one Taylor but there couldn't be two John Taylors. Christ! Memories flooded back, memories that had gone unheeded for the two years since he had left school.

It had been easy, at first – everything at Oxford was so new and exciting and there was a whole new lifestyle to absorb. It was a lifestyle that, despite the aura of freedom, brooked no deviation from the routine of wine, women and dope, the uniform of sweater and Levis, and the politics of the radical left. The pressure to conform was enormous and Peter had bowed to it. Conformity had the advantage of being enjoyable and also offering the best chance of survival – even guaranteeing it, provided you did not take the whole thing too seriously. So the occasional doubts had gone unnoticed and the memories were kept safely locked away.

The sight of John's name changed that. Comparisons were inevitable. The difference, for example, between being with John and the other night at Sally's. He shivered at the memory.

A voice within him countered this angrily. His interlude with John – it was an ordinary adolescent affair. Nothing more. 'But was it only that?' he asked himself.

'All right. It was more than that,' came his own grudging reply. 'Much more, in fact. But it all happened in a closed community where it didn't matter. Here it would be different – you'd be spotted and labelled a queer.'

'Yes, but it seemed natural at the time.'

'To love another boy at school is all right – it's part of growing up. But two men ... well, it's not natural. Everybody says so. Besides, you're not like that. So there. Stop worrying.'

'Peter! Hello!'

He looked up and his heart sank. It was Sally. That was all he needed.

Sally Dixon was, like Peter, a second-year English student. They had met early in their first term and become good friends. She was a strikingly pretty girl of medium height, with blonde hair, a lovely figure and sparkling blue eyes. In earlier times, she might have been something of a sex symbol, or even a *femme fatale*, but such possibilities were defeated by her nature, which was dominated by an outrageous sense of fun. That she had got to university at all, never mind Oxford, was a constant source of mystery to her parents and teachers, but they had missed the fact that she possessed a very good brain and enough common sense to know when to use it.

The university, particularly some of the stuffier dons,

did not quite know how to take Sally but they all would have acknowledged, if pressed, that she enriched their lives. This was particularly true of Peter.

In his current mood, though, Peter did not feel able to cope with Sally's ebullience, especially after the disastrous events two nights earlier. He thought of avoiding her but that was clearly impossible.

'I was sure you'd forget, so I was on my way to collect you,' she said.

'Forget what?' asked Peter.

'There you are, you see – I was right. You promised to take me on the river today.'

TAYLOR, *John Christopher. Warton College, Lancashire.*

'Oh, yes, so I did. But I thought after – you know.'

'Well, you thought wrong.' She gave him a long, hard look. 'God, you look *awful*, Peter. What's the matter?'

'Nothing really. I think it's mainly the weather. I slept badly last night – I had a terrible nightmare.'

'Really? Oh, you must tell me about it. I *love* interpreting other people's dreams.'

Peter smiled, despite himself. 'I will some time but not now. I feel dreadful – in fact, think I ought to go and lie down for a while. Can we postpone the river? It's not really the day for it.'

'I suppose so ... if you must.'

'Thanks. Can I buy you dinner tomorrow night to make up?'

Sally brightened. 'That would be lovely, darling. As long as you're not avoiding me because that would *never* do.'

Peter shook his head and smiled. 'I'd never do that – you're the only person in this place who keeps me sane.'

He left quickly and returned to his rooms. Another

cigarette. Breathless, he sat on the bed.

TAYLOR, *John Christopher. Warton College, Lancashire.*

'Look,' said the voice in his head, 'you are twenty years old, an Oxford undergraduate with a good career ahead of you. You have lots of friends, you're popular with the girls – look at Sally just now. What the hell are you worrying about?'

But the words did not ring true. It was useless to pretend that his memories of that summer two years ago were anything but pleasant and exciting. He felt another stab of fear.

'It can't be true. I'm not like that. There was nobody else at school – not like some of them – and there certainly hasn't been anybody since. It's wrong, anyway – disgusting, when you think about it. Two men...'

Again his memories gave the lie to his words. Temporarily, at least, he surrendered to them and lay back on the bed.

'Peter?' Thump, thump. 'Peter, are you there?'
  'Who is it?'
  'Chris. You haven't forgotten the match, have you?'
  'What match?'
  'The cricket match we're playing in half an hour!'
  'Christ! What time is it?'
  'Half past one!'
  'I must have fallen asleep again. Give me a couple of minutes.'

Peter splashed his face with cold water and immediately felt better. Luckily his gear was already packed, so he grabbed his bag and ran. 'Sorry, Chris – I had a rough night. I got up at ten but felt so bloody awful that I came back here for a lie down.'

Chris smiled. 'Hope she was worth it.'

'What? Oh, nothing like that – just this damned weather.'

Peter's college were playing in a limited-over friendly match but it was an important one because the university side was in poor shape and the selectors were looking for talent. Peter had attracted attention and was to be assessed further. He recognised some of the committee as he and Chris reached the ground; already seated, they reminded him briefly of crows sitting on a fence. He laughed for the first time that day.

The rest of the team were changing and greeted the latecomers with ironic applause.

'Sorry, chaps,' said Chris, in an exaggerated upper-class accent, the team's 'in joke' this term. 'Young Harvey's suspected of screwing again. Had to get his strength up.'

'Trust she was a belter, Harvey, old boy.'

Peter did not reply.

'Hello, he's droppin' orf again.'

Peter looked up and smiled thinly. He had not been asleep but paralysed with fear. He had found himself horrifyingly aware of ten other men in various stages of undress. One individual had caught him staring and smiled. Actually smiled! And winked! Christ, was it that easy?

The memories released earlier in the day returned. Even walking out to open the innings with Chris he was elsewhere, walking out to the wicket with someone else.

TAYLOR, John Christopher. Warton College, Lancashire.

Book One, Chapter 1

Chris took strike, planting the first ball firmly towards square leg for an easy single.

'*Howzat*?!'

Peter had not moved. Chris was stranded midway between the wickets, run out for a duck.

'Thanks, pal.'

'Sorry, Chris, I wasn't concentrating.'

'That much was obvious.' The bitterness in Chris's voice was there for the entire fielding side to hear. There was an embarrassed silence as they waited for the next man in. It was the captain, Roger Frazer.

'What the hell was that all about, Peter?'

'I don't know. Sorry, I was somewhere else.'

'Pull yourself together, mate, for Christ's sake. I want some runs out of you today.'

By a supreme effort of will, Peter managed to put aside his memories. His unbeaten seventy-nine and the subsequent victory were the cause of much celebration in the bar after the match, though he felt less and less involved as the evening wore on. Never before had he drunk so much yet remained so sober.

He made several attempts to leave, but was persuaded to stay. He remained until closing time, the alcohol worsening his mood with every minute. He walked back to his rooms with Chris Simon.

'Does our champion runner between the wickets want some coffee?'

'For God's sake, Chris! I've already apologised four times for running you out! Can't you let it drop, man?'

'Hey! What's the matter with you? It was only a joke – it happens to the best of us.'

'I'm sorry. I'm a bit off today, that's all. As I said, it's this weather – and I had a bad dream last night.'

'That all? You seem to have been down for a couple of days.'

By this time, they had reached Chris's rooms. Chris went off to make the coffee and Peter was able to avoid further comment. He sat down and shut his eyes but his head began to spin alarmingly: he was drunker than he'd thought.

TAYLOR, John Christopher. Warton College, Lancashire.

Peter shivered. The memories were becoming more familiar and less disturbing as time went on. It frightened him and confused the issue even further. He made no clear-cut decision to confide in Chris; he merely recognised that it was inevitable.

Chris returned with the coffee. 'Come on, then. Out with it. What's up?'

Peter was silent.

'You don't have to tell me if you don't want to.'

Peter began to tremble. How the hell could he? How *do* you tell somebody that you're queer? And yet if he didn't ... if he couldn't tell *somebody*...

'I do want to tell you,' he said, 'but I don't know where to start.' He looked up and laughed. 'Funny, isn't it? A student of English unable to express himself.'

'It must be bad,' said Chris, half to himself.

Peter lit another cigarette. He glanced round the room, took a deep drag, and finally found the words. 'You know this open day thing next Thursday.'

Chris nodded.

'One of the people coming is from my old school. Two years ago, I ... we ... I mean we were ... I was in love with him.'

There was a pause. Peter felt the atmosphere change. After a while, Chris spoke. 'I see. Go on.'

'The point is, I think I still am. Which makes me gay.'

There was another long pause. The atmosphere grew chillier. Peter looked up but Chris looked the other way: when he eventually responded, there was a formal edge to his voice. 'Peter, let me give you a piece of advice. That's not the sort of thing you ought to be telling too many people. They might get the wrong idea. If you think you've got a problem like that, you should be seeking professional help – and soon. Now, you've had a lot to drink tonight, and it's been a good do, so I think if you don't mind, we'll forget this bit ever happened. You must be tired after your bad night.'

Peter drained his coffee cup and stood up. 'Message received, Chris. Sorry.'

He left quickly and headed back to his own rooms. Once inside, he shut the door and leant against it, eyes shut. He had never felt so wretched in his life – not even the day he'd left school and said goodbye to John.

All the fears about what could happen to him that had been grinding around in the back of his mind all day had been fulfilled in that single, brief conversation. He went cold at the memory.

'It was your own damned stupid fault,' said the nagging voice inside him. 'Just blurting it out like that. What did you think he'd say?'

'But he was my friend!'

'*Was* is the right word. You've got to face the fact that if you're queer, you don't go around telling everybody. They might think you're propositioning them.'

'God, what a thought. And I don't even fancy him!'

Peter smiled briefly and began to get ready for bed. Glancing in the mirror as he cleaned his teeth, he was surprised to see the same face he had seen that morning. Somehow he expected the events of the day to have wrought some physical change.

He lay in bed, wide awake, the memory of the conversation with Chris Simon going round in his head like a looped cassette tape. The message was simple, he told himself: nothing – not all the love or sex in the world – was worth the humiliation and rejection that he had suffered that night.

Chapter 2

'AH! Here's the coffee.' Sally turned to the waitress and gave her a huge smile, enough to ensure lifelong devotion and first-class service. 'Thank you so much.'

Peter remained silent whilst Sally poured, and thought how beautiful she looked. He realised how glad he was that he had not cried off from their dinner engagement. He had certainly been tempted to, after the previous night. He had slept, eventually, but his earlier nightmare had returned, leaving him even more terrified.

He wrenched his mind away from that and turned again to his last evening with Sally, four nights earlier, when he had mistaken his admiration for her for sexual attraction. For the first time since it had happened – or, more precisely, not happened – he felt some element of detachment. He sipped his coffee, then raised his eyes to find Sally looking at him.

'Poor love. Did it upset you terribly the other night?'

He was ready to feel patronised by her sympathy and make a sharp retort. After all, surely plenty of people made a mess of their first time. But that was nonsense and he knew it; his lack had been of interest, not ability. And, despite his resolutions of the previous night after the abortive discussion with Chris Simon, it was time to admit it and acknowledge the consequences.

He nodded, and took another sip of coffee.

'Because you couldn't, or because of what that implied?'

God, she's sharp, this girl. 'Because of what it implied.'

She relaxed slightly. 'At least you're not kidding yourself, darling.'

'Not now, at least. Did you know?'

'I guessed. Women often do. It's something to do with not feeling threatened, I believe. And you're so like my brother Charles.'

'Is he...'

'Gay? Oh, yes. He came home one day and told us all. Just like that. I thought he was terribly brave. There was an awful row, of course, but everybody calmed down in the end. I told Mummy that it was her fault for teaching Charles how to make chocolate cakes when he was nine. We all got the giggles and it's been fine ever since. He lives with the most gorgeous young man, in Hampstead somewhere, and is as happy as a sand boy.'

'Sally, you're hopeless,' Peter laughed and immediately felt better.

She giggled. 'I suppose I am, really. But there was everybody cavorting around making this terrible scene and looking miserable and I had this sudden memory of Charles emerging from the kitchen covered in flour and cocoa, carrying this superb chocolate cake. So I blurted it out. Besides, God made him like that, so why get in a fuss about it?'

'Yes, I suppose you're right.'

'So what are you going to do about it?'

'I think events have been taken out of my hands.' He told her of John Taylor's impending visit.

Her eyes lit up. 'Jolly good! Tell me all about him.'

Peter was lost for words again but she was not prepared to let him get away with it.

'Come on. What does he look like?'

'Slightly shorter than me. Dark hair, wavy, with big brown sparkly eyes and olive skin – I think there must be some Italian blood in him somewhere.'

'He sounds gorgeous.'

'Yes, he is.' Peter blushed, surprised at his own words. He realised that in all the debates and arguments he had had with himself, the question of John as a *person*, rather than as a concept with dire consequences, had not arisen. Now, forced by Sally to talk about him – the first time that he had been able to talk to *anyone* about him – a sharp picture of his lover came into his mind. It took his breath away.

Sally watched, sipping her coffee. After a moment, she said, 'Goodness me, you are keen on him, aren't you?'

He nodded. 'Yes. Talking about him, I think I now realise how much.' The moment passed.

Sally broke the silence. 'How did it all start?'

'It was in the summer term, two years ago. I'd never really thought about sex until then. Oh, you know, we'd had the occasional experiment in the showers but no more than that.'

'Yes, I know all about those.'

'How? From Charles?'

She nodded and laughed. 'I used to make him tell me all the gory details when he came home for the holidays.'

'You horror!'

'I suppose I was, but it did him good to talk about all those things. And it doesn't seem to be doing you much harm, either.'

'That's certainly true.' Peter laughed.

'Anyway, go on. Summer term two years ago.'

'I began to notice this boy. He was in the fifth form, two years below me, but he had the room next to mine. There was something different about him. He seemed – oh, I don't know – more self-assured, more mature than the others his age – and many my age, come to that. His character fascinated me and he was, as you've gathered, rather good-looking. It all started at a cricket match.'

'Don't tell me, you did it to relieve the boredom.'

'Sally!'

'Sorry, but you know how I hate the bloody game.'

'Yes, well... It was two years ago last week. John was a very good cricketer and a natural for the first eleven. We shared in an unbroken partnership of 152, which won the match, and I scored a century. Afterwards, the two of us were alone in the dressing room and he came over and told me.'

'Told you what?'

'That he loved me. I told him not to be stupid and to stop behaving like a moonstruck kid. I said we could both get expelled – and I was the school captain.'

'Absolutely. But the idea didn't appal you?'

'No, I realise that now. Anyway, as far as I was concerned, that was that.'

'The poor lamb! You heartless thing!'

'I know – but the next afternoon, a gang of us was taken to see *Othello* at a local cinema. John sat next to me, and ... well, you can guess the rest.' He paused and looked away, strangely torn between nostalgia, embarrassment and guilt.

'He came to my room that night after lights out. It was

the most wonderful night of my life. I was hopelessly in love with him and he with me. We slept together virtually every night from then until the end of term. Looking back, it was a bloody miracle that we weren't caught.'

'Have you kept in touch all this time?'

'That's the point. Your remark about me being heartless was about right. We swore to keep in touch, of course, but I didn't. It seemed so different when I got here. Having a fling at school was all very well, but to keep it going meant—'

'That you were a raving poofter.'

'Not my choice of words, but yes,' Peter replied.

'And now he's coming to this open day next Thursday?'

'Yup, that's right.'

'Oh dear. You were a heartless sod, weren't you?'

'Yup.'

'And have you now accepted it? Being a raving poofter, I mean.'

'I think so. I tried to talk about it to Chris Simon last night but he froze me out. That was awful, because it simply reinforced my own prejudices and all that those implied – losing my friends, being labelled queer, drummed out of the cricket team. I went to sleep resolved to fight it: no way was I ever going to sleep with men again. I wasn't like that. But I gradually realised during the day, and talking to you tonight, that it's useless trying to fight it.'

'Yes, it is,' replied Sally thoughtfully. 'You're not saying anything I haven't heard from Charles. And I'm afraid that you've got to accept that some people will despise you for it. But they're probably not worth knowing anyway. And besides, you mustn't run away from it. You are what you are, and that's that. As for John ... well, you can't write a script for it, darling. If you still love him, and I don't think there's much doubt about that, and if he'll forgive you for the shameful way you've treated him, then no problem. If not – we'll cross that bridge when we come to it. Now, I would like a ginormous crème de menthe frappé to round off the evening and then you can take me home.'

'A pleasure, Aunt Sal. And by the way, you're a brick.'

'Nonsense, darling! All part of the service.'

Peter saw Sally back to her college and set off for his own. The humid weather had finally broken during the day with a spectacular thunderstorm; it was now a beautifully cool evening with a pleasant breeze.

As the clocks around him struck eleven, he revelled for a moment in the atmosphere of the city. It was easy to take the guide-book aspects of Oxford for granted when you lived in the middle of it, but the dreaming spires were apt to catch his breath at odd moments. He paused to light a cigarette and then resumed his walk, lost in thought, entering his own college grounds virtually without noticing.

'Peter!'

He jumped at the sound of his own name. The voice seemed vaguely familiar but he could not quite place it. Then he remembered; it was Mark Foster, whom he had seen giving him a smile and a wink in the dressing room the previous day. A curious nervous sensation started in his stomach.

'Sorry if I made you jump,' Mark said.

'Yes, I was dreaming a bit. It's such a lovely evening.'

'And such a relief after all that heat!'

'Quite,' replied Peter noncommittally. Despite playing cricket in the same team, he hadn't exchanged more than a dozen sentences with Mark before.

'I didn't get a chance to say how much I enjoyed your innings yesterday.'

'Oh, thanks,' Peter said, still noncommittal. 'It was a shame about running Chris out, though. He was a bit miffed.'

'Yes, you don't seem to be his favourite person at the moment – for a number of reasons.'

Peter felt a stab of fear. 'Oh? Why?'

'Look, this is a bit difficult. How about a drink?'

'Why not?' The invitation had been inevitable but Peter still felt wary.

They walked across the quad to Mark's rooms in silence. Once inside, Peter began to relax a little. There was a quality about the furnishing and decoration which was welcoming and gentle – rather like his host who was also, he realised with a slight shock, rather attractive.

A second-year history student, Mark Foster was slightly shorter than Peter, with light brown hair and bright hazel eyes that twinkled when he laughed, which was often. His white shirt was open at the neck to reveal a hairless chest, whilst his close-fitting jeans emphasised a trim waist, amongst other things.

Peter sat on the sofa as his host busied himself with the drinks, chatting amiably about the previous day's match. Peter responded at all the right moments but his mind was elsewhere. It was a new experience, this feeling of sexual attraction – very different from the all-embracing love he had felt for John two years earlier. He felt a strong desire for physical contact, a need to caress the body that moved round in front of him. The sensation was almost overwhelming and the prospect of it actually happening left him nervous and excited.

Mark turned to hand him his drink and their fingers touched lightly. The sensation was so intense that both of them jumped. The room went quiet for a moment; neither of them was quite sure what would happen next.

Mark spoke first, resuming the conversation about the match and his own job of keeping wicket to the team's rather wayward fast bowler. Eventually, the subject returned to Chris Simon. 'I gather that you were a little indiscreet last night after closing time.' Mark remained standing and addressed his comment rather diffidently to the fireplace.

Peter closed his eyes and sighed. Part of him felt fearful and depressed that his confession of the previous evening was probably being broadcast around the college; another part connected tonight's invitation with the confession and decided that it enhanced the prospect of something happening. 'I thought that's what you were going to say.'

Mark looked up from the fireplace and smiled. 'Fortunately, it was me he told and I think it was more out of genuine surprise than any malice. I gave him a good talking to about damaging people's reputations and betraying confidences, so I hope that'll keep him quiet. But who knows?'

'Thanks.'

'I thought I recognised a kindred spirit yesterday afternoon...'

'Yes, I'm sorry about that – I didn't mean to stare.'

Mark grinned then sat down. 'Not at all. I was very flattered.'

Peter began to shake. He knew what was going to happen – or thought he did – but was unwilling to make a move in case he was wrong. He was aware of Mark's hand lying on the sofa a few inches from his thigh. He moved his own leg closer.

Mark lifted his arm to scratch his ear and Peter experienced a momentary feeling of disappointment before the hand returned to the cushion, landing a little closer. He could feel its warmth on his thigh. He shut his eyes for a moment and then lifted his glass to take a sip. The action caused his leg to move slightly and contact was made. He looked up into Mark's eyes and returned his smile.

The hand now caressed his thigh and moved upwards. They kissed and Peter was aware of an intoxicating mixture of whisky and expensive aftershave. Mark's other hand joined in the exploration, closely followed by Peter's. After a few moments, they moved into the bedroom and undressed.

The sensations were wonderful but Peter's excitement was too great and it was all over very quickly. His climax acted like an abruptly drawn curtain; the brief pleasure he had experienced disappeared and was replaced by a cold dread, a feeling of guilt and distaste. He could barely bring himself to assist in his partner's pleasure and then could not wait to get out of the room. He dressed in silence and turned to go.

Mark smiled gently and said, 'It gets easier, you know. Give it time.'

Peter nodded and left.

The dream returned that night with renewed horror. This time, as the thorns forced him away from the house, the building disappeared in a massive explosion. The orange flames were so vivid that the colour remained behind his eyelids, haunting him as he tried to go back to sleep.

Eventually he abandoned the attempt and put the light on to read but he was unable to concentrate on a book. The feelings of guilt and depression were so heavy that they felt like a physical burden.

It had all seemed very easy when he was sitting there talking to Sally, an abstract thing. 'Facing up to it' was all very well, but he was not destined to face up to things like that. He was an intelligent, good-looking young man with a good education. He could look forward to a happy, prosperous future. He played cricket, was popular with his team mates; he wasn't some nancy boy mincing around a department store.

He got up and went to the window. Drawing back the curtains, he saw the sun rising over the chapel across the quadrangle. In the opposite corner lay Mark Foster's room where that sordid, disgusting *thing* had happened not three hours ago.

He closed his eyes and rested his head against the glass. For the first time in his life, he was learning to hate himself. It was not a pleasant experience.

He was aroused from his reverie by a soft knock on his door. His first instinct was to ignore it but his curiosity got the better of him. Who could it be at five in the morning? He opened the door to find Mark Foster standing there.

'I saw your light on and thought you might need some more whisky. Can I come in?'

'What the hell—'

'I couldn't sleep. You looked so bloody miserable when you left that I was worried. Please let me in before somebody sees us and ruins both our reputations.'

Peter gave a small smile, despite himself. 'Be my guest.'

Once inside, Mark produced a hip flask and two glasses from his pockets and busied himself pouring drinks. 'Here's to our mother's sons, God bless them.'

'Cheers,' responded Peter, still bemused but rather touched by Mark's concern.

'Are you all right?'

Peter shook his head.

'Thought not. Bad attack of the whymies?'

'The what?'

'The whymies. The "Oh, God why hast Thou made me like this?" syndrome. "Why me?" Hence whymies.'

'Oh, I see.' Peter nodded again. 'Yes, I suppose that sums it up pretty well.'

'I thought I recognised the symptoms. Do you want to talk?'

Another nod.

'Right. Fire away.'

'When I met you earlier, I'd just had dinner with Sally Dixon. She'd made me talk about probably being gay and somehow made it seem okay.'

'Then up pops little me with a cold dose of reality.'

'Something like that. When I sat in your room, I wanted it so badly it almost hurt. Then after I ... we ... it was over, I felt terrible. It was as though somebody had flicked a switch in my brain. I couldn't wait to get away. I'm sorry.'

Mark smiled gently. 'No need to apologise. As I said, it gets easier.'

'But should it? If the guilt is my conscience speaking,

shouldn't I obey it?'

'Oh, God, I don't know. It's the wrong time of night to debate moral philosophy. All I can say is that most of us go through this and it does get better. In any case, is it really wrong? Or have we been brainwashed, along with everybody else?'

'You might have a point there, I suppose. But it seems so unfair. There am I sailing through life and suddenly this *thing* opens up before me like a black bole. It's going to affect everything else I do.'

Mark shook his head. 'That's not the way to look at it. Nothing else has changed. You're still the same person, with the same talents.'

'But it has changed, don't you see? Everything I do from now on will be affected by the fact that I'm queer. I shall always be on the outside and ... I don't think I can face it.'

Peter put his face into his hands and began to sob. Mark moved across and took him in his arms, rubbing his back gently. After a few minutes, Peter was calm again, soothed by having somebody to hold. At moments like this, it seemed all right.

Mark made to move away but Peter tightened his grip.

Mark stroked his hair. 'Better now?'

'Thanks.' Peter kissed Mark's neck. It was soft and smooth, like the rest of his body.

'Hmm. And there are consolations as well,' Mark said with a quiet laugh.

Chapter 3

DR William Elliott, MA (Oxon), PhD, admissions tutor for the college, shuffled his papers and glanced over his pince-nez at the four students who were to act as guides for his open day. He cleared his throat and started to speak.

'Right. The programme for today is as follows: in about ten minutes, they should all have arrived. There'll be a cup of coffee in the senior common room, over which you'll have a chance to meet your respective parties. Then you'll show them round. Peter, will you start with the chapel, please? Chris with the library, Mark with the junior common room and Jim with the hall.'

They all nodded: this was spelt out in detail in their programmes but Elliott, precise as ever, had wanted to give them a final briefing.

Peter found his attention wandering. Was it only a week since he had first seen John Taylor's name on the list in front of him? The encounters with Chris Simon, Sally and Mark, the cricket match and now the news, which had reached him the previous day, that he been selected to play for the university against Yorkshire the following week.

Peter had seen Mark several times during the last few days and he had enjoyed each encounter more. As Mark had predicted, the feelings of guilt and self-reproach had lessened each time, though they had by no means disappeared. If there was anything on his conscience, it was a feeling that having sex with Mark was a further betrayal of John. Not only had he broken his promise to keep in touch after he'd left school, he was now also being unfaithful.

Mark, when tackled on the subject, did not see it that way. Like Sally, he had been told the story of Peter's last term at school and John's imminent reappearance in his life. He dismissed Peter's worries. 'I agree that you were wrong not to write to him...'

'Yes, Sally said I was a heartless sod.'

'A touch harsh,' Mark laughed. 'But I see what she means. On the other hand, you don't know how he feels now. He might have gone straight, for all you know.'

'True, but—'

'But nothing,' Mark said, pushing Peter's shoulder. 'There's nothing serious between us. It's only a bit of fun. And God knows, you needed that this week.'

'Certainly did.'

'Well, there you are then. And, besides, you're not really my type. You're a bit young for me and not nearly hairy enough, so there.'

They collapsed into giggles. 'Still,' said Mark, recovering first. 'Best friends, eh?'

Peter fixed Mark with a surprised look. 'Oh, always. And forever.'

'That's all right, then,' Mark responded. The subject of Peter's conscience had not been raised again.

Now a nudge from Mark, who had spotted his wool-gathering, brought Peter back to the present. Dr Elliott was still speaking. 'The Master will address them at one. There'll be a sherry reception at one fifteen, lunch at one

Book One, Chapter 3

forty-five. After that, they can wander around on their own for a bit and leave when they're ready.'

Peter's heart jumped as he saw the chance for a word with John.

'You should all be clear after lunch, which isn't bad. Good luck – and I hope it's not too boring for you.'

At that last remark, Peter caught himself somewhere between a grimace and a grin as the four of them walked to the senior common room. As they approached the door, his smile faded as his apprehension grew. He began to shake; his stomach felt strange – an excruciating, yet somehow pleasant, combination of nervousness and anticipation.

Peter caught sight of him almost as soon as he entered the room.

Standing alone and absorbed in thought, John Taylor was, at five foot eight, a little taller and rather thinner than Peter remembered. The classic proportions of his face had been heightened by his weight loss. Olive-skinned, with his almost black hair immaculately combed as ever, he looked very smart in school blazer and grey slacks, both fashionably cut and newly-pressed. Peter stopped for a moment, using the other occupants of the room as a shield so that he could look at him.

Whatever doubts Peter had were swept away by a surge of love. Nervousness had conquered anticipation and seemed to paralyse him. He could not move towards John and felt a strong urge to run back across the quadrangle and hide. That he did not was more a tribute to his confusion than to a conscious decision.

He's seen me now and he's walking over. What shall I say? God, but he's beautiful!

John reached him, smiling broadly, hand outstretched.

To his amazement, Peter found himself shaking the hand and speaking first. The words were automatic but nevertheless *had* been spoken. 'Hello, there! Nice to see you again. How are you?'

John was nervous too; that was obvious. 'Great, thanks – and you?'

'Oh, struggling along, you know.'

They paused.

Greetings had been exchanged. What next? There was so much to be said, but not here. Now that Peter had seen John, he was sure that the old feelings remained. But the approach – how? After all, the introduction had been polite – perhaps too polite – but there was nothing more. Or was there? That look – yes, there it was again. The eyes! It all came back in one great wave. Their eyes had met and everything seemed to click.

The silence lasted for what seemed hours but there was no particular reason to break it.

'Coffee, gentlemen?'

Peter jumped. Mark stood next to him, eyebrows raised, proffering two cups of the college brew.

'Thanks, Mark. This is John Taylor. He's ... er ... from my old school. John, this is Mark Foster.'

Juggling cups of coffee in a way that seemed certain to end in disaster, the two shook hands. Peter had the feeling they were assessing each other, rather as if, he thought with a hastily suppressed snigger, he was introducing his wife to his mistress.

Then John spoke. 'Well, I mustn't keep you two.'

Peter's heart sank. Was this all? He could hardly bear to look up from his coffee. Eventually he did and saw John smiling.

'Because you do seem to have a few other guests to look after,' he added.

Mark moved away tactfully.

'Yes,' replied Peter. 'I suppose we'd better keep them happy. Perhaps we could get together after lunch for a chat?'

'Yes, that would be great,' John replied with a smile.

Looking back on the day, Peter was sure that lunch had been very good (it usually was on such occasions) but he could not for the life of him remember what he had eaten or what had happened during the meal. He dimly recalled being forced to down a couple of whiskies by Mark Foster, with the words, 'Go for it, he's adorable.' On top of the earlier sherry, the extra drinks helped neither memory nor his digestion.

As he left the table, the feeling in the pit of his stomach returned. His mind began to race through a range of opening gambits and possible reactions, until Sally's words returned: 'You can't write a script for it, darling.'

John followed him from the table. Soon, the two were walking across the quadrangle to Peter's rooms. Neither spoke, which increased the tension. Peter was striving to appear nonchalant but it was virtually impossible. He was shaking by the time they climbed the stairs.

John, on the other hand, appeared calm. In his room, Peter shut the door and, turning round, found himself in John's arms. After a moment, they separated a little. Peter smiled. 'Hello, John.'

'Hello, Peter.'

'I'll write tonight. See you soon.' And then he was gone, hair blowing in the wind as the train gathered speed.

Peter walked slowly back from the station, humming quietly to himself. It had been a marvellous afternoon, to be near John, to touch him and hold him. It was also a comfort, a refuge, though from what he did not know.

The trouble was a nagging feeling of guilt, of having surrendered to temptation. It was stupid, he knew, and the feeling when it came was fleeting, like a target that appeared and was immediately shot down. But by what? He could not accept it was conviction, for that would have been firm and crisp like a pistol shot. This was more like a cannon: the cannon of fear, booming out, trying to sweep everything aside.

'But why fear?' he asked himself.

'Fear of more hesitation and debate,' his inner voice replied.

'But why? You are what you are and that's that, as Sally said.'

'But what am I? Answer that!'

'Oh, shut up.'

He forced it to the back of his mind. The important thing was that the gap, which he'd felt in his life for the last two years, was now filled with John. Suddenly he was happy again and resumed his humming. Celebration seemed to be in order; he quickened his pace and headed for the bar. Mark was there and greeted him with a grin and an unspoken question, to which Peter replied with a wink.

He left the bar four hours later, not without some assistance, to the strains of what certainly seemed to be *When You're Smiling*.

✣

Book One, Chapter 3

The letter arrived two days later. Peter opened it in the junior common room but put it away as soon as he realised who it was from and saved it for later. First of all, John apologised for the delay; it appeared that he had arrived back late, causing the head some anxiety. Then Dr Benson, the deputy head, had dragged him off for cocoa. Peter was amused by this; late-night conferences between the school captain and the deputy head were an institution at Warton, as he well remembered.

Next came an invitation for Peter to visit the school the following weekend, something that Peter had suggested himself when John was in Oxford. It would be easy to arrange since Peter's parents, whom he was due to visit, lived not far from the school. John said that his own parents had planned a visit but he had managed to put them off. Besides, Dr Benson would like to see Peter.

So far so good, but the next bit made Peter shift uneasily in his seat.

However, if after reading this you don't show up, I'll understand. And before I start, I want to say that I've thought about all these things and you had my answer the other day.

The temptation to skim the next bit – or even skip it altogether – was very strong but Peter carried on.

After all, neither of us is a child any more and we ought, I suppose, to be mature enough to know what we're doing. So, what there is between us is no longer simple and in its own way natural but (in terms of society) an abnormal relationship.

Our lives together could well be difficult. On top of the stresses of any love affair, we face society's scorn – being ignored, laughed at, talked about and insulted as we were to some extent two years ago. Not to mention the fact that until we're twenty-one we could be arrested and sent to prison. The question is, therefore, whether your love for me – for any MAN – could be strong enough to withstand those pressures.

Please don't think I'm trying to give you a way out because I can't think of one or haven't the courage to take one. I love you very much indeed – but feel I must have your answer.

As Peter finished reading, his first reaction was disappointment; the letter was not quite what he had expected. He felt instinctively that to rationalise love in such a way was to kill it, at least in part. But he had to accept some responsibility; after all, it was his own two-year silence that was causing John to ask those questions. For if the letter indicated anything, it was insecurity – plus an odd mixture of naïveté and maturity. It was naïve in the sense that it expected definite answers to hypothetical questions, but mature in its recognition of the pressures they would face. In the latter sense, the letter was doubly unfortunate: it amplified the doubts in Peter's mind, and stated the issues with a clarity that was both new and frightening.

'You are what you are and that's that.' *But what am I?* 'Your love for me – for any MAN...' 'Ignored, laughed at, talked about, insulted...' 'Hello, sailor!' 'Who's a pretty boy, then?' *A bloody queer. No!* 'We face the scorn of society.' *A bloody queer.*

He shivered at this parade of insults, rejecting them angrily, but still they came, implying that at least a part of him accepted them as true. A feeling of deep and bitter frustration arose within him, which he recognised from his recurring dream; the life of quiet and easy conformity for which his upbringing and education had prepared him was slowly receding, as though some giant hand were pulling him away. His white house, his wife and the kids were not to be.

He had to fight! He got up from the chair and paced up and down. He would *not* see John again. No, his love for a man could not be that strong because he wasn't really like that. He would get together with that girl again – no, not Sally, the other one – she'd seemed interested at that dance. What was her name?

Margaret Taylor heard her husband's car enter the drive, quickly checked the dinner and moved towards the lounge. She was pouring sherry by the time Stuart had garaged the car and come into the house. She turned to greet him with a radiant smile.

Stuart Taylor, QC was a round, jolly, exuberant man, with a moustache, a booming voice and, more often than not, a large cigar in his mouth. He was one of those lucky men who had turned the war to his advantage, entering the army as a raw recruit from a routine clerical job and emerging as a captain with enough qualifications to go to university and study law. Since then, he had risen to become one of the most successful barristers in the north of England, with a lifestyle to match his career: a large house on the outskirts of Harrogate; two cars; a villa in Spain, and a son about to leave public school for Oxford. He regarded all this as no more than just reward for a life of extreme hard work, but tried not to flaunt it.

He greeted his wife and accepted the sherry gratefully.

He was in a good mood and cast an appreciative eye over her. Though forty-seven, Margaret could pass for ten years younger. She was tall, with a trim figure; her dark hair was styled boyishly – hardly a sign of grey there – and she had a clear complexion and sparkling green eyes.

'You're a bit earlier than I expected,' she said. 'I only just had time to get the boyfriend out of the back door.'

Stuart grinned. 'Sorry to have spoiled your fun. Actually, I expected to be in court all day but the bugger changed his plea. Stood up and told the judge that he had murdered his wife, was glad that he had done so and would do it again!'

Margaret was taking a sip of sherry and choked with laughter. 'You're joking!' she exclaimed.

He shook his head vigorously. 'No! Old Muddiford was on the bench – he nearly swallowed his pencil.'

Margaret laughed again. 'More sherry, love? I'm afraid dinner won't be ready for another half hour.'

'Mm, please. How was your day?'

'Fine. I had lunch with Molly Hertford – she's as scatty as ever, bless her – then pottered around the shops and came home. We're playing bridge with Molly and Alec next Tuesday, by the way.'

Stuart grimaced.

'All right,' replied his wife, 'I know Molly can't play to save her life but the food's always good and Alec's a dear.'

'True,' he said between puffs on a new cigar. 'I usually enjoy myself. Any post?'

'Three bills, a postcard from my sister and a letter from John.'

'And how is our dear son?'

'Very well – he sounds more cheerful than he has for months. The day at Oxford was good fun, apparently, and he says that he can't wait to get there.'

'Are we still going to the school on Sunday?'

Margaret shook her head. 'No, he says not to bother, especially as it's Open Day the week after next. How did he put it? Oh, yes: "I know how fed up Dad gets with the day trippers' traffic all going at a two miles an hour – and if the weather's good, the road will be full of 'em."'

'Cheeky sod!'

'Well, he's right!' replied his wife. 'You're always in a foul mood by the time we get there.'

He smiled. 'Yes. I suppose that's true.'

'It would have been nice to see him, though,' she added wistfully.

'It's only three weeks to the end of term – you'll have him all summer after that.'

'True.'

'If it's a nice day, we'll go out for a spin and have some lunch somewhere. How does that sound?'

'We'll see. Now, I must go and have a look at the dinner. It shouldn't be long.'

Chapter 4

JOHN Taylor sat miserably in the sixth-form common room watching the steady rain.

He won't come now. Even if that stupid sodding letter didn't put him off, the rain will. Why did I ever say those things? He must have thought I wanted to end it – what else could he have thought? And now this rain. There might have been some hope if it hadn't bloody rained.

Despite his superficial acceptance that Peter was not going to turn up, John remained rooted to the spot, held there by a combination of hope and desperation. He kept setting time limits and then extending them; he pictured Peter sitting on Lancaster Bus Station, cursing because he had just missed the bus and had an hour to wait; then, he was getting off the bus, rounding the corner and struggling up the drive.

At one point, a bus did stop at the end of the drive and several people got off. John strained to recognise the figure that would surely turn in through the gates. One minute passed, then two, until finally he was left with the realisation that Peter was not coming.

More pictures, more excuses, flowed: the Halton bus had broken down; floods had made the roads impassable; there was a lightning strike by bus crews – all perfectly plausible and yet somehow palpably false. They were

Book One, Chapter 4

conjured up with the best of intentions, to put off the evil moment when John had to come to terms with Peter's non-arrival and the implication that their relationship was all off again.

The evil moment arrived seconds before an expensive-looking black car turned into the drive. John felt a surge of hope again until he realised that Peter could not possibly own a car like that. Then his mind returned to the contemplation of what had happened.

It was his own fault, of course. The letter had been stupid and dangerous, as if he were deliberately walking a tightrope for the first time and spurning a safety net. Disaster was certainly deserved, if not inevitable.

That car's nearly at the top of the drive now.

The questions posed in the letter had not been his to ask. Peter had surely come to his own conclusions by the time John had got to Oxford.

It's stopped.

It was unfair to attempt to reopen the debate. And if there'd been no question of a debate, then the letter must have seemed like a brush-off.

There's only one person in the car. I wonder who it is?

'What would you think if you got a letter like that?' John asked himself. 'You'd just seen somebody for the first time in two years, then he sits down the next day and starts asking you whether you love him enough. What a bloody cheek!'

He's certainly taking his time getting out of that car... Oh, he's looking for an umbrella on the back seat. Who on earth is it?

'And what are you going to do now? You spend two years eating your heart out – planning, working for another meeting by applying to the same college. Then you make a mess of it, just like a kid with a sand castle.' He paused. 'Good God! It's Peter! He's here!'

'I was sure you weren't going to turn up.'
'Why shouldn't I?'
'The weather for one thing ... and my letter.'
Peter said nothing.
'I shouldn't have sent it, should I?'
'No, John, you shouldn't.'
'I knew it as soon as I'd posted the bloody thing. I'm sorry.'
'Don't worry. It did me good in a way because it put down so clearly the things that have been worrying me ever since I knew that you were coming the other week...'
John's heart sank. So the doubts *had* been there.
'...but thinking about them clearly made me realise that we don't really have a choice in the matter.'
John's spirits rose slightly but he was already committed to his next remark. 'Some would say that if the doubts are there, the choice is too.'
'Well, the doubts aren't so the choice isn't either,' replied Peter, rather more sharply than he had intended.
'Though that doesn't necessarily stop us kicking against it.'
'That's true,' Peter said, laughing with relief as he sensed an attempt at conciliation. 'Though the sight of you certainly knocks all the fight out of me.'
John was not convinced; part of him felt that he had been right to ask those questions in the letter and that he had not yet got a proper answer.

Book One, Chapter 4

Peter, meanwhile, concentrated on driving his father's car. He felt tense, as if sensing John's doubts; worse, he felt aggrieved that his presence was not sufficient answer in itself.

The rain had stopped and the skies were clearing. They spent the afternoon in nearby Morecambe, riding on the big wheel and the big dipper, spending a fortune on slot machines and the dodgems and eating ice cream.

The only tensions now were physical: contact between them was exquisite agony, as if their need for each other was passing through their limbs. It had to be stolen in places away from the public eye: sitting, legs pressed together, on the big wheel or in the ghost train.

There was laughter born of self-mockery as two supposedly intelligent young men did everything expected of a couple of adolescents let loose at the seaside for the first time. But the afternoon was dominated by grinding, remorseless sexual frustration, serving to emphasise John's letter to the point of parody.

'Pity about the rain,' said Stuart Taylor, sipping his brandy. 'I fancied a look at the Dales.'

'It was such a nice morning, too,' agreed his wife. 'I could have sworn it was set fair for the day.'

They were sitting in the lounge of an hotel, enjoying coffee and brandy after lunch. It had been a beautiful Sunday morning and Margaret had readily agreed to her husband's suggestion of lunch out, followed by a drive and perhaps a walk. The weather had begun to change as they drove out of Harrogate towards Ripon and, by the time they reached the hotel for lunch, the first drops of rain were falling. Now it was pouring down and looked as if it would last all afternoon.

'It was lovely – much nicer than cooking.'

'Good. I'm glad you enjoyed it, love. I suppose we may as well head for home.'

'Are you sure you're all right to drive? You did have rather a lot of claret, you know.'

'Fine, fine. Don't worry – it doesn't affect me if I eat a large meal at the same time.'

'If you're sure.'

'Absolutely... I'll go and settle the bill.'

A few minutes later, they were on their way. The weather was appalling, with a slight mist created by the heavy rain; it was difficult to imagine they were travelling in the same season as they had that morning. Undeterred, Stuart proceeded at his usual brisk pace, headlights blazing. Margaret sat tensely in the passenger seat. There was a long straight ahead, and she felt the car accelerate. Finally she could restrain herself no longer. 'Must we go so quickly? You're giving me indigestion.'

She knew as soon as she had spoken that it was a stupid thing to say: it would have no effect on their speed – rather the opposite, if anything.

Stuart turned towards her and started to say something. He did not finish the sentence because in that split second they arrived at a bend just as a tractor turned out of a lane on the left.

A squeal of tyres, a rending crash, and it was over; there was only the sound of a wheel spinning, a hiss from a leaking radiator, and the rain dripping from the trees.

✢

'Why did you never write?' asked John. 'After you left, I mean.'

They were in the car driving back to Warton. Peter thought for a moment before replying. 'I don't honestly know. There was ... there was so much going on at Oxford. It was all so new, so exciting. Warton faded – it was like another world and you were part of that other world. I thought about you a lot at first...'

'Right. Thanks.'

Peter pulled the car into a layby. 'John! Try to understand. I'm a student, part of the real world – or so I thought. There was drink and politics, work ... and there were women.'

'I see.'

'You don't sound as if you see at all. What did you say in your letter? "An abnormal human and social relationship." Try to remember that. Here was I, a student at university, having little or no previous experience of life to hold onto. All I could do was conform – conform with the dress, with the politics, with the booze and—'

'With the sex.'

'Indeed, except...'

'Did you... I mean, have you...'

Peter gave a short laugh. 'Yes, I have been to bed with a girl, if that's what you're asking. Three times, to be precise.' He caught John's expression. 'It's expected! Can't you understand that? I can't say I enjoyed it. Quite the opposite, in fact. I was nervous, frightened even. I was drunk on two of the three occasions and completely failed to achieve anything at all the third time when I was sober.' He turned to look at his companion full in the face. 'It was awful, John. I was so embarrassed.'

John was trying to understand but could not. He was – angry? Jealous? He felt betrayed and frightened. He dismissed his thoughts as absurd; the important fact was that Peter was here, now, with him. 'I'm sorry, Peter, I shouldn't have asked.'

'And I shouldn't have bitten your head off. Why did you?'

'Ask? I don't know really. Insecurity, I suppose.'

Peter recalled his reactions to John's letter. 'Why insecurity?'

John sighed. 'I've spent two miserable years thinking of little else but you. Everything in my life reminded me of that summer term: the pavilion; the common room; the fact that another school captain – and then I – was standing in your place reading the lesson on a Sunday morning. And, of course, my room: the hours we had together, terrified that somebody would notice or there'd be a fire drill in the middle of the night or something. Then ... nothing.'

Their eyes met for a second then John looked away. 'I can't describe it. It was just terrible. At one point, I asked my parents if they'd move me to another school but I couldn't explain why, so they only laughed. Dr Benson spotted it and made me talk. He understood, thank God. If he hadn't, I'd have cracked up. He tried to explain your point of view rather like you've been saying this afternoon but I wouldn't accept it.

'Eventually, I calmed down and managed to lay your ghost, at least in public. But there were still times at night when I cried like a baby. Then came the thought of college; it was something to hold on to and work for. If I could get into the same college... It was eighteen months away but it kept me going.' He looked at Peter and smiled wanly.

Peter offered his hand. John took it and held it tightly. 'And now?' Peter asked gently.

'Now? I don't know. You walked out of my life once – you could do it again.' John shrugged. 'It's that simple and the prospect terrifies me. One part of me says that you will walk out and demands guarantees that you won't; another says that you won't, so there's no need to worry. And the third says that I can't have a guarantee anyway, so I may as well live for the moment.' He smiled, more firmly this time. 'I'm afraid that the first bit has been winning this afternoon.'

Peter squeezed his hand and then released it while he lit a cigarette. John noticed that he was shaking slightly as he struck the match. He felt a moment of gratification but quashed it quickly.

Eventually, Peter spoke. 'I can't deny that I was knocked off balance when I heard that you were coming up the other week. I was frightened because I'd seen what happened when you were labelled a queer. I was frightened of what it implied. I told myself that you – we –belonged to another world at another time. That I was normal. I could swill the pints, play rugger and screw women as well as – if not better than – the next man.

'There's always been a tinge of desperation about it, though. Something, somewhere was missing. When I got over the initial shock and realised what seeing your name on that list actually meant to me, it all began to fit. What I had lacked was conviction. That may sound strange but it's the best way I can put it. Life at college had become a matter of survival and, as I said earlier, the easiest way was to conform. But I began to notice that the others actually believed in it all. The beer, the football, the politics, the sex were all-important to them. Life was made up of those things and probably always would be. But not for me.

'Whatever happens from now on, that will remain true. So, in the sense that I walked out of your life from a need to conform, I can promise you that it won't happen again. You said earlier that our lack of choice in our fate doesn't stop us kicking against it, and you're right. I haven't stopped kicking against my homosexuality yet and I may never stop. But kicking against it isn't the same as running away from it. I love you, John. You've got to accept that I made a mistake two years ago, which obviously hurt you more deeply than I ever dreamed it could. But what matters now is that I've realised the mistake and I'm back – to stay.'

Saviour, to Thy dear name we raise
With one accord our parting hymn of praise...
Sunday evening chapel had not changed at all since Peter had last attended. He was particularly pleased that they were singing this hymn, always his favourite.
Guard Thou the lips from sin, the heart from shame
That in this house have called upon Thy name
The sun was still quite high and its beams slanted through the windows, picking out the boys in columns of light and dark, military in their precision. It was a sight that evoked memories, and, though Peter was not particularly religious, the simple beauty of the scene affected him deeply.
Grant us Thy peace, Lord, through the coming night
Turn Thou for us its darkness into light
From harm and danger keep Thy children free
For light and dark are both alike to the Thee.

The hymn was somehow appropriate, for the more he thought about the course John and he were embarking upon, the more he feared what could go wrong.

Grant us Thy peace throughout our earthly life...

A voice somewhere within him snorted at this, as if to say 'no chance'. He had avoided any reflections on the afternoon but accepted that there was a great deal to think about. His occasionally puritanical conscience still regarded his presence here at all as a signal failure to resist the temptations of the flesh. It was pleasant to be in love – but it was wrong. Everybody said so: God, the Bible, Society and – because both he and John were under twenty-one – the law.

An abnormal relationship. A couple of fairies. Poofs. Queers.

He shivered. No, it wasn't true. He was not a criminal. He had lived without John for two years; he could do so again. 'But what I lacked was conviction.' His own words acted like a blanket of foam on a burning match. And what of John? He could visualise only too well the suffering he had inflicted on him. The fact that it had been done unknowingly only made it worse.

Cowardice. He had dropped John because of his own spiritual cowardice. That was one in the eye for the puritan: in many ways, it took more courage to love John properly than it did to forget him.

The puritan laughed. That argument assumed that continuing with the affair was the right thing to do. Which it was not. So there.

As the religious service ended, so did the argument. Further struggles were futile. The decision was already made.

✠

After chapel, John returned to the place from where he had seen Peter arrive that afternoon. Whether in doing so he hoped to recapture the elation he had experienced then, he did not know. He was certainly feeling happy, but it was a warm glow: contentment rather than elation.

He had managed to reconnect with Peter after those two long years apart, and their relationship today had seemed as close and loving as ever. He now understood what had kept Peter from contacting him and sympathised with him over his fears for the future.

John recognised that they would face difficulties, and - in some cases downright hostility - in seeking to make their lives together, but after this afternoon he was more than ever convinced of his love for Peter.

His overwhelming memory of the afternoon was that it had felt *right*. Joking around, doing daft things, exploring feelings and explaining things, they just fitted together.

He remembered holding hands in the car, a stolen kiss, sitting close to Peter on the roller coaster and the big wheel, thighs and calves pressed together. He shivered slightly at the memory; he could not wait for them to get together during the summer holiday and then to be at the same college after October.

It was an exciting prospect.

Chapter 5

DR Arthur Benson, MA (Cantab), PhD, was nearly sixty; he had been at Warton for just over twenty-five years, fifteen of them as deputy headmaster.

He had joined the International Brigade in 1936, aged twenty-eight, a youthful idealist armed with little more than his newly acquired doctorate and a hatred of fascism. He had stayed in Spain pretty much until the end and it had not been a pretty sight. Given his feelings, it had seemed natural to jump straight into another battle against the fascists and so he immediately volunteered when war was declared in September 1939. The result was that, by the time he arrived at the school in 1943, having been invalided out of the Eighth Army in the wake of the Battle of Alamein, he had been on the losing end of one fight and been forced out of another. He had reached his mid-thirties with no more clue about what he wanted to do with his future than he had when he was fifteen.

Arthur was thirty-five when he arrived at the school. The appointment was a useful means of rehabilitation for him, and a help for the school in trying to overcome the chronic wartime shortage of teachers.

Warton, and a new wife, gave him the direction he so badly needed. He quickly realised how much he enjoyed teaching and how little he wanted to do anything else.

The Stamp of Nature

During the years that followed, he developed his own highly individual methods based on the firmly held belief that a really good teacher should not need to use physical violence as a weapon to impart knowledge.

The fact that he had not been to boarding school as a boy gave him a different view of the domestic side of school life. He defined this as the compassion of a spectator rather than the complacency of a survivor. Thus, many a new boy (or 'newt', the name applied to all first termers at Warton), who was finding it difficult to settle in, had cause to be grateful for Arthur's help and understanding. Some critics dubbed him as the 'newts' nurse' but this was an oversimplification; friendships developed with many of the young boys that survived adolescence and continued well into adult life. From these friendships the boys – including Peter and John – gained a love of Beethoven, an addiction to cocoa and a great deal of plain speaking.

Now, Arthur sat back in his chair and lit his pipe. 'It's nice to see you again, young man.'

'It's nice to see you too, sir,' Peter said.

'So how's Oxford?'

'Great, thanks.'

'And the cricket?'

'I'm in the university side against Yorkshire next week, so I suppose somebody must think it's okay.'

'Meaning you don't?'

'I've had better seasons. I don't seem to be seeing the ball as well this year.'

'Too much beer, I expect,' Arthur replied with a smile. 'By the way, congratulations on being selected for the Yorkshire game. I was really chuffed when I heard.'

'Oh, thanks. And you may be right about the beer!'

Peter retorted, laughing.

'And now you've met up with young Taylor again.'

'What? Ah, yes. I saw him briefly before chapel.'

Arthur roared with laughter, causing Peter to blush deeply. 'Oh, come off it, Peter! You don't really expect me to believe that you came all this way just to see me, do you?'

'I suppose not.'

'How do you feel about it?'

Peter's blush faded as he remembered how easy it was to talk to the old man. 'Pleased, I think.'

'You don't have to talk about it...'

'No, no. I do want to, but it's difficult to know where to start.' *And how the hell to say it.*

'Do you still have feelings for him?'

'Yes, yes. I do. Did you know? About us? Before John told you, I mean.'

'Well, it wasn't difficult to see.'

'And you didn't try to stop it?'

'Good Lord, no! I suppose if you'd flaunted it, something would have been said but you were careful – tactful would be a better word – and happy. In the end, we all have to work out our own salvation. For me to have interfered would have been unforgivable. If you'd been harassing twelve year olds, it would have been different but you were eighteen and John was a very mature sixteen. I thought the thing ought to be allowed to run its course.' Arthur paused to relight his pipe. 'If our revered headmaster had found out, of course, you'd have both been clapped in irons. Anyway, that's all in the past.'

'Yes, but now? How can you condone a Warton pupil going about with— being a qu— You know.'

Arthur's eyes were sad for a moment and he smiled wistfully. 'Sometimes, Peter, you worry me. You're so damned conventional! Can you really see me doing anything about it? Having nursed John through the last two years and seen the change in him over the last fortnight? You're both still the same people and everything I said just now holds good. John will leave here in three or four weeks' time. Good God, boy, he's old enough to die for his country; surely he can chose his own bloody sleeping partners!'

Peter blushed again.

Benson laughed. 'Sorry, that was a bit frank, wasn't it?'

There was no reply, only a cautious smile.

'Come on then: you say you want to talk. Spit it out!'

'All right. I do still love him. But I suppose what's worrying me is whether I should.'

'Does that question arise? You are what you are and that's that, surely?'

That damned phrase again – everybody's got it off pat.

'But what am I?'

'Only you can answer that, my lad.'

'I know, but I can't. One part of me keeps telling me that I'm queer. Another part of me refuses to accept it, saying that it'll pass. And a third accepts that I'm—'

'The modern word is "gay", Peter.'

'Yes, gay, and tells me to enjoy it.'

'What about when you're with John?'

'I don't know. The third bit takes over, I suppose, and I simply enjoy it.'

'That's the important bit, surely,' Arthur replied. 'If you enjoy it and feel good, then it's satisfying a need within you. There's no benefit to be had from fighting it.

You must come to terms with it.'

'Yes! But what has need got to do with love?'

'Good Lord, not the old "love sacred and love profane" thing?'

'Something like that.'

Arthur sighed. 'The man who coined that phrase has got a lot to answer for.'

Peter frowned. 'But surely it has some meaning?'

'Certainly – to repressed Victorians who thought sex was what the coalman brought every Wednesday.'

Peter laughed, despite himself.

'I've been married twice, Peter. I met my first wife while I was at Cambridge. It was an idyllic courtship. We read poetry – our own and other people's – sitting in punts among the reeds. We walked and talked and gazed into each other's eyes and every other damned cliché you care to mention. We married three months after my graduation and – not to put too fine a point on it – it was a disaster. Her mother hadn't given her any last-minute advice, let alone any facts. We spent the first hour in bed on our wedding night engaged in a biology lesson. It was terrible and then afterwards, she said, "Well, we don't want too much of that, do we, darling?" and went to sleep.' Arthur was quiet for a moment, gazing into the fireplace.

'She died nine months later bearing our stillborn child. I don't think she ever recovered from the shock of finding out what it was all about, poor girl. After that, I sat down and wrote my doctoral thesis and then went haring off to Spain to fight fascists. When I got back, I drifted about until the war came. I joined up and met my second wife on the last leave before I went to Egypt. We slept together that first night. Somehow, I ended up staying the week. We got married the week after VE day. She was everything to me: lover; friend; confidante, and helper. She was completely in love with both me and this school until the day she died seven years ago.'

There was another silence. When Arthur lifted his head, Peter noticed tears glistening in his eyes. He looked away, embarrassed.

'So that's your love sacred and profane, my dear Peter. Neither extreme represents love at all, really. One is worship of the most impractical kind; the other is just sex for its own sake. Love is somewhere in the middle – a chemistry of sexual attraction, friendship and fear of loneliness. And it ends up, like most things in life, as a compromise.'

'But that's normal love. Surely it's different for people like me and John?'

'No, Peter, it isn't! The emotions are the same, they must be. Only the sex – sorry, gender – is different. And that's something that is out of your hands, whatever you might think. Don't throw your relationship with John away because you're wondering whether you ought to love him. Whether you're gay or not is not a matter of choice, it's the way you are. God or fate made you like that and you can't escape it. Trying to hide from it will mean spinning a web of lies about your life. It will only cause heartache in the end. And, believe me, it's a damned sight easier to face whatever the world chooses to throw at you if you've got somebody with you. If you love John – and only you can decide that – then the consequences have to be accepted and faced.'

Arthur was silent for a moment. 'Now, the "Triple Concerto" and some cocoa, I think.'

Chapter 6

ARTHUR Benson strode along the corridor in a flaming temper. He had regarded the school's headmaster, Dr Roger Lawrence ('Jolly Roger') with undisguised contempt since a few weeks after the man had been appointed, ten years earlier. It was a difficult stance to take since people tended to assume that his feelings were born of sour grapes – after all, the man had been appointed over Arthur's head. Those who thought that, however, did not know Arthur well. He had given Lawrence every chance, but the first term had quickly shown that the new head was pompous, overbearing and generally incompetent. After that, the atmosphere had quickly degenerated into one of mutual mistrust, in which state it had remained ever since.

During those ten years Arthur had got used to most of the man's idiosyncrasies but to be summoned at ten o'clock on a Sunday night, as if he were a first former who'd broken a chapel window, was the limit. He could barely restrain himself from saying so as he entered the study.

Lawrence was a year older than his deputy. He was a tall, gaunt figure, one who had looked forward to a middle-aged spread only to find, to his great disappointment, that he was not going to get one. Indeed, his thin body and slightly dyspeptic nature had been emphasised by age and not helped by a painful duodenal ulcer. He sat now behind a massive mahogany desk in a study lit by one small reading lamp.

Arthur felt like a prisoner brought in for interrogation. 'Good evening again, headmaster.'

Lawrence peered over his glasses. 'Ah! Dr Benson. Do sit.'

Look at that! Not even a reference to the time of night.

'I gather that you know young Taylor, our school captain, rather better than most of us?'

That's a bloody stupid question for a start. You know damned well I do. 'Yes, headmaster.'

'I'm afraid that we've received some very sad news. I believe that it would be better if you imparted it to him.'

'I see.' *Consideration, at last? Or cowardice? Cowardice probably.* 'May I know the details?'

'Yes, of course,' Lawrence replied tersely.

On the journey to his parents' house, Peter felt more relaxed than he had done for several weeks. It was a splendid evening in which to be happy, with the bay providing one of its most spectacular sunsets. He smiled as he remembered the conversation with Arthur; it had marked something of a watershed. His doubts were at last resolved and the question: 'What am I?' answered.

'I am a homosexual.' He repeated it to himself, braced for the internal arguments that usually haunted him. There were none, so he said aloud, 'I am gay.' Nothing. 'I'm queer.' Still nothing.

He started to laugh. No more self-hatred or self-pity.

The encounters with Mark had been life changing.

Mark's experience and ability had opened Peter's eyes to a whole new concept, that sexual pleasure was something to be embraced and blended into life, not excluded as invalid or profane. Peter's only regret was that Mark had not been John.

He laughed again: the relief was as incredible as it was sudden. He wondered briefly whether it was too incredible and too sudden, but quickly dismissed the thought. He turned on the ignition and switched on the radio as the final movement of Beethoven's 'Emperor' concerto was beginning.

The music's exuberance captivated him and he burst into tears.

Then, it was over; the tears stopped and he became aware of his surroundings once more. He switched off the radio – nothing could follow that – and headed for home. His ears rang with Beethoven and his head ached appallingly but he did not care. He smiled and addressed the dashboard. 'I am what I am, and that's that.'

Chapter 7

THE sleeping tablets had done their work; John did not wake until nearly nine. It was now getting on for ten and he was still waiting for some sort of reaction.

He could remember the events of the previous night vividly. His annoyance at being woken by Arthur Benson, then sitting in Arthur's room, half-asleep and puzzled. If anything, the puzzle had been complicated further by the expression on the deputy-head's face, which was set in what was known as his 'forceful' expression: chin thrust forward and cheeks slightly redder than usual.

'John, I think you and I know each other fairly well by now...' the voice too had been different '...and you know that I'm not a man to beat about the bush.'

John had found it difficult to react; it was like a scene from a wartime film – terribly intense and rather hackneyed. It was only with a great deal of effort that he managed to keep his face straight.

'The headmaster has asked me to pass on some very sad news...'

It all fitted into place then, and John felt a slight shiver of fear. During the pause, while Arthur strained to find the words to continue, John's mind raced through a wealth of possibilities. The conception and dismissal of each one intensified the fear, like the steady closing of a vice.

'Your parents were killed in a car crash this afternoon.'

The words came in a torrent, as if their speed would somehow lessen their impact. John was silent; to his amazement, he found himself analysing both the situation and his own feelings, as though he were an observer in the room.

'Your aunt and uncle will be here in the morning,' Arthur said.

'Oh.'

'Meanwhile, Matron has suggested that you take these sleeping tablets.'

'Yes. Thank you, I will.'

'Here's some water.'

'Oh, thanks.'

Still no reaction. A delaying tactic, John supposed, as his mind tried to cope with the enormity of what was happening.

Arthur had taken him back to his room.

'Good night, sir.'

'Good night. And John.'

'Yes, sir?'

'I am so very sorry.'

'Thank you, sir.'

So, here he was the following morning, waiting for his aunt and uncle. Everything was packed; amazing how little there was, really, when it was all neatly piled up. And still the calmness persisted.

John had always found it easy to express his emotions; the fact that he had yet to shed a tear made him feel guilty.

Arthur swallowed hard and reached out to knock on John's door. He could not remember anything in the school that had upset him as much as this business. How the hell he had managed to get the words out last night he would never know. A couple of good, stiff whiskies had helped, but even so…

Now his feelings had shifted somewhat and he felt fear rather than sadness, concern rather than sympathy. For he had just met Auntie Ethel and Uncle Jack. They were incredible, it was the only word for them; caricatures from a seaside farce or a TV situation comedy.

She was a large woman with predatory features, dressed ostentatiously in black and snivelling constantly about 'our Margaret and our Stuart'. He was small and bald. He fiddled constantly with a cloth cap and resorted to such phrases as, 'Now, Ethel, don't tek on so,' and, 'There, there, luv, everything'll be awreet.' He convinced nobody, least of all Ethel, that anything he said or did could possibly affect the situation.

Arthur escorted the couple to John's room, speculating about what sort of greeting John would receive. There were two possibilities: an attempt at normality, such as, 'Ooh, John, haven't you grown?' followed by tears, or straight to the tears with no preamble. In either event, John would find himself enveloped in folds of black within fifteen seconds of Ethel's entrance, an embrace born of a sense of duty, of being seen to 'do the right thing', rather than any genuine affection.

Now, having braced himself as if the embarrassment would be a physical blow, Arthur opened the door and brought the bereaved family together. 'Your aunt and uncle are here, John.'

'Thank you, sir.'
God help you, John.

'Good luck in the match, love. And give us a ring during the week.'

'Right-o. Will do. Bye!'

The train pulled away and Peter waved briefly before turning to find a seat. Fortunately his parents had not questioned him about his late arrival the previous night and everything was perfectly normal as he prepared to return to Oxford.

When he had woken up, it had not taken long for the memory of the previous day with John to send pleasurable shivers down his spine. He had hummed the last movement of the 'Emperor' whilst shaving and then enjoyed a huge breakfast. Whenever he was about to return to college, his mother insisted on feeding him as if it were his last ever meal.

He found a seat away from the sun and settled down to contemplate the week ahead. He would have to write to John tonight; there would not be time before, with net practice this afternoon. Then the match on Wednesday, Thursday and Friday – pray God for weather like this. To actually play in a first-class cricket match! Incredible!

The train glided through the open countryside towards Preston and Peter felt a faint tug at his heart strings. No matter where he was going, he always felt a twinge at leaving Lancashire. It would always be home, whatever happened.

It had taken them nearly an hour to pack John's belongings into the car but now they were ready. There had been a few platitudes from the head, spoken in suitably lowered tones, a firm handshake and an offer of help from Arthur, and that was it.

The click of the car door could just as easily have been the slam of a prison door. For the first time in this whole nightmare, John's eyes glistened with tears as they drove through the gate and turned towards Harrogate. He craned his neck to see the main buildings disappear – virtually his whole life for the past seven years. He cried quietly in the back as Auntie Ethel talked funeral arrangements with Uncle Jack.

Chapter 8

AUNTIE Ethel organised the funeral with her customary brusque efficiency. It was ostentatious, overbearing and frighteningly alcoholic, punctuated by the organiser, large black hat askew and seventh or ninth gin in hand, proclaiming that 'we had to give 'em a good send-off' before dissolving into more floods of tears.

John cowered in a corner and got quietly drunk. He could not imagine a scene less likely to meet with his parents' approval. Their concept of style did not include a buffet of thick ham sandwiches and tinned fruit, washed down by unchilled sweet white wine and any spirits that the guests could find in the cupboards. This sort of wake would have been so painful, particularly to his mother, that he could hardly bear to think about it.

As for the actual service: well, that had been the limit. His mother had always been adamant that she wanted to be cremated. John was not so sure about his father but Auntie Ethel had ridden roughshod over such considerations. 'They'll have a decent burial, like the rest of the family, wi' a nice stone and an angel. I don't hold with this ashes and rose-tree business. Never have, nor never will.'

John had not argued. He could see that it was pointless and would only make the already strained atmosphere unbearable. But the incident still rankled and was a grim portent for the future.

When, inevitably, a distant cousin of John's mother asked, politely and merely out of interest (as she pointed out many times afterwards), whether everything had been left to John or whether other members of the family could expect a 'small bequest', a major family row ensued. It seemed entirely consistent with the rest of the proceedings and it failed to stem the flow of alcohol down anybody's throat. John staggered upstairs and passed out.

The next morning saw many sore heads and an equal number of mercifully blank memories. John awoke in a strange mood. Apart from a hangover, he had a feeling of anticipation. It could not be excitement, he decided, for there was nothing to get excited about. No, it was more a sense of impending doom. It was comforting to feel anything.

The silence over breakfast was at last broken by Uncle Jack, who gave a small chuckle. 'By gum, the Yorkshire bowlers took a pasting yesterday!'

John looked up in surprise. Peter! He had forgotten all about the match. He tried to keep the excitement out of his voice. 'Who got all the runs?'

'A new chap called Harvey. Scored a hundred and odd in his first game.'

'I know him! He went to my old school.'

'Really, how you two can talk about cricket at a time like this is beyond me.' Auntie Ethel started to clear the breakfast things noisily. Jack fell silent.

John left the room as soon as he could. He had to sort out the conflicting emotions that were confusing him so badly: pleasure at Peter's success; dread at the thought that he might never see him again; revulsion at the memory of

Book One, Chapter 8

the funeral and the company of his aunt, plus the sudden realisation that he did not know how he was going to escape from her.

Life suddenly assumed gigantic, impossible proportions. There was no weapon to fight it with – the practical side of his mind had nothing to offer, so fear predominated. The future was hopelessly uncertain and there was no mother or father to turn to, no Dr Benson, no Peter, only that insufferable, neurotic woman and her ineffectual dolt of a husband; titular relatives whose only bond with John (or his parents, for that matter) had been mutual disdain and mistrust.

As suddenly as it had arisen, the despairing moment passed. His mind switched off again. *I'll think about it tomorrow.*

'Well caught!' exclaimed a proud father. Arthur joined in the applause with a smile as the batsman returned to the pavilion. The school Open Day always left him exhausted and he usually managed a quiet ten minutes' doze during the school-versus-staff cricket match.

Today it looked as if the rapid fall of wickets would deprive him of that. He knew, though, that there was more to his inability to relax than the sound of applause. For this day, more than any other, was the school captain's. A formal speech at lunch, leading the school in the cricket match, and then hosting a reception given by the departing sixth form to staff and governors. One thing that was always borne in mind when choosing a school captain was an ability to handle Open Day; this year's choice, John

Taylor, had been automatic – and now he was not here.

Every aspect of the proceedings reminded Arthur of that fact and reinforced his sense of loss. He could not understand why he felt it so deeply; boys left every year and it caused a little sadness, but nothing like this. Even the headmaster had noticed; to Arthur's surprise, Lawrence had referred to John's absence in his speech at lunchtime.

'I suppose it's the suddenness and the tragedy,' Arthur said, heaving himself out of the deckchair and heading towards the tea tent.

He recalled the letter and frowned. The postmark and the familiar handwriting – it was definitely from Peter Harvey. There ought to be no question about it: it should be forwarded straight to John. But Arthur could not make up his mind. Could the lad cope, or was he in great need of Peter's support? Should Peter be told of John's loss? Not during the Yorkshire match, anyway.

'You're an interfering old busybody,' he told himself. But he knew that wasn't the crux of the problem; he was involved with them both and had to decide what was best. He sighed.

He acquired some tea and joined Matron at one of the tables. 'I can't settle, Dr Benson,' she said. 'It's the school captain's day and he's not here. Such a shame.'

Arthur nodded, smiling grimly. 'You too, Matron?'

Chapter 9

IT was the first day of the Varsity match at Lord's. The sun burned grass, spectators and players with a lack of mercy more appropriate to the Sahara than St John's Wood. Peter felt genuinely sorry for the Cambridge team as they took the field; he could afford to, sitting in the comparative cool of the dressing room. As third batsman, he was of course liable to be walking out there at a moment's notice and he hoped to be out there for a good long time – heat or no heat.

Nearly a fortnight had passed since his weekend at home, but nothing had happened to change his mood. He had floated through the days all but untouched by the brush of life's ripples, or even the slap of the occasional wave. His success in the Yorkshire match had made him a natural choice for this one and had been confirmed by two innings in between – less spectacular, but stylish nonetheless. His cricket was creative and free and matched his mood.

There was only one thing that concerned him: John's silence. Peter had written immediately on his return to Oxford but so far there had been no reply. Even that did not worry him unduly; he knew how hectic the last summer term could be. There would almost certainly be a letter waiting for him at home the following Wednesday.

A shout of 'HOWZAT!?' brought him back to the present

and set his nerves on edge. Here he was, at the most famous cricket ground in the world, dependent on one man's index finger...

'He's given him out! Oh Christ, that's a bloody good start!'

'Come on, Peter! You're in, old son!'

A frenzied rush – gloves, bat, last-minute adjustments to pads, good wishes from a sea of tanned faces, hurriedly hissed instructions from the captain – and there Peter was, striding, apparently confidently, down the pavilion steps, through the wicket gate and on to the hallowed turf. The applause, the cultured tones of the public address – 'Peter Harvey' – and he was at the wicket.

The scenery of the Lake District swept past, unheeded by the car's three occupants. Auntie Ethel was talking. Uncle Jack was concentrating on the road, slotting the occasional 'Yes, love' into his wife's monologue. John sat in the back and stared, unseeing, out of the window.

The funeral over, belongings had been sorted out and the process of winding up his parents' estates had been set in motion. Now they were returning to his aunt and uncle's home in Keswick. John had not been asked if he wanted to go, he'd been put into the car like an extra item of luggage. He realised that, even if he'd had the strength or courage to argue, he had nowhere else.

He was still numb. The brief moment of despair that had crept up on him the morning after the funeral had not recurred, principally because he refused to allow it. The consequences of thinking about anything other than immediate survival were far too dangerous.

They were entering the outskirts of Keswick, he noticed, and for some reason he shivered. Something to do with being off home ground, he supposed; at least home, if it could be called that now, had given him some sort of status – chief mourner or something. But from now on he sensed it would be different: he would be a guest, tolerated, but no more. It would be rather like staying in a Blackpool boarding house with Cinderella's stepmother as the landlady.

He smiled slightly at that and Uncle Jack, noticing the smile in his driving mirror, caught his eye and winked. The smile changed immediately and Jack froze at the vacant look in John's eyes. He was a sensitive man and could well understand the boy's feelings. He glanced at his wife still babbling on. It was just that he'd got used to her, he supposed.

'Clear the pitch, please, boys.' The many small cricket games going on around the ground were suspended at bidding of the loudspeaker as the fieldsmen emerged from the pavilion to scattered applause. They were hot and tired but not dispirited, since the match was evenly balanced. At lunch, the Oxford total had been seventy-five for the loss of that early wicket, of which Peter had scored forty not out. Now, as the bowler prepared to run up for the first ball after tea, the score stood at 195 for five, Harvey not out for seventy-three.

Peter was reasonably pleased. He was the first to admit that he was lucky not to have been out twice but he had survived. His job now was to hold things together, since the last recognised batsman in the side was in with him and another wicket could lead to a quick collapse. The result would be a poor first-innings total. Thus, his own innings was not the aggressive, swashbuckling affair that the Yorkshire team had suffered and, when he was eventually out at a few minutes before six, he was eleven runs short of his century.

Nevertheless, the consensus in the press box was that Oxford had a slight edge at the end of the first day and that they had this new boy Harvey to thank for it.

Oxford University 302 for nine.

Harvey eighty-nine.

'And so, with the news of that Oxford victory, we end this Sports Desk.'

Arthur switched off his radio with a smile. It was an excellent result, with Peter scoring eighty-nine and forty not out, and taking a catch as well. Those three days would be worth a place in anybody's memory.

He was also pleased that he had finally reached a decision about the letter. He had decided that morning that John ought to be able to cope again, and posted it on to the aunt and uncle's address in Keswick. It was a relief to get rid of it. Now he could enjoy the first couple of weeks of the summer holidays before time began to drag and he became impatient for the new term.

It had been the same every year since Connie died. The first few days were bliss as the most serene of silences descended on the school. But, after a week or so, the silence became oppressive; there was very little to do and nobody to see. He had even been known to get bored with his music. Still, he was used to things now and one never knew – he might get some visitors. John might come to see him.

'He certainly won't stay with that damned aunt for long.'

For at least the tenth time that evening there was a long pause in the conversation, and John became even more desperate. His companion was his cousin Pat, who had returned that day from teacher-training college for the summer. She was a pleasant, vivacious girl, very pretty and fashionably dressed. John detested her.

Back at home, Auntie Ethel and Uncle Jack had immediately plunged back into the social whirl. Tonight, it was a whist-drive at the Conservative Club. The two young people were left alone. Pat realised she was supposed to cheer John up but did not see why she should. Meanwhile, John had decided for some reason that she was supposed to lure him into marriage. It made for a difficult evening.

'What's happening about your place at Oxford?'

'I wish I knew.'

'I suppose there'll still be enough...'

'Money?'

'Yes.'

'I don't honestly know. I suppose so but everything's in a bit of a state. Dad isn't – wasn't – very organised about money.'

'And being so sudden and all...' Pat allowed her voice

to trail off, uncertain of her ground and frightened of sparking something off. There was another silence.

Finally, John could stand it no longer. 'Goodness, I'm tired! I think I'll turn in, if you don't mind.'

'Yes – I mean right, er, of course. Would you like a cup of tea or anything?'

John was half way out of the room before she had finished the question and a quarter of the way up the stairs before he uttered his refusal. Once in his room, he lay on the bed, his mind a jumble of faces, places and problems that he felt he had to sort out or go mad. Uppermost now was the phrase 'if only'.

If only all this had not happened. If only the tractor had waited. If only Dad had been going more slowly. If only they hadn't gone out to lunch. If only they'd been with me instead.

He stopped.

If only they'd been with me inst— THEY WOULD HAVE BEEN, IF I HADN'T INVITED PETER.

In a brief moment of clarity, John thought he saw the reason for his calm reaction to the news: it was his fault. His mind had switched off, unable to cope with the guilt. Now the realisation had slipped through almost accidentally.

He swung his legs off the bed and sat bolt upright. Tears poured down his face while he repeated the words 'if only' again and again until, exhausted, he fell back and slept.

Chapter 10

THE train lurched violently as it set off northwards from Euston. Peter's head magnified the lurch a hundredfold and he wished fervently that he had not accepted all that champagne the previous night. A violent stab of pain and another bout of giddiness left him vowing never to touch alcohol again. He shut his eyes to ease the pain and dozed for a couple of hours until the train pulled into Crewe. He awoke feeling much better and threaded his way to the buffet car for some coffee. He took advantage of a long stop to carry the cup safely back to his seat. Once there, his excitement began to mount.

He could visualise John's letter on the hall table: the flourish of the handwriting; the shape and colour of the envelope; the postmark, even the stamp. He thought about its contents. Would the letter be funny or serious? Neatly written or scrawled hurriedly? He smiled and put his head back.

Warrington, now Wigan, soon Preston and then Lancaster at last. There was a storm brewing over Morecambe Bay, tinting the sky a deep purple and making the atmosphere heavy, but it could not affect Peter's mood as he walked across the footbridge.

He could see his parents waiting for him at the barrier. His father, Brian, was six feet tall with bushy brown hair greying at the temples. His face was kindly and wise, or so Peter always thought, although witnesses under cross-examination in the Magistrates' Court did not always agree. His mother, Mary, was also fairly tall, with a trim figure, elegantly permed grey hair and a face that could still turn heads. At the moment she was smiling broadly as she caught sight of her son.

Brian and Mary were delighted to see him, and brimming over with pride at his success at Lord's. The journey from to their home village passed quickly as he was besieged with questions about the match; it was all he could do to think of answers as they neared the house and John's letter. Once there, Peter managed to walk calmly into the hall but betrayed his state of nerves by grabbing at the pile of mail which awaited him and dropping the lot.

Seeing the envelopes spread out on the carpet, he realised that there was no letter from John. He sorted through them twice but there was definitely nothing.

In Keswick frostiness usually prevailed at breakfast but the ice was distinctly thicker this morning. Even Pat, who was nauseatingly irrepressible as a rule, could barely raise a 'good morning'. John assumed that was to do with his rudeness the previous evening and shrugged it off.

The meal over, a tight-lipped, indignant Auntie Ethel handed him a letter. John immediately recognised Peter's handwriting, though it was overshadowed by Arthur's redirection. Then he saw that it had been opened. He felt the hairs on the back of his neck prickle with fear and anger. 'It's been opened,' he said flatly.

'Yes, of course,' Auntie Ethel replied, her tone self-justifying.

'What do you mean "of course"? It's addressed to me!'

'Now there's no need to take that tone with me, young man. This is my house. What matters is that we've – I've read it.'

'Oh, Christ.'

'You might well say "Oh Christ", you dirty little...'

'Ethel, that will do!' The totally unexpected intervention by her husband was enough to stop her in full flight. 'I told you that you were wrong to open it. Getting all steamed up about it won't change that.' He added, 'Anyway, the lad can't help it.'

Ethel recovered. 'Trust you to take his part. That's typical of you. It makes me sick to think about it. It's disgusting. Two men—' She paused for breath and emphasis. 'A nephew of mine a perverted little queer! What would his parents have said?'

'Shut up, you sanctimonious old cow! What would you know about my parents? You hardly ever came near us from one year's end to the next – and when you did come, we all dreaded it. You never had a good word to say for Dad, or me for that matter. It was always "Our Pat this" and "Our Jack that". What do you know about me or my mum and dad? You ... you just shut up and leave me alone!' It was a weak ending to a well-directed offensive and allowed for a devastating response.

'*You!* You talk about caring! Where were you when your mother lay dead and your father bleeding on the road? In your boyfriend's arms, I suppose. You were more interested in your precious Peter, weren't you? Well? Weren't you?' Ethel was screaming now. 'Answer me, you bloody queer!'

It was a random shot fired by near-hysteria but it had hit the target with monstrous accuracy, propelled by the guilt that had followed his own realisation the previous night. John stood tried and condemned in his own eyes; his aunt was now acting as executioner.

'Yes, damn you, you're right.' He collapsed into a heap of head and arms on the table.

'That's it, cry! Typical, that is. Well, you won't get any sympathy from me, my lad. I know what you are, and so do you! You're a *murderer!*'

The sound of Jack's hand across her face was like a pistol shot. John looked up, half-expecting to see blood and a gunshot wound. Jack caught his eye. 'I'm sorry about this, John, I really am.'

John left the room and fled from the house a few minutes later.

'Peter, thank you for trusting us enough to tell us.'

'I'd have had to tell you some time, Dad. Anyway, I'd rather you found out from me than through gossip or something.'

'That would have been terrible,' interjected his mother. 'I don't think I could ever have forgiven that.'

Without prompting, Brian Harvey handed his son a large whisky. He was more impressed by the boy's courage than disturbed by his 'sexual problem', which he was young enough to outgrow.

Peter took a swig from the glass and felt the warmth of the spirit calming his nervous stomach. He breathed deeply, trying to disguise a sigh of relief.

Book One, Chapter 10

That there might not actually be a letter had never occurred to him and the shock had been tremendous, forcing an abrupt change of mood. He had initially tried to pass this off as the effects of humidity ahead of the impending storm, but in the end he realised that he had to give some explanation to his parents. Suddenly the truth seemed best. He was surprised that they received the news so calmly. It could not be pleasant, he reflected, to be told that your son is homosexual, especially against the background of a raging thunderstorm.

His thoughts were interrupted by the doorbell.

'Who on earth is that?' asked his mother, her exasperation given added force by a clap of thunder.

'I'll go, Dad.'

The rain was still falling heavily, drumming on the porch roof. The figure at the door was obviously soaked to the skin. 'Poor devil's probably lost his way,' muttered Peter to himself.

Then: 'John!'

The act of ringing the bell had been difficult; John had walked past the gates of the house three times and reached the front door twice, only to turn back again. When, on the third occasion, he rang the bell it was only exhaustion that stopped him from running away again. Now, here he was, only seconds away from Peter.

'John, what on earth are you doing here?'

John tried to speak, but no words would come.

'Is there something wrong?'

Still silence.

'John, say something!'

Then at last... 'I've murdered my parents.' Then, nothing.

Peter regarded the crumpled heap on the doorstep. To his surprise, he remained calm – and grateful that he had chosen tonight to tell his parents about his love for this boy.

'Dad! Can you help me?'

'What's the matter?'

'It's John. My friend, John. He's collapsed.'

Mr and Mrs Harvey arrived on the porch simultaneously. 'Whatever's happened?'

'I don't know, Mum. He mumbled something about his parents being murdered and then passed out.'

'Let's get him upstairs. Mary, will you call the doctor? Come on, Peter, you take his legs.'

The doctor arrived and examined his new patient thoroughly. They were anxious minutes for Peter and disturbing ones for his parents as they recognised the depth of Peter's worry and hence the strength of his feelings for John. As so often before, Mary Harvey reflected wryly, her husband did not need to speak; he had a very eloquent way of raising his left eyebrow.

At length, Dr Castle's footfall was heard on the landing. Peter met him at the bottom of the stairs. 'How is he, doctor?'

'He'll live. He's in shock, with a bit of exposure thrown in. He must have been out in this storm for several hours. Have you any idea why?'

Book One, Chapter 10

'None at all, George,' replied Mrs Harvey.

'Peter said he muttered something about his parents being dead and then passed out.'

'Anyway, there's nothing more we can do tonight. From what I hear, everywhere is in chaos because of this storm. I've given him a sedative and I'll look in about ten in the morning. Perhaps we'll be able to find out a bit more then.'

'Fine. And thanks for coming so quickly, George.'

'Not at all. It's the 2 a.m. births up the valley that get to me.'

'I hope there isn't one tonight.'

'So do I. If it's across the river, I couldn't get there anyway.'

'We'll keep our fingers crossed for you.'

'Please do, Mary. Night, all. See you in the morning.'

'Good night, George. Thanks again.'

Chapter 11

WITH the morning came more wind and rain but John slept on. After breakfast Peter, who had hardly slept all night, looked in on him. He looked so peaceful lying there and it was only with difficulty that Peter prevented himself from reaching out to stroke his hair.

His mother opened the door quietly. 'Is he still asleep?' she whispered.

'Yes.'

'The doctor will be here in a minute.'

'Yes.'

'I suppose we ought to do something about letting somebody know where he is.'

'Yes. I found the letter I wrote to him the other week. It was redirected to an address in Keswick.'

'I wonder if they're on the phone.'

'*NO!*'

Both of them looked up in amazement. John was awake and looking absolutely terrified. 'Please, whatever you do, don't tell them where I am.'

'Why not, John?' Peter asked.

His mother left the room quietly.

John had been lying half-awake, dimly aware of people in the room. The word Keswick had brought him abruptly to full consciousness. Why that should be, he could not quite remember… All he was aware of now was Peter and a need to hold him.

Eventually, Peter spoke. 'Now then,' he said in a tone of mock severity. 'What's all this about?'

John did not reply immediately. He tightened his grip on Peter for a few moments and then let go. 'It's a long story,' he sighed.

'Do you want some coffee?'

'Yes, please.'

'Hang on a sec. I'll see what I can do.'

Coffee served and John introduced properly to Mary Harvey, the story came out. Hesitantly at first but later with greater fluency, John told the whole tale from the night of Peter's visit to Warton to what he could remember of the previous day. He made one crucial but necessary omission: the word 'murderer'.

Peter remained silent throughout, registering his reaction by the intensity of his grip round John's shoulders. The account of the previous morning's events left him shaking with anger, his eyes smarting with tears.

'I suppose I simply flipped,' John murmured. 'Obviously I couldn't stay there and I didn't particularly care what happened so long as I got away from *her*. I couldn't go back to Harrogate; there's nothing for me there and anyway she's got the house keys. Then I saw a coach in Keswick heading this way. and it seemed natural to get off in Lancaster.

'It was just starting to rain. I had something to eat and that used up almost all my cash. I can't remember much of the afternoon – I suppose I must have wandered around Lancaster. I think I set off for Warton at one point, but decided against it. I don't know. I probably fell asleep somewhere near the castle. I can remember it being dark and thinking of you far away somewhere. Then it clicked – you weren't far away at all! So I went to the bus station to see if I could get anywhere near you. I nearly left again. Supposing you weren't at home? What could I have said to your parents? Then the thunder started again. I was frightened, cold and wet so I decided that anything was better than wandering around all night.'

'I'm so bloody glad you didn't go away again.'

'So am I,' John said, grinning.

Peter grinned back then got up as he heard the doorbell. 'That must be Dr Castle.'

'How do we react to all this, Brian?'

Brian Harvey looked up from his book and frowned. 'What do you mean, love?'

'What about sleeping arrangements, for instance?'

'Oh. I see what you mean.'

'Difficult, isn't it?'

'Yes. It is really.' He paused, sucking at his unlit pipe. 'I suppose it all rests on whether we accept the facts or pretend to ignore them.'

'We can't pretend ignorance when Peter's told us about it. And he's probably told John that we know.'

'Yes, but remember they're both under twenty-one.'

'What's that got to do with it?'

'It makes any sexual activity between them illegal.'

'How stupid!'

'I agree, but there it is.'

'Yes, but that's not really relevant, is it?'

Brian smiled. 'Not unless they're caught.'
'Is that likely?'
'Hardly.'
'Well, then. You'd better ask Peter.'
'Why me?'
'You are his father, after all.'
'All right, dear. I think I know what he'd like, but he might not say so.'
'For fear of embarrassing us, you mean?'
'Something like that.'
'Then you'd better make it clear that it wouldn't embarrass us. It's entirely up to them.'
'Okay.' He paused again, looking at his wife as she consulted her knitting pattern. 'But would it?'

She looked up and frowned. 'Would it what?'
'Embarrass you if they slept together?'
Mary put down her knitting and stared into the fireplace. She smiled sadly. 'Of course it would, but I'll have to get used to it. He's my son, after all, and his happiness is important to me. I just wish he could... I just wish he could have been normal, that's all.'

A tear ran down her cheek. Brian put an arm round her shoulder. 'I know, love. I know.'

The letter arrived the following morning. It was addressed to Brian Harvey and upset him for the rest of the day. Had John read it, he could have told Peter's father that it was entirely in character. Brian had been inclined at first to think John's description of his aunt was exaggerated; it took only the first paragraph to convince him otherwise.

Peter's comment was brief. 'Good God.'

'Delightful, isn't it?' replied his father.

'What sort of a woman must she be to write that?'

'Evidently everything John said she was – and a bit more.'

'It's the sudden change in the middle that gets me. First of all she plays the concerned guardian worried about John and warning you of your son's naughty habits. Then it suddenly occurs to her that he might be staying here – and wow!'

'Never fear, my lad. She will receive a suitable reply. On office stationery.'

'Auntie Ethel beware?'

Brian Harvey smiled. 'You could say that.'

'Do you think we ought to show it to John?'

'No. We'll tell him that I've heard from her, but that's all. I don't think it would do him any good to read that poisonous rubbish. But what I would like is his power of attorney and an idea of what's happening about the state of the wills. Then I'll see what we can do about sorting them out and getting probate. Do you think he's up to that?'

'Yes, I think so.' Peter grinned at his father. 'You know, I always thought that having a solicitor for a father would come in useful one day.'

Brian laughed. 'Very condescending of you, I'm sure.'

Peter made to leave.

'Er, Peter... Whilst we're on the subject of John, your mother has asked me... I mean, your mother and I have talked about the pair of you and ... well ... the thing is ... about sleeping arrangements.'

Peter coloured slightly, while his father ran out of words. 'Yes, Dad, um ... I suppose we'd ... er ... like to be

... together, if you don't mind.'

'No, we wouldn't mind, providing that you two wouldn't be too embarrassed.'

'I think we'll – all four of us – get used to the idea.'

'Yes, you're probably right.'

'Thanks, Dad.'

They both became tanned and healthy looking over the next few weeks as they spent many hours walking through the countryside near Peter's home. One of their walks took them through nearby villages to the small market town of Kirkby Lonsdale. It was a perfect day, a slight breeze from the sea keeping the temperature comfortable. They had lunch in a small café in the square and wandered down to the river near Devil's Bridge.

'The river's supposed to bottomless here,' Peter remarked.

John laughed. 'You're kidding!'

'No, seriously. See how still and black it is?'

'Yes, but surely somebody must have found the bottom?'

'No. Want to try?'

'No, thanks. I'll take your word for it.'

They walked on for a while and then sat down on the bank. The river was much shallower here and raced across the pebbles. The sunlight pierced the overhanging trees to form fascinating patterns of light and shade; it was difficult to imagine that this was the same river which had caused so much havoc during the storm a few weeks earlier.

'Happy?' asked John.

'Very. You?'

'Yes, but— Yes.'

'But what?'

'I don't know, really. A sort of desperation goes with it. I feel a bit as though I'm on the *Titanic* having a great time, but the trip is ultimately doomed.'

'What's your iceberg, then?' Peter asked uneasily.

'I don't know,' replied John. 'I suppose I've lost all sense of permanence in my life. Everything seems rather...' He paused, searching for the right word.

'Ephemeral?'

'Yes, that's it.' John smiled, dismissing the subject. 'Now there's a posh word for a Tuesday afternoon.'

'Straight out of Oxford. That's what a university education does for you.'

'What? Makes you pompous?'

Peter laughed. 'You sod!'

'Come on, I'll race you back to the bridge.'

'Juvenile.'

'At least I'm not so full of big words that I can't run.'

'Right! I'll teach you...'

Chapter 12

'PETER, it's fantastic!'

Peter was delighted by John's enthusiasm. 'Have you never been to Scotland before?'

'No. My grandmother lived in Cornwall, so we always used to go there for our holidays.'

Peter restarted the car and they resumed their journey to the Harveys' holiday home on the shores of Loch Ness. It had been Brian Harvey's idea that they come to 'give everybody a break', as he put it.

'Particularly your mother,' he had added. 'Catering for two hefty eaters like you is hard work, you know. Besides which, I think she needs some more time to come to terms with it all. She – we both – like John very much, but he arrived so quickly after you'd told us. And anyway, I'm sure you'd like the opportunity to be alone together for a while.'

So here they were in Mary Harvey's car on the last stages of the journey. John was still happy, but had not been able to prevent a twinge of uneasiness when the idea was proposed. 'They want to get rid of me,' was his immediate reaction, though he quickly dismissed that as absurd and ungrateful.

Now, having seen the surrounding countryside, he was glad they were here.

The Stamp of Nature

The bungalow was more of a chalet, part of a row that had been built in the late fifties. Brian and Mary Harvey had been among the first tenants and had fallen in love with the place immediately. Brian had negotiated to buy a chalet, which was let with the others except during the months of August and September. There were two bedrooms, a kitchen, bathroom and sitting room, which had large panoramic windows over the valley.

As Peter showed him round, John tried to appear enthusiastic but it was difficult. As they had come through the front door, he had experienced a feeling of impending doom so black that it reminded him of his arrival in Keswick six weeks earlier. It was ridiculous, he told himself, but the shadow remained.

'You're quiet,' Peter remarked.

'Am I? Sorry. I'm hungry and a bit tired. You must be exhausted after driving all that way.'

'A bit tired but not too bad. But I am hungry. Let's get washed and go and find some dinner.'

'I thought we'd have to cook.'

'There's a hotel in the village. I think we'll treat ourselves as it's our first night.'

'Great!'

John picked at his steak miserably.

'Eat up, sunshine. I thought you said you were hungry.'

'Well, I'm not now.'

'Oh, all right,' replied Peter equably, as he attacked half a duckling.

John forced himself to eat, suddenly ashamed of his bad

temper. The steak was excellent and it would be a shame to waste it. Even so, it did not help his mood. He told himself it was tiredness but that was not true. He had been knocked off balance by their welcome at the hotel.

As they walked through the car park and into the garden, a stunningly pretty girl was clipping roses. She was tall and tanned, wearing a simple summer dress and large straw hat. Peter greeted her. 'Hello, Aileen.'

'Peter!' She dropped her basket and ran to him, arms outstretched. They embraced and kissed. 'Why ever didn't you tell us you were coming?'

'It was a last-minute decision.'

'Stuff and nonsense! Have you not heard of telephones? We'd have laid on a special welcome for a cricketing hero!'

'Oh, that. Don't be daft. You heathen Scots aren't interested in cricket!'

'Well, this one is,' she replied, laughing. 'Now come in and see Mum and Dad.' She grabbed his hand.

'Aileen, this is John, a friend of mine.'

'Hello, John,' she said, with a dazzling smile. 'Welcome to the Glen Arms.'

'How do you do, Aileen.'

'God, you are in a funny mood tonight.' Peter's words brought John back to the present. 'I've been talking away for the last five minutes and you haven't heard a word, have you?'

John managed a smile. 'I'm sorry. Very tired, that's all.' The smile left his face as Aileen approached the table.

'Peter, your father's on the phone. He'd like a word with both of you.'

They looked at each other, puzzled, and left the table.

'Hello, Dad?'

'Hello, Peter. You arrived safely, then?'
'Yes, about six. It was a very good journey.'
'How's John?'
'Oh, he's fine. A bit tired after the travelling, I think.'
'Listen, Peter I've got some news for him, about his parents' estate. Would you like to tell him, or shall 1?'
'Is it good or bad?'
'Fifty thousand plus the proceeds from the house. That's net of tax.'
'Fantastic! Oh, that's really marvellous news! You can tell him yourself. I'll put him on ... and Dad?'
'Yes?'
'Thanks.'
'Don't be daft. 'Bye now.'
'Right, 'bye then. Here's John.'

Peter handed him the phone and winked. John was now more puzzled than ever.

'Hello, Mr Harvey.'
'Hello, John. You all right?'
'Yes, fine thanks. As Peter says, a bit tired. And you?'
'Very well, thanks. John, I've got some news about your father's estate. That's why I'm ringing. You'll inherit fifty thousand after tax, plus the proceeds from the sale of the house.'

John was struck dumb.

'Hello? John, are you still there?'
'What? Yes. Sorry. I was a bit taken aback, that's all. I had no idea it would be that much.'
'Not fantastic by today's standards but it'll give you a bit of independence.'
'Yes, indeed. Well, thanks very much. I don't know how I can ever thank you for all you've done.'

'Nonsense, John. It was a pleasure. We couldn't let that aunt of yours get her hands on it, could we?'

John laughed. 'Certainly not. Thanks again, Mr Harvey.'

'Have a good time up there, and we'll see you in a couple of weeks. Cheerio.'

Peter could hardly get him out of the hotel quickly enough. He was brief in his goodnight to Aileen, almost to the point of rudeness, and they ran back to the chalet.

John laughed through his breathlessness. 'What was that all about?'

'I wanted so much to hug and kiss you and I couldn't in there.'

'Ha!' John laughed. 'I know you. You're only after my money!'

'You sod!' Peter chased him round the room and into the bedroom. They fell onto the bed laughing and then kissed, long and hard.

John emerged breathless again. 'God, I love you,' he said.

Peter woke up about two the next morning. The bed next to him was empty and cold. In the moonlight, he could see John sitting on a chair across the room, crying softly. 'What's up, John?'

'Nothing. Go back to sleep.'

'Come off it,' Peter said gently, getting out of bed and going over to him. 'There must be something wrong – I've been listening to you for nearly five minutes. What's upset you?'

'I don't know. I suppose it's the news about the wills.

It seems to have brought it all back. I can't stop thinking about Mum and Dad, and how they should have been with me that Sunday.'

John had been less than frank in telling his story after his arrival at the Harvey household. Even in the condition he was, he had felt his guilt was a private matter. Now, in the middle of the night when he was feeling more sorry for himself than anything else, he let it slip.

'What do you mean?' asked Peter, striving to keep his voice gentle.

'Nothing. I'm sorry. I shouldn't have said that.' But it was too late.

Peter took him by the shoulders. 'Hang on. Don't make statements that you won't explain. Are you saying that they should have been at Warton instead of me? And they wouldn't have been dead if they had been?'

'Yes.'

'Christ, John.'

'Auntie Ethel guessed, you see. That's why I was in such a state that day. She called me a murderer and she was right.'

'*No, John!*'

'Yes! I killed them, just as surely as if I'd driven that bloody tractor.' He began to cry again and buried his face in Peter's shoulder.

Peter could not think of anything to say. The lack of logic in John's argument was irrelevant; what John was feeling was cruel and unrelenting. For the first time since they had met, he felt inadequate; all he could do was to try and comfort John and help eradicate the memory. There was not much time, he realised, because the next step in this crazy situation was for John's resentment to be directed at him. From 'if only I hadn't invited you' to 'if only I hadn't met you' was such a short step.

Chapter 13

PETER was tempted to bring up the subject on several occasions. If they could not trust each other enough to discuss their feelings openly then it was a pretty poor relationship. But he held back, frightened of sparking off something that he could not control.

John, meanwhile, put thoughts of his parents out of his mind because he felt he had more important things to worry about: Aileen. Not satisfied that she and Peter had known each other for years, he was convinced that something deeper explained their easy relationship.

Despite attempts to talk himself out of it, the old mixture of doubt and fear returned.

The holiday passed pleasantly enough, as Peter rediscovered the familiar scenery through John's enthusiasm for it. The row, when it came on their last night, was something of a surprise to both of them. They had finished dinner and were washing up.

'Are you coming down for a farewell drink, then?' asked Peter.

'I hadn't thought of that,' replied John. 'Must we?'

'Aileen said something about a party and was most insistent that we look in.'

'She would be,' muttered John.

'What did you say?'

'Nothing. I'm a bit tired and I haven't started packing yet. Why don't you go?'

'Not on my own. It wouldn't be the same.'

'Don't be daft. She's your friend, after all. She's not interested in me.'

'Now who's being daft? She likes you very much.'

'Come off it, Peter. She can't stand the sight of me and you know it. It's you she's after.'

'After? What do you mean?'

'God, can't you see it? She fancies you. She's like a bitch on heat when you're around.'

'What a bloody nasty thing to say!'

Instinctively, John knew he had gone too far but he couldn't stop. He laughed sarcastically. 'Go on, Peter, you must have thought about it. After all, you are a bit AC/DC, aren't you? And you know what they say: a change is as good as a rest.'

'You bastard. You fucking bastard.' And with that, Peter planted his fist firmly on John's chin and walked out.

'John? John, are you all right?'

John stirred sleepily and looked at his watch. To his surprise, it was only ten thirty; he seemed to have been asleep for hours. Before he could reply, Peter was standing in the doorway of the bedroom, silhouetted in the shaft of light from the hall.

'John, I'm so—'

'Don't say it. Just come here.'

Peter sat on the edge of the bed.

'No, closer.'

He lay on the bed, enfolded in John's arms.

'Peter, I'm sorry. I should never have said that.'

'That's as may be, but I certainly shouldn't have hit you. There's no excuse for that.'

'Oh, I don't know. I rather enjoyed it.' John laughed as Peter looked at him in amazement. 'No, seriously. I deserved it. I am such an idiot sometimes.'

'Did you mean what you said? About Aileen, I mean.'

'Not really. I admit that I don't like her and I don't think she likes me. And the way you two get on makes me feel out of things – jealous, I suppose.'

'Well, that's my fault,' replied Peter ruefully.

'Don't be silly. It's only me and my stupid insecurity.'

'No, it *is* my fault. I should have explained. The reason she seemed to behave oddly was that she knew about us and was a bit embarrassed. I'd forgotten until we arrived and I saw her face when I introduced you. Two years ago, when we here, I was so miserable and depressed that she wanted to know why. I had to tell somebody...'

'Hmm.'

'Tonight was her engagement party. She's getting married next spring.'

John laughed. 'My God! You must despise me sometimes.'

'Don't be daft. I love you. As long as you keep remembering that, you'll be all right.'

Arthur let out a sigh of relief as he put the phone down. He had been worried sick about John, and it was really good to know that he was all right. The letter to Peter asking for news had been a last desperate throw and it had paid off; Peter had received the letter on his return from Scotland and immediately rung up to arrange a visit.

Arthur's pleasure evaporated and he winced as he looked round the cottage, realising what a mess it was. His cleaning lady was on holiday and he had never been domesticated. He tore round tidying, dusting and getting the tea things washed and ready, all at a pace that left him breathless when the doorbell announced the two lads' arrival.

'Ah. Come in, John, Peter. Good to see you both.'

'Thanks,' John said. 'How are you?'

'Oh, going along nicely, you know. Girding my loins ready for the new school year. Sit down, sit down. More to the point, young man, how are you?'

'Fine, thanks,' replied John shortly.

'And you, Peter?'

'Fine, too.'

'Good, good. You certainly look healthy enough. How about some tea, then?' asked Arthur. 'It's a bit early for cocoa, I'm afraid,' he added with a laugh.

'Tea would be fine,' replied Peter with a thin smile.

'And for me.'

'Splendid! I'll put a record on to keep you entertained.'

Arthur busied himself with the record and Peter recognised the opening chords of the 'Emperor' concerto.

Arthur bustled off into the kitchen. Once there, he leant against the door and sighed with relief. The tension in the other room had been almost unbearable.

John worried him. Superficially he looked well, but his eyes gave him away. There was a tinge of fear – almost desperation – in them and they were constantly on the move, as if to rest on one object for more than a few seconds would cause them pain. Arthur shook his head; there was something there that he would have to get to the bottom of, and quickly.

The tea-making gave him a chance to restore his equilibrium. When he returned, the two boys were standing at the window, arms round each other's waists, wallowing in nostalgia. 'Tea up!' he said brightly.

They jumped, suddenly embarrassed by their physical contact. 'And there's no need to blush, either,' Arthur added sharply. 'You don't embarrass me, so you shouldn't embarrass yourselves.'

'You don't get any less outspoken, do you?' Peter asked, grinning.

'Certainly not. It's part of my stock in trade.' Arthur began to relax for the first time since they'd arrived. 'Besides, it never did you two any harm, did it?'

'That's true,' John said, joining in the laughter. 'Though I didn't always think so at the time.'

Arthur poured the tea and sat back to light his pipe. He peered at John through a cloud of smoke. 'Come on, then. What happened? How did you two get together?'

John paused. He had realised as soon as Peter arranged the visit that he was going to have to tell his story again, and he couldn't bear the thought of reliving the whole nightmare. Yet he had also realised there was no way to avoid it.

Hesitantly at first, he told what had happened between leaving Warton and arriving at Peter's house. It was the edited version, leaving out Auntie Ethel's accusation. Arthur's reactions as the story unfolded were mirrored in his face but his eyes showed deep compassion.

Peter was angry at first, when it became clear that John was not going to tell the whole story. He recognised what John had to do; John's guilt had to be exorcised and if anybody could do that, it was Arthur.

Consequently, when John fell silent and before Arthur could comment, Peter intervened. 'There's one bit that John left out.'

'Peter, no! Please!' John interrupted, jerking forward to the edge of his seat.

'I'm sorry, John, but you've got to face it and get rid of it. And the only way to do that is to talk about it.'

'Face what?' enquired Arthur anxiously.

Peter looked at John, who sighed and nodded. 'When he invited me to Warton that Sunday,' Peter said slowly, 'he cancelled an invitation to his parents.'

'Oh, Christ,' Arthur interjected.

'His aunt guessed that and called him a murderer. Something that he had already called himself, and which he still believes.' Peter delivered the words in a monotone.

'Thank you for telling me, Peter,' Arthur said quietly. 'Now will you do me a favour?'

'Yes, sure. What?'

'Go for a walk or something for half an hour. I want to talk to John on his own.'

Peter was shocked when he returned three-quarters of an hour later. Arthur looked exhausted, suddenly an old man, and John was as white as a sheet. He looked questioningly from one to the other but got no response.

'Take him home, Peter,' Arthur instructed. 'I can't

The Stamp of Nature

convince him.'

They prepared to leave and reached the car before another word was spoken, when Arthur said quietly, 'Keep in touch.'

Peter nodded briefly and shut the car door.

'I wish you hadn't told him,' John remarked as they drove away.

'I thought it was for the best.'

'I know. But it wasn't.'

They lapsed into a silence that lasted well beyond their arrival home. Fortunately Peter's parents were out for the evening. After eating the salad that had been left for them, John asked to listen to some Tchaikovsky. They sat on the sofa, John's head resting on Peter's chest. Still nothing was said about the conversation with Arthur. They went to bed early and made love more passionately than they had for a long time. Finally John fell asleep in Peter's arms.

Peter willed himself to stay awake, and lay there watching John sleeping. He felt so *useless*. He loved John so much but there didn't seem to be anything that he could do to ease his pain and distress. He had been sure that Arthur would be able to help, but clearly not. He had to find out what had happened at Arthur's...

Eventually, he forced himself to relax. *It'll be all right in the morning. Everything will be all right in the morning.*

Finally, he slept.

It was early when he awoke but the other side of the bed was empty. Through his drowsiness, he felt a stab of panic. He found his dressing gown and wandered bleary-eyed down the stairs. There were two envelopes on the hall table, one addressed to his parents, the other to him.

Peter John Harvey had never woken up so quickly in his whole life.

He did not need to open his letter. He knew.

John had gone.

Book Two

Warton College, Lancashire.
Autumn Term 1973 – first half

Chapter 14

DR Robert Jordan sat at the breakfast table, staring into space.

'Drink your coffee, dear, or it'll go cold.'

'Hm? What? Oh, yes.'

His wife, Eileen, smiled. She knew his vacant moods: they meant worry. 'Stop fretting, Bob, everything will be all right.'

'First-day nerves, I suppose.'

Even so, as newly appointed headmaster of Warton College he had good reason to be worried, for the school was not doing well. Despite a full complement of pupils and a recently opened waiting list, morale was low among the staff and academic results were well below what they should have been. The reasons for this were complex, though many of them could be laid at the door of Lawrence, his predecessor. He had been an excessively strict disciplinarian, devoted to the preservation of the 'true public-school spirit', whatever that was. What money there had been had gone on sports facilities and showpiece buildings, such as the new theatre/assembly hall and the restored chapel, whilst the teaching facilities remained positively Dickensian.

The curriculum was woefully inadequate: only one modern language was available, and Latin and Greek were

Book Two, Chapter 14

still compulsory. The range of subjects for sixth-formers was far too limited as well. Fortunately, Bob had already managed to make a start: a second modern language was to be made available as an option to Greek, whilst A-level Economics was on the syllabus for the first time. Bob had also pulled strings and traded on friendships to arrange a business-studies course for the sixth with the local college of further education.

The governors had been persuaded to launch an appeal fund for a new teaching block, despite opposition from Lawrence who was now a governor; he wanted a swimming pool. Lawrence's appointment as a governor disturbed Bob. The early battle did not bode well for the future but he would have to live with that.

The most important change of all would be in the reform of the school rules and the abolition of fagging. Changes were being made – but would they be enough to drag Warton into the second half of the twentieth century?

Again, Eileen interrupted his thoughts. 'You're in *The Times*, dear.'

'Really?' he replied, wrenching himself away from the school. 'What do they say?'

'"Dr Robert Jordan, MA (Oxon), PhD, 37, takes up his appointment today as Headmaster of Warton College, Lancashire, following the retirement of Dr Roger Lawrence, BSc, PhD. Before his appointment, Dr Jordan was Senior Lecturer in Education at the University of Westmoreland, and a frequent contributor to both *The Times* and *The Times Educational Supplement*."'

'Nice to know you're appreciated, I suppose.'

'Yes, I think it's very good of them.'

Bob looked at his watch. 'It's nine thirty, love, and the

first of the new staff is due in a quarter of an hour. Time for work.'

'Okay. I'll clear away these pots and then I'll be in reception if you want me.' Eileen knew that he had not heard her; he was off in his own world again.

One thing that boded well for the changes, reflected Bob as he headed for his study, was the attitude of the staff. The eighteen survivors of the old regime had, by and large, detested Jolly Roger, and two of the four newcomers had been pupils during his time and therefore were unlikely to be admirers.

Barbara, his secretary, greeted him as he reached the study. 'Good morning, Dr Jordan. Lovely day, isn't it?'

'Yes, beautiful. Good start to the term. Any post?'

'Nothing urgent. There's confirmation from the agency that they've found a temporary replacement for Mr Royston. He should be here by lunchtime today.'

'Excellent. That is fast work.' Bob was relieved. One of his earliest problems had been the sudden illness of the head of English, Mr Royston. Bob had been anxious to secure a temporary replacement since the new timetable was tightly drawn.

'Yes, funnily enough he's another old boy of the school— Blast the phone, it's not stopped ringing this morning.' Barbara went to the switchboard. 'Oh by the way, the files for the new staff are on your desk.' His secretary was certainly one of the better things he had inherited from Lawrence.

Bob sat down in his study and lit the first cigarette of the day. He reached for the first of the files and read the label. *HARVEY, Peter John (Old Wartonian) ENGLISH/Assist Games.*

⁜

Book Two, Chapter 14

Peter rounded the bend, crossed the familiar canal bridge and pulled the car into a layby. To the right, across the fields, lay the school. From a distance, nothing much had changed.

He smiled, reflecting that the same could not be said of him. Seven years had passed since he had left, five since he was last there during term time – a fateful weekend that had probably done as much to shape his life as his entire time at Warton as a schoolboy.

He was still not sure that he was doing the right thing by going back. What had he to offer? True, the last year at college studying for his teaching certificate had been enjoyable; teaching was a challenge to which he had risen with no difficulty and much pleasure. But the four years before? The best that he could say about them was that they had started badly and did not get much better.

He could still vividly remember that August day, five years earlier. He had arrived at the school, brandishing John's letter and accusing Arthur of breaking them up and ruining their lives. Then he had listened to Arthur's patient explanation of why he had advised John to leave.

'I was shattered when you two arrived yesterday afternoon. John was like a time bomb that had gone wrong at the crucial moment: the slightest knock could set off an explosion. Oh, I know he looked healthy enough, but it was in his eyes. I shouldn't need to tell you how steady they are normally. But after you left school – I expect he told you – he went through a very bad time and that showed in his eyes, too. They darted about the room, never still, and he was always blinking. Well, it was there again yesterday. When you told me about his feelings of guilt, it all fitted. They are driving him mad, Peter – literally. When I asked you to go for a walk, I thought I might be able to talk him round but I didn't stand a chance.

'I hate to say it but you are the problem. You are a constant reminder of what happened to his parents. And despite that he still loves you, which makes him feel even more guilty. The final straw was that he didn't have anywhere to go if he *did* leave you. Add that little lot together and there was enough conflict to tear him apart.

'My nephew runs a private clinic down in Kent. John agreed to go as a voluntary patient if I could get him in, so I rang Bill and arranged it. He's on his way there now.'

Peter fought to retain his self-control. 'So I've lost him?'

'No,' replied Arthur quietly. 'Not necessarily. But you've got to give him time. If he gets over this and still wants you, fair enough. But I must warn you that the chances are fairly slim. If you want my advice, get on with living your own life.'

Arthur's advice had not proved easy to follow; back at Oxford, there were so many reminders of John's visit. Bouts of depression meant that Peter gained a mediocre degree rather than the good one that had been forecast. Arthur's regular bulletins on John's progress did not help, though Peter insisted on receiving them.

After university, Peter gravitated towards London. He had no clear idea what he wanted to do, so he drifted into the civil service. The job was undemanding but the same could not be said of his social life. He discovered the gay scene and set about exploring it fully.

Looking back now, he did not regret the experience but he felt no nostalgia for it. He met some interesting people and he spent some enjoyable nights, but in the cold light of day the fulfilment – the sense of *rightness* – he had felt with John was missing. Peter came to understand the gulf between a casual pick up and making love to somebody who you cared about. What he had lacked was commitment; he was not ready to commit himself to anything or anybody until he and John could plan their lives together.

The problem had been pointed out, several times and with increasing force, by Mark and Sally, his two closest friends from his university days. Mark had seen him through his last major crisis. It was not long before Christmas and Peter had not seen John for nearly two and a half years...

The weak December sun shone from a cloudless sky but there was a bite in the wind which blew down The Mall. Peter tugged at the collar of his overcoat. He had left Kevin, who he had met in a disco the previous night, at Victoria tube station with a promise to meet again that evening. Kevin was a nice boy, and might turn up...

Peter shrugged; there were more important things at the moment. That morning he had received his regular letter from Arthur. It was in his pocket, unopened, waiting until he could settle down somewhere and read it on his own. John had left the clinic almost a year ago and was making good progress with an external degree. For some reason, Peter was convinced that this letter would contain a message from John.

He removed the letter from his pocket, opened it and started to read. Suddenly he felt blood rush from his heart, flushing his face, and then just as quickly drain away. During the past few months, he had been prepared for

The Stamp of Nature

almost every eventuality. Except this one.

John was to be married.

Peter was in a daze as he walked back to Victoria and returned to his flat in Earl's Court. Once there, he went straight to his local. 'Whisky, please, Tom. A double.'

'Hello, Peter. Whatever's the matter? You look as if you've seen a ghost, mate.' Tom placed the drink on the counter.

Peter downed it. 'No. I've lost one,' he said and gave the sign for another drink.

Mark came into the pub about an hour later and found Peter absolutely plastered. He took him home and put him to bed for the afternoon. When Peter awoke, the first thing he saw was Mark's face. 'Hello, Mark. Where am I?'

'My flat. When I walked into the pub, you were on your seventeenth scotch, so I thought I ought to take a hand.'

'Christ, I must have spent a fortune.'

'Very probably,' replied Mark severely. 'But that's not my major concern. You promised, after the last one—'

'Oh, Mark, not now please! I feel so bloody awful.'

'What you need is a shower and something to eat. Help yourself, while I cook you an omelette. Then I want a serious talk with you.'

Fed and watered, Peter felt a great deal better.

'Now, you can start telling me why you were so drunk.'

Peter said nothing, but handed him Arthur's letter. Mark read it. 'Mm-hmm. That rather puts the cap on it, doesn't it?'

'You could say that.'

'Good.'

'What do you mean, good?'

'I mean just that – good. I'm pleased that John is now

properly and completely unattainable. And I bet Arthur's pleased as well, if all you tell me about him is true.'

'Thanks very much.'

'Oh, for God's sake, Peter! Stop feeling sorry for yourself!'

'What do you mean?'

'It's simple. When the Great Drama happened, it knocked you off balance. Right?'

'Right.'

'And you decided to wait for John, despite all the advice you were given.'

'Yes.'

'So you got a rotten degree, came down to London, drifted into a mediocre job and went on the scene.'

'We've been over this.'

'Right or wrong?'

'Right.'

'Well, now it's finally over and you've no hope of seeing John again. Right?'

Peter shrugged. 'I suppose so.'

'So now you've got to stop hanging around and start building a life for yourself, haven't you?'

'Yes, but where?'

'That I don't know, except to say that it's not in the gay pubs of Earl's Court. You can't let the fact that you're gay dominate your life. There's nothing wrong with having a good time – but there's got to be something else as well. Three years ago you were at university and doing well. You got your cricketing blue. You've still got the same mind and the same talent, so why not use them?'

Spurred on by Mark's advice, Peter had decided to try teaching. The vacancy that had arisen at Warton seemed heaven sent, a chance to get back to basics – or even perform an act of exorcism. So here he was, due to report to Dr Robert Jordan in ten minutes' time, to take up an appointment to teach English and help with games at his old school.

'At least,' he said to himself, glancing heavenwards, 'the weather's on my side.'

Chapter 15

BOB finished reading and glanced out of the window, noticing Peter's car. He had obviously been a very able and popular chap, reflected Bob. Strange that he could only manage such a poor degree at Oxford, though.

The intercom from reception buzzed. 'Yes, Eileen?'

'Mr Harvey has arrived.'

'Right. Could you send him up, please?' He shut the file and put it in his desk drawer. Peter knocked. 'Come in.'

Peter walked in, not knowing what to expect. The changes in the lower part of the house had started to unnerve him – and then he had met Eileen Jordan. Her frank, welcoming smile had knocked him off balance and seeing the new head completed the process. Peter expected headmasters to be old and venerable, kindly or irascible. This one dramatically failed to fit the bill: he was youngish, certainly no more than forty, over six feet tall, with a handsome, open face and a full head of dark-brown hair.

'Ah, Mr Harvey! Welcome – or should I say welcome back?' They shook hands.

'How do you do, headmaster?' Peter's mind was racing. *Christ! How on earth did he get the job? He's actually under sixty! The governors must have had a brainstorm!*

'Take a pew.'

'Er, thank you, headmaster.'

'Before we go any further, do you mind if we drop this "headmaster" business? I'd prefer Dr Jordan in public and it's Bob in private.'

Peter emerged from the study ten minutes later, thoroughly pleased with life. The head's ideas were unorthodox and would certainly encounter opposition, but Peter was sure that Bob's ease and charm would see him through.

The only slight worry was the sixth-form teaching; he had not been expecting that, and he was sorry that it had been caused by old Royston's illness. Royston had been largely responsible for Peter's love of English literature and he had been looking forward to learning more from him.

'You arrived safely, then, young man.'

Peter recognised Arthur's gruff tones, and turned to greet him. They strolled into the quadrangle together, chatting generally, before the older man asked the inevitable question. 'And what do you make of him, then?'

'The head? I think he's great – exactly what this place needs.'

'Hasn't wasted much time in turning it upside down.'

Peter smiled. 'Yes, but he's making changes you've been after for years, isn't he?'

Arthur grinned suddenly. 'Yes, and bloody glad I am to see them too.' There was a pause. 'I think ... I think he's going to be the sort of head that I would like to have been. I can't say fairer than that, can I?'

'No,' Peter said, impressed. 'You certainly can't.'

'My last year before retirement is certainly going to be an interesting one.'

Book Two, Chapter 15

By tradition, the staff assembled in the common room before lunch for a sherry reception on the first day of term. Peter and Arthur were the last to arrive. The room was relatively full – there were some wives as well – but even so, Peter's eye fell straight on him. Framed by the backs of two men talking in different groups, John Taylor was sitting on a sofa chatting amiably to Martin Fisher, another contemporary of Peter's.

He was dimly aware of a muttered 'Oh my God' from Arthur beside him, and then felt a tight grip on his arm. 'Stand fast, my lad. Stand fast.'

Peter's mind had stopped working as he attempted to grasp the horror of the situation. All he felt was an overpowering need to get out – out of the room, out of the school – anywhere, just out. But any move was forestalled by Arthur's grip on his arm and the announcement of lunch.

'He must be the temp for Royston,' muttered Arthur. 'I didn't know his name, only that he was an old boy of the school.'

Peter laughed bitterly. 'Now there's fate for you.'

They moved into lunch. Arthur had to leave him to sit next to Eileen, but it did not matter because Peter's conditioning had taken over. He ate his lunch, conversed briefly but politely with those sitting near him – but most important of all, he stayed. It happened against a background of whirling, unconnected thoughts and a churning stomach. But he stayed.

At the first decent interval, he mumbled an apology and headed for the quiet of his room. Whatever happened, he must not lose his grip; he had to allow himself time to absorb John's presence and form a plan of action. He was not left alone for long, though; there was a perfunctory knock at the door and Arthur rushed in, breathless and worried.

'God, Peter, I'm sorry. I wouldn't have wished this for the world.'

Peter looked at him and managed a wan smile. 'Don't worry, Arthur. It's not your fault. I should never have come back here. It was tempting fate.'

'Bloody nonsense. The same coincidence could have happened anywhere.'

'Yes, but it didn't, did it? It happened here at Warton. That has to be fate.'

Arthur sat down heavily. 'Yes, I suppose you're right. What are you going to do?'

'Leave. What else can I do?'

'Lots of things. In fact, the one thing you must *not* do is leave.'

'Why on earth not?'

'Well, for a start, what would the head say? For that matter, what would you say to him? Secondly, where else would you get a teaching job after only staying here for a day? Thirdly – and here's the real point – you've got to make a stand. Your affair with John is over. It was over five years ago. You do accept that, don't you?'

Peter nodded.

'Come on then. You can't let what happened dominate the rest of your life. Remember the happy bits, by all means, but don't let it ruin this part of your life as well.'

Chapter 16

Lord, behold us with Thy blessing.
Once again assembled here…

ARTHUR could not help smiling as he sang, reflecting that he must have sung this same hymn at least seventy times before in this same chapel. His eye ran over the people singing with him and he wondered whether Peter was right about fate; it certainly seemed to have brought Peter and John back together, opening at one stroke wounds which had taken such effort to heal.

Why did they all they come back? Besides Peter and John there was Martin Fisher, also starting this term, Ian Palmer now in his fourth year, and Stanley Sharpe. A return to the scene of the crime, perhaps. A search for the security they had lacked since leaving.

Come on, now. Your mind's wandering. Getting senile. Concentrate on the hymn.

Speed our labours day by day
Mind and spirit, mind and spirit
With Thy choicest gifts array

It was no good. There was too much to think about. Peter had calmed down considerably in the twenty hours or so since he had spotted John, and had at least decided to stay. Apart from anything else, he needed the money and he had admitted that it would have been impossible to give Bob Jordan a logical explanation for leaving so quickly.

Nevertheless, the decision did little to quiet Arthur's fears.

There was John to consider as well. Though Arthur did not particularly approve of the marriage, and had therefore rather drifted away from him, he still felt responsible for him and was worried about the new term. Remembering so vividly the traumatic events five years earlier, he did not relish a repeat performance. But he *knew* that something of the sort was likely, if not inevitable.

Across the chapel, John Taylor was also finding it difficult to concentrate on the service. The situation was embarrassing, to say the least, and his own reactions – a disturbing jumble of guilt, fear, affection and anger – did not help.

He was no stranger to guilt but this was new: a reminder of his abrupt departure from Peter's home with only a short letter of explanation. Fear and affection went together; he still felt something for Peter; that was obvious from the choking feeling that had hit him as soon as he saw Peter the previous lunchtime. However mild, this resurgence of affection was frightening since it only added to the doubts he felt about the months of treatment that he had endured in the clinic. His anger was directed at Arthur, who had dissuaded John from applying for the job that Peter now had. Now it was clear where Arthur's preference lay, and John was shocked at the extent of his own jealousy.

Being in the school with Peter would have been bad enough, but to be working closely in the same department … there would be some nasty moments ahead.

A few rows behind, Peter was equally unhappy. He had

made the decision to stay on Arthur Benson's admittedly sound advice but that advice was based on practicalities; his emotional repugnance remained. He dreaded his first face-to-face encounter with John; nothing good could possibly come of that and subsequent encounters. His peace of mind had been cruelly dissipated by John's reappearance. Having taken five years to put the ghost to rest, he would now have to start all over again.

The religious part of the service was over and Dr Jordan addressed the school for the first time. His tone was brisk, authoritative. 'Gentlemen. As you know, I visited the school several times last term and had ample opportunity to see it at work. Frankly, I did not like what I saw.'

A frisson ran through the congregation. Backs straightened, heads were raised as the whole school became alert. Even Arthur, John and Peter forgot their own worries.

'The school ran on the flimsy pretext of being, to quote my predecessor, "a bastion of true public-school virtues and the true public-school spirit", seeking, and again I quote, "accomplishment in team sport, the creation of a true esprit de corps and, of course, academic achievement". You will note, gentlemen, the order of priorities: sport first, the abstract concepts second, and academic achievements a very poor third – almost an afterthought.'

A ripple flowed through the chapel. One of the juniors whispered to the boy next to him, 'He's going to abolish games!'

'Don't misunderstand me. I attach great importance to sport and sporting achievement, and would never seek to restrict or abolish games.' The sigh of relief among the audience was audible. 'I would merely ask the question:

The Stamp of Nature

what are you here for? My answer would be that you are at Warton to gain an education. It is my job, and that of my colleagues, to see that you get that education. Of course, we must include the cultivation of a certain esprit de corps. We live in a complex society and we must work and cooperate with one another if that society is to survive.

'But, in addition and far more importantly, we must seek to equip you for your life after school. The world is no longer sharply divided into classes. You will not automatically become the leaders of your generation as so many public school boys have in the past. You will have to fight hard for your place. Now, it is fashionable to question the examination system and to question the value of the pieces of paper you get at the end of it. I share some of those views but I am a realist. As long as those pieces of paper have a value, I will see to it that you get as many as possible, and at as high a grade as possible.

'Therefore I would give you a revised list of priorities. Academic work, and the maximisation of each boy's talent and ability, will come first. Secondly, I want to introduce a new concept: self-discipline. It's a concept that will be of immeasurable value to you, particularly if you go on to university, where the exercise of self-discipline to sit down and do the work is often as demanding as the work itself. Thirdly will come athletic and sporting achievement.

'Towards these ends, I have already instituted several major reforms. The number of subjects available to you is to be increased, with the objective of broadening both your outlook and the scope for the best possible exercise of your talents.

'Next, I am instituting a major review of the school rules. This will bring about a considerable relaxation of

Book Two, Chapter 16

those rules, with a view to promoting self-discipline and self-realisation. I shall announce the results of this review after half-term.'

There was a stirring within the ranks of the sixth form and a brief hum of pleasure from the lower school.

'These are my initial reforms. They will, I believe, provide the basic framework for an education of a vastly higher standard than was previously available to you at Warton. I hope, gentlemen, that you will take advantage of those opportunities.'

The headmaster sat down and the chaplain rose to complete the service, but few were interested in the blessing or the dismissal hymn. Discussion and dissection of the speech were far more important. Conversation rose to a roar as the quadrangle filled: the witty imitated the headmaster; the flippant laughed; the traditionalists stamped, and the younger school whooped with joy at the prospect of more freedom. If Bob's objective had been to make an impression, he had certainly succeeded.

During the ten minutes between the end of chapel and the start of teaching, the excitement increased as breathless accounts were relayed to those boys not in chapel. In the staff common room there was a stunned silence, eventually broken by Ian Palmer. 'So, we're to have some new tablets of stone, are we?'

'Yes,' replied his fellow historian, Terry Fowler. 'Presumably the whole school will echo to the sound of carving for the next few weeks. Do you think we ought to pinch a "Caution, Loose Chippings" sign for the head's door?'

'It's all very well joking,' interrupted Stanley Sharpe. 'But you can't run an outfit without discipline. The army taught me that.'

Ian sighed. 'Ah, the SS has spoken.'

Arthur was amused but whispered, 'Careful, Ian. Let's not have a row on the first day of term.'

'Don't worry, Dr Benson,' retorted Sharpe pompously. 'I shan't allow myself to be provoked. Time will tell. Time will tell.'

'Personally, I agree with Mr Sharpe,' chimed in Martin Fisher eagerly. 'This was a fine school when I was here. I'd hate to see all it stands for being thrown away.'

Arthur looked at Peter and rolled his eyes. Peter winked, but said nothing.

'Well, it must have gone downhill bloody quickly,' remarked Ian. 'Because it's been bloody awful since I've been back.'

'From what I've seen, that's probably not a coincidence,' said Sharpe, leaving the room quickly.

'Ha-ha! Who's been having sarcasm lessons during the hols?'

'Terry, stop it,' snapped Arthur. 'We had enough of this sniping last term. At least let's try to get behind the new head.'

'Oh, I'm with him one hundred per cent,' replied Terry. 'It's the other buggers.'

'Yes, same here, Arthur,' said Ian. 'Though I can't help feeling that the attack on his predecessor was a little ill advised.'

'That's the understatement of the year!' said Fisher. 'Poor, I call it. Jolly Roger's a fine man and he was a good headmaster.'

Terry choked on his coffee. Fisher walked out.

'That's two against,' remarked Ian. 'Could be an

interesting term. Now, forward, Fowler! We have Our Message of Hope Through History to impart.'

'Good Lord,' remarked Terry, as he picked up his books and prepared to follow. 'He's waxing lyrical on the first day of term. Whatever next?'

Ian Palmer grinned. 'Don't worry. My enthusiasm won't survive the Lower Fourth.' He picked up his gown and swept out.

'Come to that,' remarked Arthur, 'very little does survive the Lower Fourth.'

There was considerable division in the sixth form as they prepared for the first lessons of the new term. 'I obeyed all the bloody rules when I first came, so why shouldn't this lot?' was one remark.

Another youth, Ian Thomas, was more severe. 'He had no right to say those things about the Jolly Roger – you should never attack a colleague in front of the whole school. All these reforms smell of socialism to me. If my father wanted me to have a socialist education, he'd have sent me to a bloody comprehensive! He'll have something to say about all this!'

'Yes, that's it, Thomas. Write to Daddy and he'll have the whole of the Monday Club marching up the drive.' This last came from a newcomer to the room. Standing no more than five foot six, with straight blond hair and a mid-Atlantic accent, Alan Kelly was the school captain.

'I might have known you'd support him. You always were an arse-licker,' retorted Thomas.

Kelly beamed at him and turned to the others. 'Look,

we've been at this school six years or so now and seen it get steadily worse. Now we've got a new head with new ideas. We might not like them all, but we've got to give him a chance. Just remember all the names we used to call the Jolly Roger before you start condemning Jordan too.'

Most of the others nodded in agreement and left for their lessons.

Chapter 17

FOR Peter, agonising about John's presence had given way to straightforward nervousness as he faced the prospect of taking his first class at Warton. He was not looking forward to it; for a start, it was with the sixth who would very quickly spot his shortcomings. And then there was the head's speech, discussion of which was bound to be more important than Chaucer.

As he neared the classroom, the Ian Thomas–Alan Kelly argument had resumed and was getting heated. Peter paused for a moment to listen. On hearing the words, 'Why, you arrogant little bastard,' he reached for the door handle and breezed in as if completely unaware of the situation, but noting the face of the aggressor.

'Good morning, gentlemen. Allow me to introduce myself. My name is Peter Harvey, and I am your new English master.'

'Morning, sir,' came a few muffled replies.

'Right,' continued Peter with false brightness. 'Can you tell me who you are? We'll start by the window.'

'Alan Kelly, sir.'

'Don't worry about the "sir". You're in the sixth form, not the first year.'

'John Williams.'

'Frank Wright.'

'Stephen Yates.'
'Arthur Frost.'
'Pater Baxter.'
'Ian Thomas, sir!'

Peter, who was noting the names down on a desk plan and attempting to put names to faces in between, put down his pen and looked up properly. 'I asked you not to use "sir", Ian,' he said mildly.

'Sorry, sir. It's what I've been taught to do, sir. By the way, I said my name was Thomas, sir.'

The rest of the class sat spellbound. Peter, shaking with anger, strove to remain calm. 'Who are you trying to make a fool of? Both of us, or only yourself?'

The boy remained silent. There were a few titters, quickly silenced by a glare from Peter. 'Mr Thomas, I asked you a question. Please answer.'

'I'm not trying to make a fool of anybody—'

'That's not how it looks from where I'm sitting.'

'I'm not, sir, honestly. We've been taught to be formal in class and I think that ought to be maintained.'

'I see. You're a believer in discipline and respect for authority, are you?'

'Yes, sir.'

'Good. So am I. Which is why I expect to be obeyed when I issue instructions. And why any further repetition of your insolence will be punished severely. Understood?'

No reply. The rest of the class were clearly enjoying the spectacle.

'Understood?'

'Yes.'

'Good. Right, let's get on with it. I understand that Mr Royston had progressed as far as the Chaucer and one of the Shakespeare plays. What I want to do today is to settle the choice of the remaining set books.'

'Ah, John. You're free now, aren't you? Could you pop up to my rooms for a minute?'

'Oh, er ... yes, certainly.'

Arthur found John's confusion rather amusing. 'Come off it, lad. I'm not going to eat you!'

John smiled nervously but remained silent until they reached the deputy head's rooms. Then he said, 'I suppose you want to shout at me.'

'Not really. It's happened now. And in any case, you weren't to know.'

'I would have done if you'd been frank about the job in the spring.'

Arthur glowered at him. 'What do you mean frank?'

'If you'd said that you didn't want me to apply because you wanted Peter to get the job.'

'If you choose to believe that, John, that's up to you. But it happens to be untrue. I advised you against coming back here because I thought it was asking for trouble, what with the memories you must have of the place. Peter got the same advice but went ahead and applied anyway. I didn't know until I saw his name on the interview shortlist.'

John looked crestfallen. 'I'm sorry.'

'That's better. Now, what are we going to do?'

'God knows. I haven't recovered from the shock yet.'

'I suppose that's understandable,' Arthur replied. 'I don't think Peter has either. How do you feel about him?'

'You still don't pull your punches, do you?' John

The Stamp of Nature

responded with a brief laugh. 'I hadn't thought about him for – oh, two years? – yes, two years. Then I saw him yesterday and I was choked, so I suppose there's still something there.'

Arthur looked at him steadily then said, 'So, what do you want to do about it?'

'Obviously the ice has got to broken sometime – and quickly. We're in the same bloody department so we can't ignore each other. I'd like – I'd like us to be friendly. Nothing more. But we can't have embarrassed silences all the time.'

'No, I agree. I think the first move ought to come from you.'

'I thought you might say that,' John replied. 'How about an invitation to dinner next week? I've found a bungalow to rent, so Kate'll be up at the weekend.'

'That's a bit strong, isn't it?'

'Oh, I don't know. Demonstration of domestic bliss but offering the hand of friendship. That sort of thing. You can come and referee.'

'All right – but I'm not convinced.'

'Neither am I, Arthur, but there it is. We've got to do something. If we don't, life will be impossible for both of us. And don't forget there are still a few people around who remember how close we were – Martin Fisher, for one. Don't you think they'll begin to wonder?'

'I hadn't thought of that. I must be getting old. Yes, you've got a point there.'

'How about next Tuesday?'

'It's okay with me. You'd better ask Peter.'

John looked crestfallen again. 'I thought maybe...'

'Yes, I dare say you did – but no. You've got to do the

asking or it won't work. I'm not sure it will anyway, but still...'

'Right, gentlemen. We've only got ten minutes left, so we'd better get a move on. We've got to choose two from three – *Luther, A Portrait of the Artist as a Young Man* or *The Caretaker*. Which is it to be?' He paused for consultation, which quickly got bogged down. 'Let's have a vote on it then. Those for *Luther* ... fine. Those for *A Portrait* ... great. And who votes for *The Caretaker*? Thanks. So, it's *Luther* and *A Portrait*.' The result was greeted with general approval.

'Let's have a look at the Joyce first. Has anybody read it?'

To Peter's amazement, Ian Thomas's hand shot up first.

'Good. What did you think of it?'

'It's disgusting. It's all about little kids and sex and masturbation and prostitutes. And it mocks religion. I think it ought to be banned.'

Peter's mouth dropped open as he listened to the tirade, but he noticed that the rest of the class sat back and relaxed; they were obviously used to this sort of thing. Mercifully the bell rang to signify the end of the period and Thomas was cut short.

Alan Kelly met Peter in the doorway. Peter shivered slightly at the boy's attractiveness, but managed to speak first. 'You're the school captain, aren't you?'

'That's me.' They shook hands.

'It's nice to meet you, Alan. I hope you'll enjoy the course.'

'I'm sure I will.'

'Hm, arse-licking again.' It was Ian Thomas.

Peter didn't have time to think about remaining calm this time. 'Mr Thomas! Come here, please.'

Heads turned in the crowded corridor. Thomas strolled over, smiling slightly. Peter deliberately remained in the corridor and the boy's smile faded.

The second form emerged from the room opposite as Peter spoke. 'I suggest,' he said loudly, 'that in addition to apologising to Mr Kelly for that last remark, you get hold of a copy of the Joyce we were talking about and write out the passages which offend you five times each. By nine thirty tomorrow morning, please.'

Thomas went scarlet.

'If you wish to be treated like a second former,' Peter continued, 'I'm perfectly willing to oblige.'

Thomas marched away angrily. Alan Kelly muttered his thanks and followed at a more leisurely pace. Peter smiled to himself, realising that he had rather enjoyed the confrontation, and set off for the staff room.

Terry Fowler fell into step with him. 'I must say that was beautifully done, Peter.'

Peter grinned. 'Thank you.'

'If you can quell Ian Thomas with a few well-chosen words, you won't have much trouble with the rest of the school.'

'I don't know about that. All you've got to do is remind him of his so-called respect for authority and he collapses. What happens when they haven't got any respect?'

'Thump 'em!'

They laughed but Peter's laughter faded as he caught sight of John coming towards them. There was a brief exchange of pleasantries before Terry excused himself.

'How was your first period at Warton?' asked John.

Peter sensed a heartiness in his manner which was new, and which he suspected was false. The thought of John's tension was strangely comforting but nevertheless he stammered and his voice was strained when he replied. 'Uh, um ... fine. Thanks ... John.' Should I call him John, or is that too familiar? Don't be so bloody ridiculous! 'How was yours?'

'Haven't had one yet. On my way now.'

'Best of luck, then.'

'Thanks. By the way, I thought you might like to come to dinner next Tuesday, with Arthur.'

'Oh ... er...' Christ! What do I say now? 'Er... Yes. That would be ... um, lovely.'

'About seven thirty?'

'Fine.'

'Great. See you then, if not before. I must dash, got the lower fourth now. Cheers!'

Again, the heartiness that was so obviously forced. Peter suddenly realised how difficult it must have been to issue the invitation and felt guilty at even having considered a refusal.

'Hello, Peter.' It was Martin Fisher.

'Ah, morning again, Martin,' replied Peter, recovering. 'How does it feel to be back?'

'Oh, very nostalgic – especially seeing you two together again.' Fisher's smile did not reach his eyes and he strolled off.

Peter stood open-mouthed and terrified for a full minute before retiring to the staff room for the strong black coffee and cigarette he urgently needed.

Chapter 18

'RIGHT, boys, come on now – into the pavilion and get changed.'

Thursday afternoon meant first-form games: sixty youngsters about to be introduced, or re-introduced, to the delights of rugby union football. Peter would be assisting Stanley Sharpe in these sessions, which was all very well in September but would pall on a foggy November afternoon. Still, it was all part of the job.

'Er – excuse me, sir.' Peter looked down to find a small, timorous first former thrusting a battered envelope at him. He took the envelope and opened it.

'I'm not supposed to play games,' the small voice explained. 'It's my heart,' it added sadly.

'I see,' Peter replied. There was a note of confirmation from Matron, countersigned by the boy's housemaster, Ian Palmer. 'Then you'd better nip back to school and report to somebody – Mrs Jordan first, I think. She'll know what you're supposed to be doing.'

'Yes, sir. Thank you, sir.'

The boy disappeared and Peter went towards the staff changing room. On the way he passed Stanley, already changed and running on the spot, a whistle bouncing heavily on his chest. 'What? Not changed yet, young Harvest? This won't do, you know! Got to be out here first or the little buggers'll run riot!'

A brusque reply sprang to Peter's lips but he contented himself with a brief nod. He changed quickly and returned to find the boys lined up, parade fashion, and being counted.

'Fifty-eight, fifty-nine.' Stanley frowned. 'Should be sixty. One missing.'

'Oh, yes,' Peter responded. 'One boy's excused games, Mr Sharpe. He's called Bailey, I believe. He had a note from Matron, so I sent him back to the school.'

'Excused Games, Harvest? Nonsense! Nobody's excused games in this school!'

'The note said he had a heart condition.'

'Pah! You're too easily taken in, Harvest!'

'The name is Harvey,' Peter snapped. 'And with all due respect, Mr Sharpe, I don't see how you're in a position to judge.'

'Judge? Twenty years in the Army taught me to spot a slacker when I see one!'

'I'm not going to argue in front of the boys, Mr Sharpe. I suggest we leave it for the moment.'

'We'll leave it for the moment, Harvest. But I shall see this boy when we return to school.'

Peter shrugged. 'Very well.'

Peter was exhausted by the end of the afternoon, drained by the combination of warm September sun and more running about than he had done for a long time. Not being on duty, he decided to miss tea and go down to the village pub later for a snack. He dozed for an hour and

The Stamp of Nature

then roused himself to do some preparation before setting off for the pub.

It was a glorious autumn evening, and the walk down the drive to the village was delightful. If only John had not been around... But he was, and that was that. Peter sighed; strangely, it was not as bad as he had expected. Bad enough, but the situation had not taken him over completely. They had spoken two or three times since the initial confrontation in the quad and it had been easier each time, though the matters they had discussed had been purely professional. Peter longed to ask questions like 'Why?' and 'Are you happy?' but it would have been wrong and achieved nothing. As for the rest of the time, there seemed to be more important things going on.

'Well, if it isn't young Harvest!'

Peter looked round in surprise. It was Terry Fowler. He was with Ian Palmer – the History Twins, as Arthur had dubbed them.

Peter chuckled. 'Don't you start! I've had enough with the SS getting my name wrong.'

'Oh, not wrong, sunshine,' replied Ian. 'It's your new nickname – Harvest Gold, after your shining locks apparently.'

'You're joking! Whoever came up with that?'

'Dunno,' said Terry. 'But it's stuck. Presumably the SS got things wrong as usual and thought it was your real name.'

'Would you by any chance be heading in the general direction of the local hostelry?' asked Ian.

Terry looked shocked. 'Mr Palmer, how could you suggest such a thing?'

'Easily, Mr Fowler. Harvest has a car, which he is not

using. He is therefore walking to the village and there's nothing there that could possibly interest him except the pub.'

'In the face of such logic I'd have to go now, even if I hadn't intended to!' Peter responded.

'Which you had,' said Ian firmly.

'Which I had,' agreed Peter.

The three of them set off together and established themselves in what the regulars called 'School's Corner' in the local pub.

'How was your first session with the SS, then?' asked Terry.

Peter shook his head. 'Don't remind me! The man's a bloody lunatic! I thought we were going to play rugger but he had everybody – me included – tear-arsing up and down the pitch for two hours.'

'Standard practice,' said Ian. 'Trying to find the boys with speed.'

'Yes, but why me?'

Terry laughed. 'Presumably you had a difference of opinion?'

'Yes, actually.'

'Hm. True to form, as ever. He's done it to me. The trouble is, you can't very well refuse in front of the boys.'

Ian glowered. 'I bloody would.'

Terry grinned. 'Yes, I bet. How did you upset him, Peter?'

'Oh, something and nothing. First of all I didn't change quickly enough, and then I sent a boy back to school because he was excused games.'

Terry laughed. 'Fatal! Presumably you got the "nobody's excused games" line?'

Ian did not seem to see the joke. 'What was the boy's name, Peter?'

'Christ, now you're asking. Boyle? Bowles? Barley? Bailey! Yes, that was it, Bailey.'

Ian looked grimmer than ever. 'I thought so. Did the SS say he'd see him when the period was over?'

'Yes. But why all the questions?'

'The boy had to be excused prep tonight. He wasn't at all well and was obviously upset about something. I thought it was probably homesickness but that seemed odd because he'd been settling in okay. It all fits now. You'll have to excuse me, gentlemen.'

'Where are you going?' asked Terry,

'To see the head.'

'What, now?'

'Yes, now. I want a showdown over this. The SS has done this to me before but Lawrence always sat on the fence. We'll see how the new man shapes up.' He walked out.

Terry raised his eyebrows. 'The shit, as they say, has really hit the fan.'

Peter felt nervous, though. 'I should have kept my mouth shut.'

'Oh, don't worry about that, Peter. There's been a row brewing between those two for over a year now. If it hadn't been this, it would have been something else. At least Ian's on solid ground with this.'

'I suppose so – but I'd rather it hadn't involved me, especially in my first week.'

'I can understand that but I'm afraid you'll have to get used to the idea. There's going to be a fight over the reforms and everybody's going to have to decide where they stand.'

Their food arrived before Peter could reply and the subject was dropped. They divided Ian's meal between them and ate in silence. Peter ate quickly and nervously, worried about the repercussions of the Bailey business. He would have liked to go back to the school and find out what was going on but it was none of his business and it would have been rude to dash off and leave Terry.

He finished eating long before his companion and sat back to look around. He found himself looking at Terry properly for the first time. In his late twenties, he had longish brown hair, a dark complexion and hazel eyes, which held a sadness but sparkled brightly when something amused him. A drooping moustache would have made him look every inch the Mexican bandit. Peter allowed himself a brief flutter of attraction but quickly slammed a door on the thought.

Terry looked up, caught Peter's eye and smiled. Peter blushed slightly and looked away, searching his pockets for a cigarette to cover his confusion. Terry accepted a cigarette, still smiling, eyebrows slightly raised,

'So,' Peter asked. 'How long have you been at the madhouse?'

'Three years, now. Just starting my fourth.'

'You arrived at the same time as Ian?'

'Yes. We were interviewed on the same day too and we both came in here to drown our sorrows, certain that we'd blown it. We met again on the first day of term and we've swapped insults on a daily basis ever since.'

'So I've noticed,' Peter replied with a chuckle. 'You seem to keep Arthur entertained.'

'Don't you believe it. He keeps us supplied with most of our material. Talk of the devil. Good evening, Dr

Benson, sir.'

'I see,' Arthur remarked. 'I might have known you'd be in here, Fowler, leading my protégé astray.'

'If he's your protégé, Arthur, he won't learn much from me.'

'Touché.'

'Pint?'

'Alas, a swift half only, thanks, Terry. I've really come to collect Peter. The head wants to see him over this Bailey business.'

Terry went off in search of Arthur's beer.

'I wish I'd kept my mouth shut,' remarked Peter.

'Don't be daft, lad. I'd have been damned annoyed if you'd said nothing.'

Terry returned. 'Here you are, Arthur, one half-pint. So the illustrious Dr Jordan is displeased, then?'

'Yes,' replied the deputy head. 'As soon as Ian told him what happened, he started a full inquiry and sent for me to help.'

'Anybody would think there'd been a murder.'

'If that boy had been forced to play games, there would have been.'

Bob sat in his study. He was facing a difficult situation and annoyed that it had cropped up in his first week. He and Eileen had been sitting quietly over the remains of dinner when Ian Palmer arrived, breathless and in high dudgeon. Though comparatively young to be a housemaster, Palmer took his job seriously. He had already impressed Bob.

After he'd calmed down and been plied with brandy, Ian

made his complaint. When he had finished Bob, though inwardly sharing his anger, questioned him closely. 'You say that Sharpe told Peter Harvey that he would see the boy when he got back. Do we know that he did?'

'Not yet. But it's virtually certain; our Stanley's nothing, if not a man of his word.'

'Yes, but I think we need to establish the facts. You say that the boy's in Matron's charge?'

'Mm – she came to me.'

'Had the boy said anything to her?'

'No. She said he was so upset that she couldn't make head nor tail of what had happened.'

At that point, Matron was summoned. No, she said, the boy was not so upset now. Yes, she had been able to find out what had started it. Mr Sharpe had summoned Bailey after tea, and told him that nobody was excused games at Warton and that he was going to be made a man whether he liked it or not. No, she had not spoken to Mr Sharpe about it and yes, the boy should be all right in the morning.

Bob was pondering his next move when Arthur arrived in response to an earlier invitation for a drink. Hearing what had happened, he expressed his lack of surprise. 'We'd better have a word with Peter as well,' he added.

'That's a good idea, Arthur.'

'He's down at the pub with Terry,' Ian interjected.

'Are they on the phone?' asked Bob.

'Don't bother calling. I could do with stretching my legs,' Arthur said.

Peter confirmed Ian's version of the afternoon's events, all of which left Bob with a potentially explosive problem that required careful handling. He was thinking through his tenth different solution when Arthur returned, as promised, from a late-night patrol of the dormitories.

'All quiet on the western front,' he remarked.

'Good,' replied Bob. 'Would you like a drink?'

'Yes, please. Straight Scotch, if I may.'

Bob returned with the drinks and sat down. 'Any thoughts?'

Arthur laughed. 'Plenty. And none of them likely to improve the health of our beloved games master.'

'Quite.'

'Still, that won't get us anywhere.'

'No, but it wouldn't half make me feel better,' Bob said, grinning.

'You realise, I suppose, that this is the culmination of a long battle between Sharpe and Palmer?'

'I gathered as much. Ideally, I'd like to remain neutral and bash heads together when staff fall out with one another but obviously I can't in this case.'

'No, I agree. Sharpe's clearly in the wrong, but telling him so will only make matters worse.'

'He'll see it as me taking sides, you mean?'

'Certainly – and he won't forget it.'

'The last thing I want to do is make permanent enemies at this stage.'

'I can understand that, but I wouldn't worry too much in this case.'

'How do you mean?'

'Sharpe's already made it clear that he's against any relaxation of the rules, and he's got wind of the fact that you put the kibosh on his beloved swimming pool.'

'How the hell does he know that?'

'Your predecessor?'

'Oh bloody hell.' Bob paused to finish his drink. 'Another?'

'No, thanks,' Arthur said.

'Well, I need one tonight.'

'I don't blame you.'

Bob returned with his replenished glass. 'What you're really saying is that since Sharpe is agin me anyway, I might as well give him good reason?'

'Something like that. Though I can see that it could be dangerous.'

'Yes, especially since carpeting him now would amount to a public slap in the face.'

There was a silence, which Arthur eventually broke. 'How about a staff notice?'

Bob frowned. 'I don't follow you.'

'You issue a notice saying that there are certain boys who, for various reasons, are not permitted to engage in certain activities. You list the names, including the various boys who don't attend chapel, the Jewish boys who are excused Saturday prep, and so on. Then you slip Bailey's name in.'

'Arthur, you're a marvel!'

Arthur became bashful. 'One does one's best.'

'Yes, that's it! Purely for information, that sort of thing. But what if Sharpe doesn't see it?'

'Don't worry. I'll make sure he does.'

'What about Ian, though? Won't he see it as another climb down?'

'You can leave him to me. He'll see reason.'

'You make that sound sinister,' Bob said with a smile.

'No, not at all. I'll threaten to put the pub out of bounds. No, seriously, he's behind you one hundred per cent on these reforms and he'll understand your dilemma.'

'Good.' Bob shook his head. 'You're a devious old bugger, you know. I'd hate to think what it would be like if we were on opposite sides.'

Chapter 19

IT was Tuesday evening of the second week, and the school was settling into the routine of the new term. Arthur's suggestion of a staff notice had successfully defused the first major row, though it had taken some intensive lobbying of both Palmer and Sharpe to ensure that the issue was well and truly dead. Arthur could not help feeling that it was only a temporary reprieve; things would get worse before they got better.

'Take tonight, for instance,' he said to himself, rummaging through a drawer in a fruitless search for his cufflinks. 'Nothing good will come from this dinner party, that's for sure.' He groaned as the doorbell rang announcing Peter's arrival. 'Hello, Peter. Won't be a minute – can't find my bloody cufflinks.'

Peter grinned nervously. 'That's all right. Take all night if you want to.'

'That bad, eh?' Arthur replied with an ironic smile. 'Well, I can't say I blame you. I'm not looking forward to it myself.'

'I can't think why John invited us. I was so confused when he did that I decided to refuse and then accepted!'

'I'm bloody glad you didn't refuse – that would have been fatal. At least this way I can say "I told you so". Aha! Found them.'

'Pity.'

'Come on, let's get it over with. You never know, you might even enjoy yourself.'

'No chance.'

The bungalow that John had rented was about three miles from the school, on the way to Morecambe. The drive took about ten minutes, during which time Peter's stomach tied itself into ever more complicated knots. According to Arthur, the estate was made up of retirement dream homes for Bradford fish-and-chip shop owners. It was difficult to tell one house from another and the concentration required to find the place relaxed the tension a little. Peter felt it returning as Arthur announced that they had arrived.

'Pity,' Peter said again.

'Best foot forward. Stiff upper lip and all that. Chin up, stomach in. By the left, quick march! Up, two, three, four. Left, right, left, right.'

'Arthur, stop it. John'll think we're laughing at him.' Peter pressed the doorbell. 'For whom the bell tolls?' he asked.

As John opened the door, Arthur spoke loudly. 'Ah, John! Sorry we're a little late! Couldn't find my damned cufflinks. By God, there's a good smell coming from the kitchen!'

John was bowled over by Arthur's ebullience and could only manage a brief nod in response before Kate appeared and the volley was resumed.

'Kate, my dear! How nice to see you again! It must be – oh – nearly two years! Still as beautiful as ever, I see.'

'Dr Benson, you're too kind. And this must be Peter. How do you do? I've heard so much about you.'

Oh, my God. Peter managed a half smile, gritting his teeth. 'Hello, it's nice to meet you.'

John took his cue from Arthur, clapping his hands and rubbing them together vigorously. It was, thought Peter, a grotesque gesture.

'What's everybody having to drink?' John asked, adding hurriedly, 'Sherry okay?'

'Yes, fine,' Arthur beamed.

'Lovely,' remarked Peter. 'Thank you.'

Kate disappeared to the kitchen. John poured the sherry, his hand shaking slightly. Arthur winked at Peter, who spluttered as he tried to light a cigarette and smother a giggle at the same time.

'Ah, thanks so much, John!' Arthur said, grimacing slightly at the dark, syrupy liquid.

'We don't drink much these days,' explained John. 'We've had this since Christmas.'

Peter took his glass with a nod and a smile.

'Oh,' John said flatly. 'I think we've got an ashtray somewhere. I'll go and ask Kate.'

'I should swallow your ash,' muttered Arthur.

Peter almost choked, trying to hide his amusement. 'Stop it, Arthur!' he hissed.

'I thought I was doing rather well.'

John returned with the ashtray. 'Rather well at what?'

'Oh, er ... rather well at – er – canasta. Yes, canasta. I've recently taken it up.'

'Really? How funny! That's how Kate and I first met! We used to play a lot.'

Arthur gulped. 'Really,' he said, closing the subject firmly.

John sat down at the opposite end of the room from Peter

and stared at the curtain rail. There was a silence. Kate came into the room and smiled regally. Another silence.

'Dinner won't be long.'

'Oh good,' Peter said helpfully.

'Well, isn't this nice?' enquired Arthur hopefully.

'Yes, isn't it?' enthused Kate.

'Mm,' remarked John.

Peter nodded.

'I'd better go and check on things in the kitchen.'

'Yes, I'll open the wine.' John followed his wife into the kitchen like a frightened rabbit into his burrow.

'Wincarnis?' pondered Arthur.

'Presumably,' Peter agreed. 'Medicinal purposes only.' He paused. 'You know, it only requires the vicar to arrive and lose his trousers for this to become the complete Whitehall farce.'

'Dinner is served, gentlemen,' John announced solemnly.

'I don't think I could stand television tonight, Bob. Do you mind?'

'Not at all.' It was rare for Eileen to ask him not to watch something, so Bob could hardly object. He got up and switched the set off.

'I seem to have seen so little of you this last week or so, except in the office,' she added.

'I know, love. It's been a bit hectic, hasn't it?'

'Yes, but things are beginning to settle down.'

'It's early days yet. I don't think we'll get into a proper routine until the new rules are bedded down. If then.'

Book Two, Chapter 19

'Bob, don't be pessimistic. Of course we will.'

'You may be right but I've got an uneasy feeling in the back of my mind. I suppose that letter from Ian Thomas's father started it.'

The letter had arrived that morning and at first Bob thought that somebody was playing a practical joke.

Dear Sir,

I have today received a letter from my son, Ian, informing me of the nature of his English course for the new academic year. He tells me that the course is to include a close study of A Portrait of the Artist as a Young Man *by James Joyce. Both my son and I have read this book, which we consider to be pornographic and sacrilegious.*

I would remind you that I pay considerable sums of money for my son's education. I do not do so in order to have him taught perverted rubbish of this nature. Therefore, I must ask you to arrange for this book's immediate withdrawal from the syllabus, so that reference of this matter to the school's governing body may be avoided.

Yours etc.

Col R L Thomas, JP (Retd)

Reading it that morning, Bob had laughed. Now, he was not so sure; it was frightening rather than funny.

'Yes, but the governors will back you. You said so yourself.'

'Sure. But ... oh, I don't know... I keep picking up little hints. And Arthur tells me that young Fisher has been openly critical a couple of times. I suppose what worries me is that we might end up with a formidable opposition party inside the school.'

'Yes, but surely you'd win?'

'Probably, but that's not the point. I don't want the school divided because things certainly won't settle down if it is. The latest round in the battle will always be more exciting than the next lesson.'

'Well, I think you're wrong,' Eileen said firmly. 'There are too many people around who can see how much good you're doing. They wouldn't allow that to happen.'

Bob smiled, dismissing his fears. 'We'll see. Now, how about a cup of tea?'

'Kate, that really was delightful.'

'Thank you, Dr Benson. It's a pleasure to cook for such an appreciative guest,' Kate replied, glaring at Peter, who had hardly eaten a thing.

Peter blushed and kept his head bowed. Kate had watched him relentlessly throughout the meal and he had never felt so uncomfortable in his life. He tried smiling back but that had not worked – his smile had been frozen by the ice in her eyes. Then he had glared back but his eyes had faltered first.

Arthur kept up his mood of expansive bonhomie throughout the meal and John had done his best, but the effort had been too much for both of them and they been unable to stop the slide towards disaster. And there was still coffee to get through. Peter shut his eyes in silent prayer.

Kate rose from the table. She decided to make one last effort. 'John, why don't you fetch that photograph album?'

'Which one?'

'You know, the school one. I'm sure Peter and Dr

Benson would enjoy it.'

The blood drained from Peter's face. He glanced at Arthur, who coughed and shifted uneasily in his seat.

John grimaced. 'Oh, I don't think so.'

'Nonsense! I'm sure they would.' She turned to Arthur. 'Wouldn't you, Dr Benson?'

'Er...'

'There you are, you see!'

John looked panic-stricken. 'Not now, love. Besides, I don't know where it is – I don't think we've unpacked it yet.'

'Yes, we have, I was looking at it the other day. There are lots of shots of Peter in it.'

'Good God,' muttered Arthur.

Peter glanced up to find John looking appealingly at him. That confused him even more. There was silence. Kate disappeared into the kitchen.

John found his tongue. 'I'm sorry. Tonight didn't turn out as I'd hoped.'

'No. Quite,' Arthur responded. 'Come on, Peter, I think we'd better go.'

Chapter 20

NEITHER Peter nor Arthur spoke on the way back to Warton and their goodnights, when they arrived at the school, were brief to the point of curtness. Peter was deeply hurt and very upset. He went up to his rooms automatically but took one look inside and left again; the idea of staying there, either to work or to sleep, was abhorrent. He returned to the car and set off towards Morecambe.

His immediate thought was to go to John; it seemed the only way to sort things out properly otherwise they would get worse and somebody would get hurt, probably badly. But what was there to sort out? John gave every appearance of being a happily married man; the tension between them was the result of something that had happened a long time ago.

Suddenly a remark that Chris Simon had made about one of the college barmen came back to him. 'I can tolerate queers so far,' he had said, 'but not when they get pathetic.' The memory made Peter shudder; it had been a horrible thing to say, but he understood what it meant. Now the cap was in danger of fitting.

He drove past the turning for the Taylor bungalow and continued through Morecambe towards Heysham. It was a drive full of memories: of Sunday afternoons with John, riding on the big wheel and eating candy floss; of childhood wonder at the illuminations, winking now in faded glory on to an empty promenade; of indulgent affection for a seaside resort which tried hard but never quite made it.

With no sense of purpose, he turned off the main road into Heysham Village and parked the car by the nettle wine shop in the village street. From there, he walked through the churchyard, climbed the steps and arrived at the top of Heysham Head, by the ruin of St Patrick's Chapel. It was a perfectly clear September night. Peter sat down on a rock and stared out to sea. Perhaps the only escape would be death. He smiled at the stray thought.

'But why not?' he asked himself. 'John seems to follow you about without being attainable. Suicide would certainly stop him following.'

'Yes,' replied another voice inside him. 'But you're too much of a coward to commit suicide.'

'What has cowardice got to do with it?'

'A great deal. Here you are; admittedly you've got problems but suicide would be no solution. It's an escape, and to achieve that escape you're prepared to inflict pain and suffering on yourself and other people. But escape into what?'

'Yes, better the devil you know, etcetera. I agree, but...'

'But nothing. Look on the positive side. You enjoy teaching. You're part of a team that's going to do great things with the school. You've got friends. You can be happy if you put as much effort into it as you put into thinking about John.'

Peter smiled suddenly. If anybody heard him sitting on top of the Head arguing with himself at midnight, they'd lock him up. Still, it had done him good...

The Stamp of Nature

To be or not be. That is the question.

He laughed, struck by the similarity of his own debate to Hamlet's. Only Shakespeare had put it much better than he did. And look what a sticky end Hamlet had come to.

Kate Taylor emptied the washing-up bowl and slammed it back into the sink. John braced himself. The washing up had been accomplished in fraught but merciful silence. He sensed, though, that he was now about to receive his wife's verdict on the proceedings.

'That was a bloody disaster, wasn't it?' she said

'Yes.'

'You didn't help. All those long silences. Couldn't you have talked about work or something?'

'I'm sorry. I couldn't think of anything to say.'

'And as for that Peter…'

'You didn't help there. You kept glaring at him.'

'Only to avoid looking at that horrible Dr Benson,' she countered petulantly.

'Come off it! He was charming to you tonight.'

'Rubbish! He tried but he certainly didn't mean it. He didn't like me from the start. You told me that yourself, didn't you?' John did not reply. 'Come on now, didn't you?'

'All right! Yes – *and* he advised me against marrying you, if you must know.'

'Oh, did he? Perhaps he's got some sense, after all.'

'And what's that supposed to mean?'

'Surely you – even *you* – can't pretend that our marriage is a success!' She swept past him into the dining room. He remained silent. 'God,' she said returning with a full ashtray. 'If I'd known that Peter smoked, I wouldn't have let him in.'

'Don't be daft.'

'Look at this, just look. It's revolting! You know, there's something odd about him.'

John blushed. 'Odd? I don't know what you mean.'

'I don't know myself, really, but there is definitely something odd.'

He retreated into the dining room but she followed. 'Yes,' she continued. 'Very odd.'

John did not respond to the taunt. 'I'm going to bed.'

'Still,' she remarked, as John reached the door, 'we can't have helped your chances of staying in this God-forsaken hole much longer, can we? I suppose that's one good thing.'

'Some help you are. Is that why you wouldn't shut up about the album?'

'Oh, were you trying to shut me up?' she asked innocently. 'I'm sorry, darling, I didn't realise.'

John snorted. 'You bloody well know I was.'

'I'm glad I didn't shut up. Tonight has taught me a lot.'

He blushed again. 'What do you mean by that?'

'Oh, nothing.'

'Don't say nothing like that! You meant something. Now – what?' He returned to the centre of the room and faced his wife angrily.

She smiled and patted him on the head as if he were a naughty schoolboy. 'Poor John,' she said and left the room, smiling sadly to herself.

John remained where he was for a moment, then went off to the spare room and slammed the door.

✧

The Stamp of Nature

Peter drove back to Warton and, to his surprise, met Terry Fowler in the car park. 'Hello, Terry. You're here late for a non-resident.'

'Hello, young Harvest! I'm on my way home. I've been doing a spot of house-sitting for Ian. He's courting, you know.'

'Really?' Peter replied, thinking that that was one theory out of the window. 'Is she nice?'

'Don't know – haven't had the honour yet.'

Peter nodded, then said, 'Fancy a nightcap?'

'It's a bit late but why not?'

They went up to Peter's rooms and retrieved a bottle of Scotch, a good-luck present from Peter's father.

'So how was your evening with the Taylor household?' Terry asked.

Peter shivered involuntarily. 'A disaster. Absolute, unmitigated disaster.'

'Too many skeletons in the cupboard?'

'What do you mean?'

'Shall we say that some of our older colleagues ... have ... um ... long memories. They've dropped gentle hints – and I tend to be rather perceptive about these things.'

'Oh,' Peter said flatly.

Terry shook his head. 'I'm sorry. That was pompous of me.'

'Yes, it was a bit.'

'What I wanted to say,' continued Terry quietly, 'is that I'm gay too and if you need any help – well, it's not far away.'

Peter paused, then smiled. 'Coffee?'

'Fine. Thanks.'

In his small kitchen, Peter leant against the door for a

Book Two, Chapter 20

few seconds, breathing deeply. He made the coffee and returned to the sitting room. Terry had decided to join him on the sofa. Peter raised an eyebrow but said nothing and sat down.

'Do you want to talk?' Terry asked.

Peter thought for a moment. He nodded but paused to finish his whisky and offer a cigarette. 'It started here – in my last term.' He told the story quietly and unemotionally, surprised at his own detachment. At one point, Terry's arm moved round his shoulders. He relaxed into the embrace and continued his story, finishing with his sighting of John in the staff room the previous week.

'And how did you feel last week when you saw him again?'

'Panic-stricken. I just wanted to run.'

'Understandably. But how did you feel about *him*?'

Peter paused before replying. 'Do you know, I haven't really thought about that? It was the horror of the situation that bothered me more than anything.'

'Try thinking now,' Terry commanded quietly.

'I don't know. I suppose that, if he were attainable, I'd go running after him. But he isn't.'

'Would you?'

'What makes you ask?'

'It seems to me that John's always taken the initiative – at school, and then when he came to Oxford. Whilst you were in London, you were waiting for him to make a move.'

'Yes, you're right. So?'

'If he's not going to take the initiative now, it shouldn't worry you. You can get on with the rest of your life. If he *does* come to you at some point in the future, you'll have to decide. But meanwhile…'

Peter nodded. 'Yes, that's what I've been telling myself, but tonight didn't help.'

'Ah, yes. But tonight was a monumental mistake. John should never have invited you. Don't you see – it was another initiative? And you certainly shouldn't have accepted. As for Arthur – well, I'm surprised at him.'

'I agree. But hindsight is the most exact science and all that.'

'True.'

'Anyway, it's over now. I went up to Heysham Head earlier on and gave myself a good talking to. And you've completed the process very nicely.'

Terry smiled and moved his hand to stroke Peter's hair. He pressed slightly, inclining Peter's head towards his own. They kissed.

'Are you going to stay?' whispered Peter.

'No, that would be dangerous. I know it's a bit sordid to remind you, but we do have to be careful. Are you free tomorrow night?'

'After nine.'

'I'll meet you in the pub and I can return your hospitality. You can stay the night at the bungalow, if you like.'

'Okay.'

They kissed again. Terry got up to leave. He smiled. 'Thanks for the drink.'

Peter went to bed and fell asleep, smiling.

Chapter 21

THREE weeks passed after the disastrous dinner party. As Bob had foreseen, the school was unsettled; everybody was waiting for the new rules to be announced and implemented.

Peter's morale was high. He had reached – and passed – his crisis on Heysham Head. Of course, the growing relationship with Terry helped, though both insisted that it should be kept at a friendly rather than passionate level.

He was also enjoying teaching. The sixth-form work was particularly rewarding, despite his initial nerves and Ian Thomas's obvious hostility. The rest of the group were intelligent and challenging to work with. They had taken to Peter and he saw a lot of them socially.

The keenest in this aspect was Alan Kelly, the school captain. Peter had many dealings with him as teacher, as a colleague in running Washington House, a fellow sportsman and eventually as a friend. It occurred to Peter that Alan might be seeking more than friendship, but he rejected the idea as out of the question.

When it did become clear that Alan was indeed seeking more from their relationship, it was not, therefore, a total surprise. It happened on a Wednesday evening. They had been playing squash, and were strolling back to the school. After a minute or two's silence, Alan spoke. 'Since we established last week that you're an incurable romantic, will you answer a question for me?'

Peter's romanticism, which he hotly denied, had become something of a standing joke between them. 'Okay. Fire away,' he responded with a smile.

'Where do you draw the line between friendship and love?'

The smile disappeared from Peter's face. 'Is that a question or a declaration?'

'A declaration.'

They stopped and faced each other. Peter found the frankness behind Alan's eyes terrifying. 'Yes, I was afraid it might be.'

'Aren't you going to answer the question?'

'Yes, but not here. Dump your kit and come to my rooms.'

Alan smirked. 'All right.'

'And you can wipe that look off your face as well.'

'Oh.'

When Peter got to his rooms, he poured a large drink, sat down and lit a cigarette. He was striving to get his thoughts into some sort of order. It was not every day that he was propositioned by such an attractive young man, and he knew that he should refuse the offer lightly. But it had to be refused – there could be no question of anything else. The question was how. Not by denying that he was gay, that was certain, and not by pretending that he found Alan unattractive. And certainly not harshly, because he did feel something for the boy.

There was no chance to think it through any further as he heard a knock on the door. 'Come in, Alan. Sit down.'

The school captain was surprised by Peter's cold tone.

'Well, young sir.' Peter gave a small smile.

Alan relaxed. That was better.

'You don't mince your words, do you?'

There was no reply.

Peter took a deep breath. 'Look, Alan, cards on the table. Yes, I am gay. Yes, I am attracted to you and could cheerfully take you to bed right now.' Alan brightened. 'And, no, I'm not going to.'

'Can I ask why not?'

'Yes. That's simple. Point one, you're a pupil at a school where I'm a teacher. Point two, you are under twenty-one.'

'So?'

'So I'd be breaking a trust. And if anything were discovered, I'd lose my job and probably end up in jail.'

'In other words, you're scared.'

Peter smiled gently. 'Yes, you could put it like that. I'd call it realistic.'

'What's realistic about that? The only things that are real are our feelings.'

'Ah, if only life were like that.'

'Well it is – or it can be, if you let it.'

'Of course it can be, and a part of my life has been like that. But you've got to make a choice sometimes and this is one of those times. During the past couple of years, I've built myself a rather nice life. I've got a job which I enjoy, a belief in myself and a belief in the future. Now you're asking me to risk losing all those things – and for what?'

'Love.'

Peter shook his head. 'No, Alan. For sex, for an hour of tumbling about on that bed in there. Because that's all it could be. Love's not about that, now is it?' Alan remained silent. 'Oh, come on, Alan. This isn't easy, you know.'

Alan laughed bitterly. 'I'm sorry. I realise that I should accept your pearls of wisdom and go away like the naughty boy I am.'

'I didn't mean that,' snapped Peter. 'All I'm trying to say is that you could at least recognise the facts when they're presented to you.'

'But I don't think they are facts! Look, let's be honest. If I want sex in this place, I can have it – there are plenty of horny young adolescents who wouldn't mind a quick wank with the school captain. And it wouldn't do them any harm, it's all part of growing up. But I don't want that.'

'Point taken. But let me ask you a question: how would you feel if you were chucked out because you'd slept with me?'

'I'd be upset, naturally.'

'Is that all?'

Alan shrugged. 'All right – more than that.'

'And your parents?'

'Furious.'

'And?'

'Angry – with you, probably.'

'And ashamed?'

'Yes.'

'Well then. Is it worth the risk?'

'Yes.'

'Bloody hell, Alan! Act your age!'

'I am doing! I'm not prepared to submit my love and happiness to an audit by the rest of the world. Especially when I know what the outcome'll be before I start. If you've reached your age without realising that, then I'm really sorry for you!'

'Stop it.'

'Ha! Getting a bit near the mark, am I?'

Peter saw red. 'What a fucking nerve you've got! You come up here with a great "I love you, sir, can we have it off, please, sir?" routine. Then when I refuse, you start telling me how to run my life!'

'Yeah, but I didn't know I'd fallen for a sodding coward.'

'Oh, get out! You don't know what you're talking about.'

Alan left. Peter swore loudly and slammed about his bedroom for a few moments before he left too, in search of some solace at the pub.

'So what's all this about a mysterious visitor, then?' asked Ian Palmer eagerly.

He and Arthur were seated comfortably in School's Corner, having got embroiled in dominoes when they arrived. Arthur had started to tell the story on the way down from school and Ian, always interested in hearing – though not passing on – the latest gossip, had been burning with curiosity ever since. He had played dominoes appallingly as a result.

'The visitor was only Martin Fisher,' replied Arthur, grinning.

'Oh,' replied Ian. 'How disappointing.'

'You wouldn't have said that if you'd been there.'

Arthur had been sitting quietly doing some marking when Fisher arrived. Their contact had only ever been brief and official, though this had never prevented Arthur from disliking the man intensely; his arrival was not, therefore,

The Stamp of Nature

a pleasant surprise.

'Hello, Martin. Come in.'

'Thank you, sir.'

'What brings you up here, then?'

'I wanted to ask your advice, Dr Benson.'

'Oh,' Arthur had replied, rather taken aback. 'You'd better sit down and tell me about it.' He recognised a note of condescension creeping into his voice but did not bother to stop it.

'You've been at Warton for a long time, sir.'

'Yes.'

'And presumably you're fond of the place?'

'Very.'

'Good. Then you'll help.' Fisher sat back and relaxed.

Alarm bells rang in Arthur's head. 'Help? Help with what?'

'To fight Jordan and his reforms, of course.'

'What did you have in mind, Martin?'

'First of all, I want to get as many of the staff as possible to oppose the new rules. If we fail to back the head, he's almost bound to resign.'

'Ah, I see.'

'I want to see the school under somebody like Jolly Roger...'

Arthur noted the tone of reverence Fisher used even with the man's nickname.

'...and not as a comprehensive school, which might as well be under the local council.'

'You don't feel that's a bit of an exaggeration?'

'No,' Fisher replied hotly. 'Why, do you?'

'I didn't say that. Just testing.' Arthur waited, wondering how he could get out of this.

'So, will you help?' Fisher asked again.

'One or two more questions before I commit myself. Tell me, what was the most important thing you learned here as a boy?'

'To be a man.'

Arthur frowned for a moment in genuine wonderment. 'I see. Could you elaborate on that?'

'Well ... how to be a sportsman, to work in a team, be a good loser, and so on.'

That really took the biscuit. In Arthur's experience, the boy had been the worst loser the school had ever produced. 'And why did you come back here to teach?'

'Because I loved the place so much. Nothing outside was ever the same.'

'But surely, Martin, that's the point,' Arthur responded.

Fisher frowned. 'I don't follow you.'

'How many other people have left here with the same unrealistic view of the world?'

'Many, I expect.'

'You're probably right. And wouldn't that seem to imply that there's something wrong?'

'With the world, yes.'

'Not with the school?'

'No.' Fisher's reply carried supreme conviction.

'And are you really saying that we should spend our time forcing boys into a mould of nineteenth-century values and ethics, then fling them out into the twentieth century and expect them to survive?'

'Well, I did!'

'No, you didn't! You came running back here at the first available opportunity!'

Fisher blushed deeply as he realised his mistake. He was

angry with Arthur for leading him on, but also with himself for making a major tactical error. 'I think I'd better leave.'

'Very well.' They walked to the door. 'I'm sorry to disappoint you, Martin, but I believe wholeheartedly in what Dr Jordan is trying to do.'

'He didn't reply,' Arthur now told Ian Palmer. 'Simply stamped off down the corridor.'

'Christ,' said Ian quietly. 'He's even more of a nut case than I thought.'

'I'm inclined to agree – but he could be dangerous.'

'Do you think he'll get much support?'

'From the staff? No, not enough to achieve a rebellion – he'll get the SS and perhaps a couple more, that's all. But add to that a sixth-form clique and one, possibly two, governors and you've the beginning of trouble. And talking of trouble...'

'Good evening, Dr Benson,' Peter said, with mock formality. 'And if it isn't Mr Palmer. Well, what a surprise!'

'Stop wittering, young Harvest,' replied Ian, 'and get the beer in.'

Peter groaned. 'Timed it wrong again, have I? Oh, well.' He disappeared to the bar.

'Hm,' muttered Ian. 'Where's the other half of the partnership, then?'

'Terry? He's on duty,' replied Arthur. 'Do I detect a note of jealousy?'

'Me? Jealous? Not at all,' replied Ian defensively. 'But I feel that they are a little too inseparable at the moment. Don't you think so?'

It was Arthur's turn to be defensive. 'I don't know what you mean.'

Ian grinned maliciously. 'So you've noticed too. Perhaps

you might counsel a little restraint?' Arthur was silent. 'Arthur, I've rendered you speechless for the first time ever!'

'No, it hadn't occurred to me before, that's all.'

'Oh, don't worry. I'm not going to make it banner headlines in the school mag. Terry's still a good friend – so is Peter, come to that – even if I don't share their sexual tastes.'

'Good,' growled Arthur.

'I'm slightly concerned that blackmail might be a useful weapon to the opposition. That could sink us, mate.'

Peter returned with the drinks and the subject was dropped.

Arthur was still bothered about Fisher's visit and related his story to Bob, but he only laughed. 'Well, they can't be a co-ordinated opposition yet,' Bob said.

'How do you know?'

'Because Lawrence has put the subject of rules on the agenda for tonight's governors' meeting and my soundings indicate that the governors will back me. I don't think the staff would risk an all-out fight.'

'I thought the meeting wasn't till next week.'

'No, it's been brought forward.'

'So Fisher will be presented with a *fait accompli*?'

Bob nodded. 'Caused by a miscalculation on the part of his idol.'

'Splendid.'

'By the way, you know that Dr Royston is not fit to come back?'

'Yes, I had heard.'

'I thought that I'd suggest making John Taylor's appointment permanent. What do you think?'

Arthur's immediate thought was for Peter; how much easier it would be if John quietly disappeared at the end of term. On the other hand, John was a good teacher and would be an asset to the school. 'Yes, fine,' he said out loud. 'I think that's an excellent idea.'

Chapter 22

BOB glanced quickly round the room and began to speak. 'Good morning, gentlemen. I'm sorry to interrupt your lunch but I thought it wise to hold a staff meeting before half-term so we can familiarise ourselves with stage two of the reforms, which, as you know, we plan to introduce after the break. I've undertaken, together with the school captain and Dr Benson, a complete review of the school rules and circulated a copy of our proposals. I should say that the governors discussed these proposals at their meeting last week and the document has their full backing.'

Several amused pairs of eyes turned in Martin Fisher's direction. He glanced at the ceiling and blushed.

'You will see that there will be a considerable relaxation of the disciplinary standards. As you will be aware, many of the existing rules have proved unenforceable or have been allowed to lapse. So, the relaxation will not be as great as it seems.

'Our aims during the review were twofold. Firstly, we wanted to get rid of the petty restrictions that go with age. All boys are equally important members of the school and it seems absurd that, for example, a first former should not be allowed to put his hands in his pockets. The second aim was to establish a framework within which to promote self-discipline. For example, compulsory prep periods will

The Stamp of Nature

be abolished. These periods tend to mean that most pupils do the minimum amount of work, since they don't want to spend more than the compulsory prep period on it. Instead, we have increased the penalties for late or skimped work.

'Before I throw open the meeting, I want to refer to what will probably be the most controversial aspect of the changes: the abolition of fagging. We were unanimously against fagging for several reasons. Firstly, the older boys need to became domestically self-reliant. Secondly, fagging places restrictions on the junior boys in both their academic and extra-curricular activities. Finally, the servant/master relationship has no place in a modern school.'

Bob glanced quickly round the room. He knew that most of the staff were in favour of the changes, but it did no harm to remind them of the arguments in their favour. He recognised the opponents easily by the grim set of their jaws. Would they speak out? Now was their chance. 'That's enough from me,' he said. 'Can we have some comments from you now, please?'

Arthur spoke first. 'I would just like to confirm, headmaster, that these proposals have my full backing. What we are about to introduce is long overdue.'

Bob noticed Fisher's face redden slightly and smiled. It could almost have been a deliberate trap to get Fisher to speak, because he now stood up. 'And I'd like to say, in case anybody thinks my youth signifies an automatic acceptance of change, that I consider these proposals to be dangerous in the extreme. I shall fight them all the way.'

'Could you elaborate on that statement, Mr Fisher?'

'Certainly, headmaster. They are dangerous in two ways. You propose to change another aspect of school life in a term that has seen far too many changes already. Secondly, easing the rules and abolishing fagging will inevitably lead to a relaxation of the tough discipline and standards of good behaviour for which the school is famous. We must be wary of becoming nothing more than an expensive comprehensive school.'

'I can't agree with that,' said Ian Palmer. 'It seems to me that the best results in terms of commitment and effort – which is all that we can expect – will be achieved by boys who appreciate our efforts and respond. We won't get that response while we are regarded as "the enemy", to be outwitted by breaking petty rules.'

'That's all very well, Mr Palmer,' interjected Stanley Sharpe in a surprisingly conciliatory tone. 'But my experience has taught me that discipline is a very important aspect of life. You can't run a place like this without it.'

'I think we ought to be aware of drawing too ready a comparison with state education.' This was John Taylor. 'I did my teaching practice in a London comprehensive and, whilst I agree with Mr Sharpe, I can assure him that these new rules are very strict compared with those that were applied there. If we had tried to enforce even some of these new rules in the comprehensive, there would have been a riot. Surely what we are trying to do here is to strike a balance – retaining rules that are necessary and enforceable whilst getting rid of the nonsense. And it's the nonsense that leads the boys to call the whole system into question. We have a chance to get them to respect our system of discipline, and that respect is an extremely important part of their education.'

His words were greeted with a chorus of muttered assent, which died down as Stanley Sharpe rose again. 'I feel that I should come back on that, headmaster, since Mr Taylor and I are not as far apart as some of you might think.'

Arthur's eyebrows shot up. He glanced at Bob, who winked. Terry nudged Peter and they both looked at Ian Palmer, who shrugged.

'I was about to add,' continued Stanley, 'that there is a middle way. If you expect unquestioning obedience from a body of human beings, you've got to show that you're at least halfway sane. I would get precious little respect from my cricket team if I told the bowlers to bowl long hops and full tosses all the time. I was opposed to this review when it was announced – no point in saying anything else since most of you know that – but it seems to me now that these proposals are a brave attempt to find that middle way. There are some things I disagree with, but no doubt there'll be a further review after a term or so…'

Bob nodded.

'…so I think we've got to give 'em a go.'

By now, Fisher had gone bright scarlet, furious with Sharpe's desertion. He had made the mistake of assuming that Stanley would be on side, but he had failed to secure his man and been outflanked. He knew that he was beaten but he tried to remain calm, fighting his anger and bitter frustration. 'Well, I'm sorry, headmaster,' he said, 'but I cannot agree. I consider the reforms dangerous and nothing will convince me otherwise.'

'Your opposition is noted, Mr Fisher,' replied Bob. 'But I think you'll agree that you're heavily outnumbered. The new rules will be introduced after half term. If there's nothing else, gentlemen…'

Book Two, Chapter 22

As Peter emerged from the meeting, he saw Alan Kelly hanging about waiting for somebody. Their contact since the previous Wednesday evening had been brief and formal. Peter had decided that he was certainly not going to be the one to attempt to heal the breach; any approach might be misinterpreted and start the row again. Even so, he was bothered by the estrangement and pleased when he realised that Alan was waiting to see him.

'Can I have a word in private?'

'Yes, certainly,' replied Peter with a smile. 'Do you want to pop up to my rooms?'

'Er ... no, if you don't mind. I thought a quick stroll in the grounds.'

Peter nodded. 'Okay.'

They left the building and walked across the quadrangle in silence. Only when they were well out of earshot did Alan speak. 'I wanted to ... apologise for the other day.'

Peter did not reply, sensing that there was more to come.

Alan continued to stammer for a few moments, and then: 'I behaved very badly.'

'Yes. You did. But don't worry, it's not important.'

'It is to me,' Alan interjected forcefully.

'All right,' Peter said gently. 'But what's done can't be undone.'

'No, but... God, I've felt so bloody awful since.'

The boy was trembling and near to tears. Peter wanted to reach out and comfort him but knew it was impossible. 'Hey,' he said gently. 'You mustn't get too upset.'

'I've gone over and over what you said,' Alan continued, recovering a little. 'I've tried to understand how you feel – and I do. But I still can't accept that you're right.'

'But you realise that it's got to be my decision?'

'I do. That's why I feel so guilty about all those things I said last week.'

'Don't worry,' Peter replied with a smile. 'We all say things in the heat of the moment that we don't mean and regret afterwards. I'm equally to blame because I flared up as well. I should have been more patient.'

Alan smiled back. 'Thanks for that, anyway.'

They reached a bench by the rugby field and sat down. Peter lit a cigarette and stared vacantly across the field. Eventually, he spoke. 'You know, the trouble with our lives is that, whatever we do, we can't win. We can never get away from the fact that we're different.'

'Surely...'

'No, wait. Let me finish. We can either live a so-called "straight" life, pretending to be "normal", with the sex bit tucked away in a nice little corner. Going about in a private world of lies and deception, living in fear of discovery and having secret, short-lived affairs. Or we can be honest, in which case we accept limitations on the type of jobs we can do and friends we can have. By coming back here to teach, I'm trying to find a compromise between the two. I'm not going to be excessively secretive but on the other hand I'm not broadcasting it. I'm trying to build a life that's not dominated by the fact that I'm gay. All right, it may not work in the end but I've got to give it a chance because I won't go back to either of the extremes.'

Alan was taken aback by Peter's vehemence. He was tempted to suggest that changing social attitudes made those views appear simplistic but something held him back. His experience had been restricted to Warton, after all. So, he merely nodded. 'And having a relationship with me would betray that attempt?'

'Exactly,' replied Peter.

Stanley Sharpe was approaching, complete with the third form. Their *tête-à-tête* was over. Alan grinned. 'Well, all right then – but I reserve the right to play Satan to your Wilderness.'

Peter laughed. 'The pleasure will be all mine.'

They walked slowly back to school. Peter had a free afternoon and planned to go for a walk so he left Alan in the quadrangle, headed down the drive, through the village and up on to the Crag. He found a rock and sat down to admire the view. For some reason, it made him think of John. Despite the disastrous dinner party, it had proved possible for them to co-exist. Maybe now that John was joining the staff that might lead to a rekindling of their friendship. It didn't matter that there would be nothing more. In some ways, being able to have contact with John without it hurting had been the greatest achievement of the past few weeks.

Of course, it was Terry who had made the difference. Though their relationship could never be described as romantic and involved no commitment, it was based on friendship, a shared sense of humour and similar interests. Sleeping together occasionally was a pleasant bonus but not the *raison d'être* of their relationship; therein lay its great strength.

And then there was Alan. His apology had been a welcome relief, and Peter was pleased that they would remain friends. Most of all, he was proud to have resisted such strong temptation – a resistance that would have been much more difficult two or three years earlier. More than ever, he appreciated the wisdom of Mark Foster's advice that December Saturday in London. He had built himself a life based on something other than his sexuality and it was a good one.

Book Three

Warton College, Lancashire.
Autumn Term 1973 – second half

Chapter 23

THE return to the school after the half-term break was greeted by a vicious gale that lasted for three days. Lessons were punctuated by rattling windows; voices were almost drowned by the noise of the rain. The breaks between lessons, usually leisurely strolls across the quadrangle, became frantic dashes round its edge as staff and pupils tried to stay dry. Outside games were suspended and the games periods became nightmarish attempts to keep upwards of seventy boys out of mischief.

It was against this background that the new rules were introduced. Bob announced them to the whole school during chapel on the Monday morning. Every boy received a copy of them during the first lesson of the day, for which he was made to sign.

Most of the sixth form were caught in a neat trap: their own interests were obviously being harmed by the abolition of fagging but, on the other hand, fagging went against the liberal instincts that these children of the sixties were developing.

Ian Thomas was unfettered by liberal thought and thus uniquely equipped to lead the opposition. 'I fagged for two bloody years when I first came here. The only thing that kept me going was the thought that in four years' time some other poor bastard would have to do it for me.'

Book Three, Chapter 23

He was confronted by the school captain. 'So because you were wronged, everybody who comes after has to be as well. Is that it?'

'It's not only that, it's the principle of the thing. As I said at the beginning of term, the head wants to turn the place into a bloody comprehensive.'

'As usual, Thomas,' countered Alan, 'you don't know what you're talking about.'

'Oh, suddenly the education expert, are we? Look here, Kelly, I'm not interested in your arguments. You only got your job because you acted as bum boy to half the staff so don't keep on at me about right and wrong—'

He was interrupted by Alan's fist. They sprawled on the floor, grappling and striking at each other viciously, until Thomas was eventually defeated and forced to apologise. At that point, Peter bounced exuberantly into the room. He was totally unprepared for the scene of upturned desks and chairs with two sixth-formers laid out in the middle of the floor. 'What's this?' he exclaimed.

They were still too busy arguing to hear him.

'All right, Kelly – I'll take back what I said about you being school captain. But I'll tell you this – I shall call a fag in the normal way, and anybody who refuses will get the same treatment I'd have got if I'd refused – a flogging.'

'In that case,' replied Alan, 'don't blame us when you get sacked.'

'If I go, mate, there's a lot I'll take with me.'

Peter, having recovered his composure, intervened. 'Er, gentlemen? Might I remind you that boxing is taught during PE lessons and not during English?' There was a hurried shuffling, as order was restored to the room. 'I hope I don't need to remind you both that this sort of exhibition hardly befits your position in the school.'

'No, sir,' they replied in unison.

'I'm pleased to hear it. Perhaps you could try to remember that in future.'

'He struck the first blow,' said Thomas.

'I've no doubt he had suitable provocation, Ian. Now, if either of you wish to make any further comments about the incident, you may do so in the headmaster's study. Otherwise, I suggest you forget about it and we carry on with the business in hand.'

The boys resumed their seats and said nothing more. Peter breathed a sigh of relief. He was disturbed that the reforms should provoke such controversy, and by the prospect of trouble from Ian Thomas whose capacity for stirring things should not be underestimated. It promised to be a difficult six weeks.

John Taylor was not teaching for the first two periods of the morning. He was always grateful for this Monday morning respite – but never more so than today. He went to the staff room after chapel and poured himself some coffee; he had been so anxious to get out of the house that morning that he had gone without breakfast.

The crisis that now faced him had come as a severe shock, though he was coming to realise that something of the sort was probably inevitable. It had started on Saturday night, with one of his increasingly frequent rows with Kate; as usual it blew up over nothing but somehow managed to become more serious than ever. It had ended with Kate storming out of the house and going alone to a party to which they had both been invited.

That in itself was not all that terrible, since John loathed parties. He had spent a pleasant evening reading and listening to a concert on the radio before going to bed about eleven but he had been unable to sleep, largely because of the noise from the party. It had eventually died down and he was dozing off when he heard Kate's key in the door. From all the shushing and giggling, it was obvious that she was not alone.

Wide awake again, John listened with growing horror to the sounds coming through the thin walls. The clink of glasses, muttering, then silence for a while. The creak of furniture growing steadily more rhythmical, the small soprano groans and bass grunts, which grew in volume until they suddenly stopped.

John lay in bed paralysed. He despised himself, not only for his inability to go in and stop them but also for the surge of excitement he experienced. He wondered who he was more jealous of, Kate or her partner, but quickly forced his mind away from the question. The sounds changed and became those of departure. John pretended to be asleep; mercifully pretence became reality before Kate came into the bedroom.

He woke early the next morning and left the house before Kate rose, leaving a curt note to say that he had gone for a walk and would not be back until late. He walked for most of the day, stopping only for a snack at a wayside pub, and reached the outskirts of Kendal at dusk. He tried not to think about the previous night but that was impossible; he was immersed in a vicious circle of thoughts and memories as inconclusive and repetitive as the theme of Ravel's 'Bolero'.

A Lancaster bus lumbered towards him out of the November gloom. He bought a ticket for Carnforth, where he could connect with the bus home. Only when he sat down did he realise how tired he was; sleep again provided an escape.

The driver woke him at the Lancaster terminus with a peremptory demand for more money.

'Why didn't you give me a shout at Carnforth?' John asked.

His question was met with a blank stare and shrugged shoulders. 'Not a bleedin' alarm clock, am I?' The sullen London accent seemed out of place but it made John realise that further argument was futile. He paid the extra fare and left the vehicle.

There was a gale coming and a gust of wind blew across the virtually deserted bus station. It reminded John of another stormy day in the same place, five years earlier. The memory helped a little because nothing could ever be worse than the way he had felt that day. But then he remembered the sequel: the welcome he had received from Peter and his parents and the magical few weeks that had followed. There could be no happy ending this time... At least not yet, his mind added hurriedly.

The wind blew again, harder this time, then the rain began to fall. He remained under cover, watching the streets transformed by the downpour. The dull, sinister light of the blue street lamps was relieved a little by the reflections in the wet tarmac. A solitary car passed, its engine noise drowned by the hiss of water and the rhythmical beat of the windscreen wipers. The rhythm reminded him again of what he had heard last night.

A lone pedestrian walked from the bus station, his

footsteps echoing in the quiet street. John envied him his sense of purpose. In the distance, a clock struck seven, the chimes varying in pitch as the swirling wind carried them in different directions across the city.

After ten minutes or so, the rain eased slightly and the bus station suddenly became busy as people made a dash for it from doorways and shelters. In all, no more than three dozen people arrived, but they made the place seem crowded and John didn't like it. He had a sudden inspiration: seven o'clock meant opening time.

He installed himself in the nearest pub, drinking steadily and allowing the conversation and laughter to pass over him, as if he were some unseen observer. Two or three people sat at his table and tried to strike up a desultory conversation but, deterred by his monosyllabic grunts, they eventually left him alone.

Closing time arrived all too quickly but by then John was sufficiently drunk to contemplate going home. Reeling slightly in the fresh air, he found a taxi. Kate greeted him at the door, concern written all over her face, but she was only in time to escort him to the bedroom where he promptly passed out. He awoke about six the next morning and, for the second time, left the house before his wife stirred.

Now, in the cold light of a November Monday morning, he faced the situation. His marriage was an illusion, a means of proving to himself that his cure had worked and he was no longer queer. Kate's behaviour on Saturday night marked a turning point. Surely, it could only now be a matter of time...

And yet. Maybe it was an aberration – too much drink or something. Everybody made mistakes. Perhaps they could come to some agreement. Yes, that was it. It was too soon to give up. They could stay together but go their separate ways. There had to be something in the marriage worth preserving. It might work; there was no harm in trying.

Martin Fisher banged his fist on the desk, shocking the class into silence. Despite his belief in discipline, this was the first time in six weeks that he managed to achieve order with the fourth. 'Just because the school rules have been relaxed, you lot needn't think you're going to get away with murder. You will behave yourselves in my class or sit here every evening until you learn how to.' He glowered at them, daring anybody to defy him. Silence. Good.

'Now get out your textbooks and learn the next ten lines of *Gallic Wars* off by heart. Any of you who can't recite them at the end of the lesson without a mistake will write them out twenty times.'

There was a rustling and banging of desk lids, then silence reigned once more. Fisher smiled briefly, savouring the sense of power. Until this morning in chapel, he had not really believed that the new rules would come into force. He could not accept that another piece of his beloved school would be ripped away like some rotten fabric – but it had happened. Worse still, he now recognised that open opposition would not work; he would never get a majority of the staff to back him. He would just have to await his opportunity.

He looked up angrily, distracted by a rustling of pages somewhere in the room. He found a boy leafing through his Latin dictionary and making notes. 'Turner!'

'Yes, sir?'

'What are you doing, boy?'

'Looking words up, sir.'

'I can see that! Why?'

'I wanted to see what the passage meant, sir.'

'What did I tell you and the rest of the class to do, Turner?'

'Learn the next ten lines of *Gallic Wars*, sir.'

'Then why are you translating it?'

'Because it helps me to learn it better, sir, if I know what it means.'

'Are you trying to be clever, boy?'

'No, sir!' came the aggrieved reply.

'When I want you to use your enquiring mind, such as it is, Turner, I will tell you. And when I want you to use your memory, I will tell you. Is that clear?'

'Yes, sir.'

'Now, since you're obviously so fond of translating Caesar, you may translate the next hundred lines for me by tomorrow morning. Understood?'

'Yes, sir,' Turner replied with a sigh.

'Good. Now get on with the task I set you.'

The boy resumed his study of the book, blushing furiously. Fisher sat back and smiled. That would show them he meant business.

Chapter 24

ALAN Kelly sighed and looked at his watch for the fourth time in as many minutes. Twenty to seven, another twenty minutes to go before his patrol duty was over.

Even though the compulsory prep period had been abolished, Bob was anxious that peace should still reign during the evenings so that the pupils could work. He had insisted that boys who were not working should be in the recreation block and maintained the traditional study patrol by prefects and masters. It was one of the few prefectorial duties that Alan hated. Still, at least Peter Harvey was sharing the duty tonight. That helped.

The thought of Peter made Alan sigh again. It was so bloody frustrating, knowing that Peter was gay but would not respond to his advances. It had been a relief, though, to get his apology out of the way before the holiday. He still felt guilty about his behaviour that Wednesday; although he remained convinced that Peter's attitude was wrong, he now recognised that it was not born of cowardice. Part of him admired Peter for the stance he had taken. It would have been nice, though...

He reached the end of the corridor and was about to go back when a noise stopped him. Passing this room earlier, he had thought he heard crying but assumed that it was a junior boy feeling homesick. He had not intervened for fear of embarrassing him, but now the sobs were louder and he clearly had to do something.

Alan knocked quietly and entered. He was surprised to see a fourth-form boy, his desk littered with Latin books, his head in his hands. 'Hello, Turner,' he said gently. 'What's the trouble?'

Turner gave him a garbled account of Fisher's lesson that morning, ending with more tears. 'And I've done fourteen lines and it's taken me an hour and at this rate I'll never get it finished,' he added.

Alan was silent for a moment, then asked, 'Are you sure he said a hundred?'

Turner nodded vehemently.

'Haven't you got a crib?'

'No, he confiscated them all.'

'He did what?'

Turner nodded again. 'That's right.'

Alan hesitated once more. Fisher was clearly in the wrong. The question, though, was how to proceed. The punishment of a hundred lines of translation was excessive at any time, but for this type of so-called offence – and to a boy who had spent three years in the school with a good record of behaviour – it was bloody criminal.

Technically, it was none of Alan's business unless... He had found a boy in distress, which he should report to the duty master. Yes, that was it. And Peter was the duty master.

Alan patted Turner reassuringly on the shoulder and prepared to leave. 'Don't do any more, Keith. I'll be back in about ten minutes.'

The boy nodded and smiled crookedly.

Peter was in his rooms, stealing a quick smoke between

patrols. He smiled as Alan came in. 'Hello! What can I do for you?'

'You'd be surprised.'

'After the last couple of weeks, I doubt it.'

'Well, there's a thing... No actually, Peter, this is serious.'

Peter listened with amazement to the story and could only think of one suitable riposte. 'The stupid bastard.'

'My sentiments exactly,' observed Alan grimly.

'Which house is Turner in?'

'Furness.'

'Ian Palmer's. Excellent.' Peter glanced out of the window towards Furness, the third largest and most modern of the school's four houses. 'And he's in. Right, Alan, will you go and fetch Turner? Meet me by Mr Palmer's rooms, will you?'

Alan grinned. 'Anything for you, sir.'

'Get out,' retorted Peter, laughing.

Kate Taylor sighed with relief as she heard John's key in the front door. She had wondered if he would come home at all after yesterday – and she had spent the afternoon wondering if she would care if he did not. Somewhat to her surprise, she had decided that she would – a little. After all, they had been married for nearly three years and that must mean something – certainly more than Saturday night's little episode. That was the trouble, though: Saturday night had happened. Nothing could ever be the same after that.

Yesterday had been strange. John's abrupt departure meant that he probably knew about what went on in the lounge. And for that she had, and still, felt guilty but she also despised John for his weakness in not putting a stop to it. Then again, she was glad he hadn't. Recalling it again, she shivered with pleasure but then tried to shut it out. That was impossible. It had happened and she had enjoyed it. She wriggled at the memory.

'Hello, Kate.'

John's voice made her jump, and she looked up in surprise. How long had he been watching her? Again, guilt threatened to overwhelm her. 'Hello.' she said, managing a smile. 'Good day?' She was not going to be the first to say anything.

'Not bad, thanks. Bit tired.'

'I'm not surprised, after—'

'Yes. I'm sorry about yesterday. I just felt I had to go out and – think.'

'About what?'

'Us.'

'And Saturday night?'

'Yes.'

'You heard then?'

'Yes.'

'Why didn't you stop us?'

'I don't know, really. I suppose I thought it was none of my business.'

'What the hell's that supposed to mean?' Kate felt her anger rising. He didn't even care. She had had it off on the lounge carpet with another man while he was in the next room – and it was none of his *business*!

'I've never been starry-eyed about being faithful,' John continued. 'So I thought if you were having a good time, I'd let you get on with it.'

'Oh. I see.' His tone was so reasonable that it should have defeated her anger but it only served to fuel it. A voice inside her insisted that his attitude was born of weakness and she despised him for it. But she forced her emotions back: what could she say? 'That's all right then.'

The subject was closed. John gave a small sigh of relief; he had taken the right line, after all.

Arthur sipped his whisky and peered at Bob over the top of his glass.

'I'm afraid we can't get away with a memo on this one, Arthur,' Bob remarked.

'No, it's a clear breach of the guidelines that were issued with the rules.'

'To give a boy a hundred lines of Caesar to translate in less than a day would breach any bloody guidelines,' Bob retorted feelingly.

They lapsed into silence. Arthur took another sip, reflecting that it was the formula much as before: the need to criticise without delivering a public slap in the face, and to ensure that the boy did not suffer in the future.

'I suppose,' Bob said, 'that we can safely assume that it was deliberate.'

'Defiance, you mean?' Arthur sighed. 'I think we must. After all, it's not as if Fisher was in the habit of doling out this sort of punishment – or any sort, come to that – before half term. From what I can gather, he couldn't have kept them quiet enough to tell them what to do.'

Bob laughed for the first time that evening. 'So I gather. Another drink?'

'Please.'

There was silence while Bob replenished their glasses. Sitting down again, he took a sip and put his glass down firmly. 'So, there's nothing for it. Fisher will have to be seen and given a rollicking.'

'I'm afraid so.'

'Formally?'

'Well, if he chose to defy you again, you'd want rid of him, I suppose?'

'Certainly.'

'Then it's got be a formal interview.'

'Bloody hell. That means union representation, the lot.'

Arthur shook his head. 'He's not a member, as far as I know.'

'How convenient.'

'Indeed.'

'Right, I'd better write to Fisher tonight, to cover young Turner. We don't want him beating the living daylights out of the boy for not handing the work in on time.'

'So, Fisher's fired the first shot, has he?' remarked Terry.

'Looks like it,' replied Peter.

'Very interesting.'

'Yes, but hardly wise in the circumstances.'

'I agree. But put yourself in his shoes – what would you do?'

Peter shrugged. 'I don't know, it's never really occurred to me.' He thought for a moment and then brightened.

'Hello.' Terry grinned. 'A pearl of wisdom is about to issue forth.'

'Not really. All I was going to say is that I'd have waited until something really serious came up then given the boy a stiff punishment. If that happened, it would put Bob on the spot; he couldn't stop a punishment in those circumstances without running the risk of undermining the new rules.'

Terry smiled and inclined his head. 'Very good. I'm glad you're on the right side.'

'But Fisher's too stupid to think about it like that.'

'I wouldn't say that. Fisher is single-minded and too impulsive, but don't underestimate him. This business – followed presumably by a rebuke from the head – will drive him underground.'

'Literally, I hope.'

Terry laughed. 'I'll second that.'

'Anyway, enough of Fisher's doings. How was your week at home?'

'Oh, don't! It was awful. Poor Dad's so deaf now, I was hoarse within ten minutes of getting there. And the silly old bugger won't have it. I'm sure he could have a hearing aid but if you so much as suggest it – once you've got through to him, that is – he goes up the wall!'

'Poor old man,' Peter said with a laugh. 'I'm sure you're unfair to him.'

'Unfair be damned. He always was obstinate. I'm afraid I've got very little patience with him.'

'You missed me then?'

Terry turned away to hide the sparkle of amusement in his eyes. 'No,' he said, addressing the window. He turned and saw Peter's crestfallen look; laughing, he ruffled Peter's hair. 'I declare, young Harvest, you're getting too serious.'

'Me, serious?' countered Peter, taking his tone from Terry. 'Not at all, Mr Fowler.'

'Good.' The sparkle suddenly disappeared from Terry's eyes. 'Because it won't do, you know, Peter. Getting serious about things.'

Peter was momentarily floored and wondered why; after all, his own thoughts the other week on Warton Crag had been down to earth rather than romantic. 'Friends with benefits', they called it. Anything more was clearly absurd.

Terry watched with wry amusement, eventually saying, 'Your silence is in danger of betraying you, young Harvest.'

The use of his nickname relaxed the sudden tension and Peter felt comfortable again. 'You flatter yourself,' he said. 'What makes you think I could possibly take *you* seriously?'

Terry was clearly not expecting that and he was disconcerted, much to Peter's gratification. 'I think it's dangerous to rationalise feelings like this,' Peter responded. 'The risk is that they're either deeper than you thought, or shallower than you hoped. Either discovery isn't very comfortable.'

Terry recovered. 'What a perceptive remark, young Harvest. Except that the deeper feelings are usually less uncomfortable, as I suspect we might be finding out.'

'I think that, in your usual pompous way,' Peter said, amused, 'you've just conceded the round to me.'

'More like game, set and match.'

Chapter 25

MARTIN Fisher was admitted to Bob's study by Eileen, who was standing in for the school secretary. She immediately resumed her seat at one end of the desk. Bob rose to greet Fisher, as did Arthur, who was sitting at the opposite end of the desk from Eileen.

Bob shook hands formally. 'Mr Fisher, do sit down.'

'Thank you, headmaster.'

Bob resumed his seat, glanced at and then shuffled some papers. After a few moments, he removed his glasses and looked up. 'Mr Fisher, as I indicated in my note last night, this is a formal disciplinary interview held under the agreement reached between the school governors and the appropriate staff representatives. You were given a copy of that agreement when you took up your employment here, I believe?'

'That is correct, headmaster.' Fisher appeared calm, even arrogant, but his feelings were running high: a combination of anger, resentment and fear.

'And you understand the procedure set out in that agreement?' Bob continued.

'I do, headmaster.'

'Very well. I should say at this stage that Mrs Jordan is standing in for my secretary, who is off sick, and will merely take notes. Dr Benson is here as an observer, at my request.'

Fisher inclined his head, but said nothing,

'Now, I understand that you are not a member of a trade union. Is that correct?'

'That is correct, headmaster.'

'Do you wish to be accompanied by a third party?'

'No – thank you.'

'Right, then. We will proceed to the case itself.' Bob paused, unfamiliar with the formality that this business required. He longed to thrust it all aside, give Fisher a good bollocking and get it over with but he could not do that. 'The case against you rests on reports that yesterday, Monday the fourth of November, you set an imposition, namely translation of one hundred lines of Caesar's *Gallic Wars*, to a fourth-form boy named Turner. Such an imposition exceeds the guidelines and is, in all respects, unreasonable.' Bob looked up from his notes, but Fisher's face was a mask. 'Is that clear, Mr Fisher?'

'Yes, headmaster.'

'Very well. Now, at my request – and I wish to emphasise that it is at my request – those parties involved in yesterday's incident have submitted written reports. I shall now read them to you.'

Arthur listened uncomfortably to the accounts from Turner, Kelly, Peter and Ian Palmer. This massive assault on Fisher's dignity was not likely to end the man's opposition to Bob, and the possible consequences were alarming. Like Terry Fowler, Arthur worried about Fisher's capacity to stir up trouble. Even so, there was no alternative; apart from anything else, Bob had to demonstrate that his reforming zeal had not made him soft; that if he issued instructions, he would enforce them. Arthur glanced at

The Stamp of Nature

the clock: it was still only quarter to ten but it had already been a long morning.

'That,' concluded Bob, 'is the evidence on which this hearing is based. Is there anything in those reports that you wish to dispute?'

'No, headmaster.'

'Okay. Have you anything you wish to say in your defence?'

Fisher had spent most of the night trying to decide on a defence, ranging from a servile retreat to a vitriolic counter-attack. He had been unable to reach a firm decision; consequently his mind now was full of uncoordinated thoughts. After a few moments, he managed to find coherence. 'I considered Turner's attitude yesterday morning to be insolent, headmaster. He answered my questions with a distinct grin on his face...'

Liar, thought Arthur. Turner had never been known to grin at a master, even on the most relaxed of occasions.

'...and he was disobedient in that he was translating when he had been told to memorise. I decided to punish him as an example to the rest of the class. I should add that I have found the fourth form to be a particularly difficult class in which to instil any sense of order or propriety.'

Eileen coughed, smothering a laugh at the idea of fourteen year olds having a sense of propriety. Arthur raised an eyebrow. The corners of Bob's mouth twitched dangerously but he managed to avoid smiling.

Fisher was undeterred, however, and carried on. 'I admit that Turner has not been conspicuous as a ringleader in the class but I felt that the incident might presage an attempt to assume such a role. As a consequence, it needed to be stamped on...'

'I...' started Bob.

'...firmly,' concluded Fisher.

'...see.' Bob tried to ignore Arthur, who had gone very red in the face and was almost bouncing with suppressed anger. Bob shared his feelings; Fisher's defiance, pomposity and self-satisfaction were intolerable and so reminiscent of Lawrence as to be almost a caricature. He realised now what an implacable an enemy Fisher was – and how bad he was at his job.

When Bob spoke again, there was an acidity in his tone that surprised even Eileen. 'I take it you received a copy of the staff guidelines, which I issued with the new rules?'

'Yes,' replied Fisher tersely, responding to the change in atmosphere.

'Did you read them, Mr Fisher?'

'I glanced at them, yes.'

'Do you recall the paragraph on impositions?'

'Not specifically.'

'Obviously not, judging by your behaviour yesterday.' This first outward sign of hostility took Fisher by surprise, and he blushed slightly. 'I'll read it to you,' continued Bob. 'it's paragraph five of the document. You should perhaps make a note of that. I quote: *"Impositions. Provided that they are not used to excess, impositions can prove a useful means of punishment, particularly for those boys whose academic performance may profit from a little extra enforced effort. However, the amount of work set should never impair his ability to do the required work in other subjects. Therefore the following upper limits should be observed."*'

Bob looked up and glared at Fisher over the top of his glasses. 'Note the word "upper", Mr Fisher. I quote again: *"One. An essay should not exceed five hundred words.*

The Stamp of Nature

Two. Translation should not exceed twenty lines. Three. A requirement to learn by heart should not exceed ten lines, though this may be varied where poetry is involved. Four. In all the above cases, and any other variants you may use, the time required to complete the exercise should not exceed one hour. Thus, in setting the punishment, staff should take into account the mental capacity of the boy and the seriousness of the offence. Finally, lines of the 'I must not lock Matron in the loo' variety should not be given." Is there anything in that paragraph you don't understand?'

'No, headmaster.' Sensing defeat, Fisher allowed his deferential tone to return.

'Good. I think you will agree that the imposition that you set Turner yesterday exceeded those guidelines by a considerable margin.'

'I would say, Headmaster, that the severity—'

'Yes or no?'

'Yes, headmaster.'

'And you do not dispute my right to issue such guidelines?'

'Certainly not, headmaster.'

'And you would accept that it is not unreasonable to expect them to be observed?'

'I would accept that, certainly, but—'

'Have you anything further to say?' Never had an invitation to speak sounded so much like a closing remark.

'No, headmaster.'

'Very well. We shall have a short adjournment to consider the points I have made. Would you wait in my secretary's office please, Mr Fisher?'

⊹

Book Three, Chapter 25

Peter was teaching first-form English. He was worried; one of the boys, Perkins, was obviously not well. Usually a robust child, he looked pale and there were signs of bruising over his left eye and on his right cheek. His lower lip was also swollen. Peter wondered why the injuries had not been noticed at breakfast then concluded, correctly as it turned out, that the boy had probably skipped the meal. After about ten minutes, he decided that he would have to do something.

'Perkins, come here, please.'

The boy immediately looked defensive. 'Sir?'

The rest of the class watched his progress to the front of the room closely.

'All right. The rest of you get on with your work.' Peter turned to the boy and spoke in a lowered tone. 'You're in a bit of a state, aren't you?'

'No, sir. I'm all right.'

'What happened?'

'I ... er ... I ... fell down the stairs, sir.'

'Did you now? Are you sure you haven't been fighting?'

'No, sir.' Suddenly, the boy's face crumpled and tears rolled down his normally rosy cheeks.

Peter's mind swept back to Ian Thomas's threat a day earlier and he shivered. No, surely not. One thing was certain, though: the matter could not be pursued in front of the rest of the class. Peter glanced out of the window, wondering what to do. He could not leave the class unsupervised but he wanted Matron to see Perkins as soon as possible; perhaps together they could get the truth out of the boy.

Suddenly, he had an idea. 'Stay there, Perkins – and keep quiet, the rest of you.' He dashed out of the room and

The Stamp of Nature

into the next, where he knew Terry had the sixth. 'Terry, sorry to butt in, but can I borrow a prefect to look after my lot next door?'

'Surely. What's up?'

'A bit of a crisis. I'll fill you in later.'

'Fair enough. Arthur Frost do you?'

'Great. Arthur, can you look after my class until the end of the period, please? They've got some work to do, so they shouldn't be any trouble.

Peter returned to his own class, where a buzz of conversation quickly died down. 'Right, Mr Frost is going to look after you for the rest of the period so behave yourselves.' Then he said quietly to Perkins, 'Come on, young man. We're off to see Matron.'

'Right. Mr Fisher, sit down again, please.' Bob was gratified to note that Fisher had lost some of the outward assurance he'd show at the start of the interview. 'You will have gathered that I take a very serious view of this matter, hence my decision to deal with it on a formal basis. I must say that your actions yesterday and your attitude this morning have not improved my confidence in your abilities.

'I consider that you have been guilty of a serious breach of the guidelines. In the circumstances, I have no alternative but to give you a formal written warning to the effect that any repetition of such misconduct will lead to more serious disciplinary action including, possibly, dismissal. Is that clear, Mr Fisher?'

'Yes, headmaster.'

'Of course, you have the right to appeal to the school governors if you are dissatisfied with my decision. Should you wish to exercise that right, advise me in writing within seven days of this hearing.'

'I shall not be appealing, headmaster.'

'Very well. That will be recorded in the notes. Finally, I wish to emphasise that this matter is now closed. I do not expect any retaliatory action, either covert or overt, against anybody involved. Understood?'

'Yes, headmaster.'

'Good. That's all, Mr Fisher. You may go.'

Chapter 26

EILEEN left the room shortly after Fisher to make some coffee. As she returned with it, a knock on the door announced Peter's arrival. He was looking very grim.

Bob had just been entertained by Arthur's imitation of Fisher and his sense of propriety, and found it difficult to stay serious. 'Hello, Peter. Whatever's the matter? You look as if you've lost a shilling and found sixpence.'

Peter delivered his news. 'Ian Thomas has beaten up a newt for refusing to fag for him.'

'Oh my God,' Arthur said quietly.

'Who?' asked Bob.

'Perkins is his name.'

'When?'

'Last night.'

'Why weren't we told?'

Peter shrugged his shoulders and sat down, suddenly exhausted. He lit a cigarette. 'Apparently it happened about eight. Alan Kelly and Pete Baxter tried to put a stop to it. It ended up in a brawl between the three prefects before Kelly and Baxter managed to overpower Thomas.'

Bob turned to Eileen. 'Track down Alan Kelly for me, love. Tell him I want to see him now, if not sooner.'

Eileen left the room while Bob and Arthur continued to question Peter.

'How did you find out?' Bob asked.

'I noticed Perkins during first period this morning. He didn't look well and there was some bruising on his face. I took him to Matron to get him patched up a bit and we managed to get the story out of him. He was frightened to death, poor little devil. Matron's sent for the doctor because his ribs are bruised as well.'

'You're joking!' exclaimed Arthur.

'I wish I was.' Peter sighed as he helped himself to some coffee. 'It's true, though, and Perkins' story fits. I broke up a fight between Kelly and Thomas yesterday morning—'

'You did *what*?' Arthur interjected.

'Two prefects were fighting over the new rules, or something stemming from them. It was settled eventually – but not before Thomas said he would call a fag in the normal way and beat the first kid who refused.'

Bob shook his head in disbelief but said nothing. He picked up the phone. 'Eileen, have you found Kelly yet? Oh, he's on his way? Fine. Can you get Ian Thomas up here in about five minutes? And fetch me his file, please. Thanks.'

He put down the receiver and paused for a moment, taking a deep breath. Then he smiled. 'This is certainly turning out to be some morning – my first disciplinary interview and now possibly my first expulsion.'

Eileen came in with Thomas's file, followed by Alan Kelly who was sporting a large plaster over one eye. 'What the hell happened to you?' Bob asked tersely.

Alan registered surprise that the question should be necessary but confined himself to saying that he had been trying to stop a beating.

'Who was beating whom?'

'Ian Thomas had got young Perkins for refusing to clean his shoes.'

'Did you stop it?'

'Eventually, yes. But it was a bit of a scrap. Didn't you know?'

'What do you mean, "didn't we know"?' interrupted Arthur.

'We reported it. Pete Baxter went to see Martin Fisher soon after it happened. He said he'd deal with it and not to worry.'

'Why Martin Fisher?' asked Bob.

'He was on duty from eight till ten last night – he took over from me,' Peter said.

'Christ, this gets worse!'

Eileen came in. 'Ian Thomas is on his way. Here's the second post, by the way,' she added. 'I think the top one's rather ironic. I'll give you a buzz when Ian arrives.' She left again.

Bob read the letter silently then passed it to Peter. 'Somehow I don't think we need to worry about that any more.'

Peter took the letter, which had been forwarded to Bob by the chairman of the governors. It was from Ian Thomas's father.

Dear Sir

I am writing to lodge a formal complaint against the headmaster of Warton College and Mr P J Harvey, a member of the English Department at the school.

The complaint is twofold: (a) that Mr Harvey continues, despite protests from my son, to teach impressionable teenagers that A Portrait of the Artist as a Young Man *is worthy of the title great literature; and (b) that Dr Jordan supports him in this, refusing to take any notice of my complaint, to which he replied briefly, to the point of curtness.*

I attach copies of the correspondence. I will be glad to be of further assistance should you or your colleagues require it.

'My God, he must be mad,' Peter replied. 'I could understand it if we were teaching *Ulysses* but even then – to pretend that that class is a collection of impressionable teenagers!' He grinned at Alan. 'They know more about a lot of things than I do.'

Alan blushed slightly but only Peter noticed amid the amusement that his remark caused.

'Well, I think events have overtaken it,' Bob remarked. The phone rang, announcing Ian Thomas's arrival. 'Right, gentlemen. Would you like to disappear into the boardroom? I'll call you if and when I need your testimony.'

Arthur, Peter and Alan nodded and left.

They were not required, however. Thomas admitted the charge, maintaining that he had merely exercised his rights as a prefect to give a disobedient boy a good thrashing.

He was expelled and left the next morning.

'Ah, Mr Fisher. Sit down, please.'

'Thank you, headmaster.'

Fisher was much less calm than earlier in the day. He had been summoned peremptorily, and could not think why. Because it had all happened so quickly, and Bob had acted so decisively, the school grapevine had been slow to catch on to the Thomas sensation; though wild rumours were beginning to circulate, they had not yet reached

The Stamp of Nature

Fisher's ears.

'I'm sorry to have to interview you twice in the same day, but this is an informal discussion since the events with which I am now concerned took place before your warning this morning.'

Fisher frowned. 'I'm afraid I don't understand, headmaster.'

'I asked you to come and see me about Ian Thomas.'

'Yes?'

'He has been expelled, with immediate effect, following an incident last night in which a first-form boy, Perkins, was rather badly beaten up.'

'Oh?' said Fisher. His puzzled look became a facade as he recalled the events of the previous evening.

'The school captain tells me that Ian Thomas was reported to you last night for using undue violence on a junior boy. Is that so?'

'Yes, headmaster.'

'And also for using the same degree of violence against two prefects?'

'Yes, but I really don't—'

Bob's anger erupted. 'Just answer my questions, Mr Fisher. I'm not interested in your excuses. Now, what attitude did you take to the report?'

'I thought it was either a prank or yet another sixth-form wrangle.'

'So, you didn't act on the information?'

'No, headmaster. I don't like tale-tellers, especially among supposedly mature sixth formers who are supposed to be exercising self-discipline.'

Bob ignored Fisher's attempt at sarcasm. 'I see. So, you are not aware that a first-form boy was badly beaten up in the school last night?'

'Really, aren't we getting a bit extreme over a minor matter?'

Bob went dark red in the face but managed to keep his temper. 'I'm surprised that you consider expulsion to be a minor matter – especially when the cause is a beating, after which the victim needed prolonged medical attention.'

Fisher paled noticeably.

'However,' continued Bob, 'I have not asked you up here to continue investigations but to say that I regard your conduct last night as totally unsatisfactory. And to find it so for the second time in the same day is disturbing, to say the least. What am I to make of it? On the one hand you oppose relaxation of the rules and demonstrate your opposition by giving a boy a draconian punishment. And on the other hand, you decline to investigate a serious incident when it's reported to you.'

Fisher still said nothing.

'Let me make this clear. Any breach of the school rules reported to you must be investigated and help sought to deal with it, if necessary. Of all the staff, I didn't expect to have to remind *you* of this – and I certainly don't expect to have to remind any member of staff that he must remain impartial.'

'Really, headmaster, I...'

'If you wish to argue any further, Mr Fisher, please do so in a letter of resignation. Good night.'

Chapter 27

AS the term went on, the close working relationship that had developed between Bob and Arthur deepened into a firm friendship. Bob learnt to trust the older man's judgement. For his part, Arthur prized the friendship with both Bob and Eileen as highly as any he could remember; it was almost like having a family again. His zest for life, and particularly Warton life, was restored to heights he had not thought possible after the death of his wife Connie.

The three of them now sat over the remains of Sunday lunch. Arthur was speaking. 'But I still don't see why you're uneasy, Bob, especially now. You've initiated the new rules, you've got rid of Thomas without too much bother and Fisher's lost all credibility. It seems that the opposition's been routed.'

Bob laughed. 'I suppose that's the trouble. It's been easier than I expected and a little voice keeps telling me that it's been too easy.'

Arthur grunted. 'I wouldn't have thought easy was the word after this week.'

'Understood. Of course, I would never say that I enjoyed rollicking Fisher or expelling Thomas but, if you think about it, the opposition has played straight into my hands. Jolly Roger tried to upset the governors over the rules before half term and that backfired on him. Fisher deliberately ignored the guidelines twice, and then Ian Thomas got himself chucked out for making a futile gesture of protest. With enemies like that, who needs friends?'

'But you've just answered your own case,' insisted Eileen.

'I know but I still can't get rid of this feeling.'

'But it's so stupid,' replied his wife. 'Arthur, can't you stop him worrying?'

'I can't stop him feeling uneasy, love,' Arthur responded wistfully. 'Any more than I can defeat a woman's intuition when—'

'Yes,' interrupted Bob. 'That's the word – intuition. It tells me that this is fundamentally a political battle. If all the opposition forces get together and go to a governors' meeting, they might just win.'

'If they told enough lies,' Arthur added.

'Exactly.'

Eileen frowned. 'But how *can* they get together? Thomas has been shunted off home to Reigate, having admitted a serious offence. Fisher is stuck here – and we've no evidence that he ever really knew Thomas – whilst Lawrence couldn't act without the pretext for a meeting.'

'Yes, I know all that,' her husband replied. 'I've been through it a hundred times, but I can't stop myself worrying.'

'All I would say, Eileen,' Arthur said carefully, 'is don't underestimate Fisher. He might be impulsive and he might be a bloody useless teacher, but he's no fool.'

Martin Fisher sat on the promenade, watching the sun setting over Morecambe Bay. It had been a disastrous week. First the new rules, then the Turner business, the Thomas expulsion, and finally his second interview with Jordan.

Life at Warton was getting steadily worse; it was so bloody frustrating. He wished his mother was still alive, she would have known what to do. Years of experience in the diplomatic corps had given her a superb talent for infighting. She would have relished this situation.

'First,' she would have said, 'list all the points and forces in your favour. Second, think of all the innuendo you can – it should be as near the truth as possible but, if there isn't any truth, invent some. And lastly, find somebody else to fire the bullets for you.'

He began to follow the procedure step by step and was surprised at how much material there was. The germ of an idea emerged and he started to pace up and down the promenade as the details fell, or were forced, into place. Suddenly he clapped his hands and set off quickly to find the nearest telephone box. He picked up the phone and dialled directory enquiries.

'Which town, sir?'

'Reigate, Surrey, please.'

Terry, Peter and Ian were not literally banging on the door of the pub at opening time but they were definitely the first customers, a fact that Harry, the landlord, remarked on. 'Shouldn't you lot be in chapel?' he asked.

Ian grinned. 'One of the first changes the head made was bringing Sunday chapel forward half an hour.'

'At your suggestion, presumably,' replied Harry.

'Dr Benson's actually,' Terry intervened.

Harry laughed. 'I might have known. I'm half expecting him to move in here when he retires next year.'

They took their beers and established themselves in the usual corner, which now boasted a notice proclaiming it to be 'Wart's End'.

'What have you two been up to this afternoon?' asked Ian, with a malicious grin. 'Or shouldn't I ask?'

'You shouldn't ask,' replied Terry.

Peter blushed, much to Ian's delight.

'It's been quite a week,' remarked Terry, trying to cover Peter's embarrassment.

'Certainly has, eh, young Harvest?'

'Yep. Nice to see the back of that bastard Thomas, though.'

Terry agreed. 'Yes, he was a particularly unsavoury character.'

'Do you think we've seen the last of him?'

Peter shivered at the implication behind Ian's question. 'Why shouldn't we have done? Surely he confessed.'

'Confessions can be retracted.'

'Come off it, Ian,' exclaimed Terry. 'It's not as if Bob put the thumbscrews on him, is it?'

'No, I'm not saying that. It's just that I witnessed a rather touching farewell scene on Wednesday morning between Thomas and Martin Fisher.'

'Palmer, you're getting devious. Why didn't you tell us before?' asked Terry.

'Because it was only last night that it struck me that there was anything odd about it.'

Peter frowned. 'Why odd?'

'They didn't know each other.'

The Stamp of Nature

'They must have done.'

'They didn't, Terry.' Ian was warming to his subject. 'Think about it for a minute. Thomas was in my house and had nothing to do with Fisher, who's in Keswick House. Thomas didn't do Latin, which is the only thing that Fisher teaches.'

'Yes, but surely they'd have come across each other,' Peter said. 'Thomas was a prefect, after all.'

'Perhaps. But were they close enough to exchange addresses?'

'Exchange addresses?'

Ian nodded. 'That's what it looked like to me.'

Terry frowned. 'Why the hell would they do that?'

'You tell me, Terry.'

Terry turned to Peter. 'He's right, you know. There is something odd about that.'

For some reason, Terry's remark reminded Peter of the second morning of term and meeting John in the quadrangle, Fisher appearing and then his sickly smile as he had said, 'Oh, very nostalgic, especially seeing you two together again.' He shivered. The conversation drifted away from school but the memory remained with him and rather spoiled his evening.

John awoke with a start. He'd heard a gunshot but realised that it was from a film on the television. He glanced at his watch and saw that he had been asleep for over an hour. Why had Kate not wakened him? He rubbed his eyes and then stretched, grimacing at the furry taste in his mouth.

'Kate?' No reply. 'Kate, where are you?' Silence. 'That's

funny.'

Still feeling unsteady from sleep, he turned off the television and walked into the kitchen. He turned on the light but the harsh glare of the fluorescent light hurt his eyes, so it was a few seconds before he saw the note. *Gone for a walk*, it said.

He frowned and turned to switch on the kettle. Then he stopped. 'But she hates walking.'

He made himself some coffee. Returning to the lounge, he remembered what had happened in the room little more than a week earlier. He shivered. Only a week? It seemed a lot longer, what with the goings-on at school. Still, at least Kate had been grateful for his attitude and promised that it wouldn't happen again. But could he trust her? And had he actually any right to expect... He dismissed the thought quickly. She had not been asked to promise, after all. But where was she?

A car drew up outside. It only stopped long enough for somebody to get out and then drove off again. Steps on the path, key in the door...

He met her in the hall. She was looking slightly dishevelled and flushed. Eyes bright, lipstick smeared. 'Hello,' she said with a nervous smile.

'Do you normally go for a walk in people's cars?'

She shrank from his tone.

'You've been with him.'

It was a statement and required no answer. John turned away and ran for the bathroom. He was violently sick. Afterwards, he sat on the edge of the bath and cried.

The Stamp of Nature

Terry woke suddenly and glanced at the clock. Two a.m.

Peter was asleep but dreaming, thrashing about. Then he started to shout. 'Let me go! I want to go home! Let me go!' Suddenly he woke up, wide-eyed with fear and sweating,

'Hey,' said Terry. 'That was some nightmare.'

'The road stopped me again, it wouldn't let me go home.' Peter shivered and started to cry.

'Peter, get a hold of yourself. What are you on about?' Terry held him close and stroked his forehead.

Suddenly Peter recovered himself. 'God,' he said. 'I haven't dreamt like that for years.'

Chapter 28

'ARTHUR, do come in. Take a pew.' Bob finished signing his post then looked up and smiled. 'I wanted a word with you about Christmas. I meant to mention it yesterday afternoon but I was so busy playing the prophet of doom that I forgot all about it.'

Arthur grinned. 'Does that mean you're feeling a bit more optimistic today?'

The younger man nodded. 'A shade. Eileen had another go at me after you left and it made me feel a bit better.'

'Good. Now, what about Christmas?'

'I wanted to ask you whether there any good old Wartonian traditions that I ought to know about.'

'Not really. Jolly Roger didn't approve of Christmas. It – ah – offended his sense of propriety.'

'Not that word again.'

Arthur laughed. 'That's where Fisher got it from, you know.'

'I might have known. Well, what about before Lawrence's time?'

'Oh, yes, there were plenty then.'

'Perhaps we can try to restore a few.'

'There was the pantomime, of course.'

'Yes, we've already decided to put one on, as you know.'

'Mm. Bloody good idea. Then there was the carol service.

That was always on the morning of the last day, following the panto the previous night. Jolly Roger changed it and had the carol service on the last Sunday of term – I think he felt people might be too jolly on the last day of term to take it seriously enough.'

Bob laughed. 'Back to propriety again?'

'Absolutely.'

'Okay, so we move the carol service to the last morning of term, followed by Christmas lunch?'

'Yes, that was the way we did it. Lunch tended to last the whole afternoon – but of course Jolly Roger insisted on normal lessons on the last afternoon.'

'Well, I'm not having that. We'll lay on a special tea and have one big party from lunch till bedtime. I think we'll all deserve it after this term.'

'You're not kidding,' replied Arthur feelingly. 'Alec Prebble – Jolly Roger's predecessor – he always used to say—'

The telephone interrupted.

'Excuse me.' Bob lifted the receiver. 'Hello? Okay, put him through.' He put his hand over the mouthpiece. 'The chairman, no less.'

Arthur raised his eyebrows.

'Hello? Hello, Jim! What can we do for you?... Yes?... Oh Christ!... On what grounds?... Victimisation? How the bloody hell do they work that one out?... I see... Yes... Hmm... Oh, bloody hell... Yes, I know it's not your fault... When do they want to meet?... Twenty-third? Let me check.' Bob leafed through his large desk diary. 'Hello? Yes, that's all right with me, worse luck. What time?... Ten o'clock. Okay, then... What?... Oh, a written report. Yes, I'll let you have it by Friday... Okay, Jim, thanks for ringing... Yes, I'll speak to you again when you've read the report... Fine, fine... 'Bye.'

As he put the receiver down, Bob's gaze remained fixed on his desk. Then, he sighed and reached for a cigarette.

'Bad news?' asked Arthur.

There was a nod in reply.

'Thomas?'

'Yes. I was right, I'm afraid. Thomas's father has appealed against his son's expulsion. The governors will meet on the twenty-third to consider the case.'

Kate Taylor glanced out of the kitchen window into the deepening November gloom. Catching sight of her own reflection, she looked away quickly; she was in no mood to look at herself. With an angry gesture she moved away from the sink, abandoning her preparations for the evening meal.

'I need a drink,' she said to herself. Going into the dining room, she poured herself a large gin, added a splash of tonic and sat down at the table.

Something had to be sorted out. They could not go on like this. When she had promised John that it would never happen again, she had been sincere; despite her husband's meek acceptance of her adultery, she really had felt guilty. But when the phone had rung last night, and she had heard that voice, all her resolutions went out of the window. But afterwards! She had never hated herself so much in her life. It was not as if she loved the man, it was only ten minutes in the back of a car – satisfaction of an animal lust. She shivered.

But she needed sex. That had to be recognised. After all, this wasn't the Victorian age, when women weren't supposed to enjoy it. She had rights as well, and since … since…

Her spirits lifted a little as she made her decision. The choice was clear. Whether to carry on like this, torturing both herself and John, or go. There could only be one answer, really. The suddenness was frightening but the decision was made. And it had to be done quickly or not at all.

'Bloody hell!' said Peter.

'Exactly what I said,' replied Bob, with a brief smile.

'Why the week's delay?'

Eileen answered. 'Apparently Thomas's father told Jim Stewart that he had originally been prepared to accept the decision but he has now received "new evidence" that casts doubt on the matter.'

'Martin Fisher,' Peter said flatly.

'So it would seem.' Bob sighed. 'Arthur warned us not to underestimate him.'

'Strange, though,' Peter remarked. 'I wouldn't have thought he'd have the guts.'

'Arthur says,' interrupted Eileen, 'that Fisher is a desperate man.'

'Yes, I suppose so. Still… When's the meeting, Bob?'

'The twenty-third.'

'Surely there's no question of anything going wrong?'

'That depends on how many lies they're prepared to tell. Apart from Jim Stewart, the chairman, there are five other governors. Two of them – my revered predecessor and his pal Forbes-Smith – opposed my appointment and were against me from the start. It's a question of how many others they can sway, and what they'll do to sway them.'

'But what are the grounds for appeal?'

'Victimisation.'

'That's good. How do they work that out?'

'They're claiming that I forced Thomas into confessing because I wanted him out of the school after he stirred things up over the Joyce book and the new rules.'

'But surely even Jolly Roger realises that an assault like that has to be punished severely?'

'Oh, yes,' interjected Eileen. 'But remember that Thomas is now denying that he assaulted Perkins and also that Fisher didn't take the incident seriously when it was reported to him.'

'That's the sort of evidence that could sow doubt in people's minds,' Bob mused. 'All they need to do is to discredit one or all of the witnesses by innuendo, and we could be in deep trouble.'

'Yes, I see.' Peter was silent for a moment as he weighed up the implications. 'So, you don't think we stand much of a chance?'

'I wouldn't go that far. All I'm saying is that we've got to be prepared for things to go wrong.'

'I see.'

'Another drink, Peter?'

'No thanks, Eileen. Actually, I must go in a minute. I'm on duty from eight till ten.'

They rose and moved toward the door. 'Don't be too depressed about the twenty-third, Peter,' Bob said. 'Just remember that things could go awry. Meanwhile, if you think of anything they could use against you, let me know and we'll prepare a suitable answer.'

Bob's farewell remarks brought home the full import of the news. Peter stammered his goodnights and left quickly. On the way downstairs, he laughed bitterly. *Can they smear me? That's the laugh of the year! They've probably got enough material to discredit me four times over.*

He opened the door, turned into the quadrangle and walked straight into Arthur Benson. 'Oh sorry, Arthur.'

Arthur grunted. 'Don't worry. I'm on my way down the road. Fancy a quick pint?'

'I'm on duty in five minutes,' Peter replied ruefully.

'Oh, right. Been to see Bob, have you?' Peter nodded. Arthur looked grimmer than Peter had ever seen him. 'Bad isn't it?'

'That's the understatement of the year!' Peter responded with a bark of laughter.

'Oh, I don't know. Bob's worried, but—'

'He'd be a bloody sight more worried if knew about me!'

'Good Lord, I hadn't really thought about that.'

'Neither had I, until Bob asked me to warn him if there was anything they could use against me.'

'Did you tell him?'

Peter shook his head. 'Of course not. How could I?'

'Forewarned is forearmed, as they say.'

'Yes, but there's not only me to consider. There's Terry – and possibly John, as well.'

'That's true, I suppose.'

'In any case, if it came out at the meeting that Bob was employing two – possibly three – gay teachers and *knew* they were gay, it might make his position even worse.'

Arthur remained silent, watching his breath rise in the

crisp night air. Peter wanted to cry. Arthur caught his expression and patted him on the back. 'Never mind, lad – we may be exaggerating, you know.'

Peter shook his head. 'No, Arthur. Somehow I don't think so.'

John Taylor parked his car in the drive and slumped in his seat. He could not remember a time before when he had felt so tired. Of course, last night had done it. It was his own fault; he should never have tried, but the attempt had been essential. If he had succeeded in making love to Kate, everything would have been all right. If only...

He hadn't, so that was that. The question was, what happened now? He had lain awake all night trying to work that out and failed miserably – as in everything else. He smiled ruefully; a tired failure. Not bad for twenty-four. Took some doing, when you thought about it.

He roused himself and got out of the car. He glanced at his watch: eight o'clock. Kate would be furious. He quickened his step and opened the front door. 'Kate?'

Silence. Oh, not again!

'Kate, I'm home!'

The bungalow was clearly empty. Then he saw the note on the hall table. As with Peter, five years earlier, he did not need to open it. He knew.

Kate had gone.

Chapter 29

WORD of the meeting spread rapidly and the topic became the main interest of many people as the days wore on. Letters home were full of the subject so Bob had to spend considerable time reassuring anxious parents. His main supporters assessed the prospects quickly, concluded that they were not good, and thereafter avoided the subject.

Peter, in particular, was worried. He became irritable and introspective, much to Terry's dismay. Ian Palmer was deeply angry about the whole thing and was in a bad mood for a week. Bob had four rows with Eileen in as many days, something unheard of in their fifteen years of marriage.

Of all the people involved, Arthur bore the brunt. He alone knew everything that could be used to smear his friends, even though he was not directly threatened himself. He alone was detached enough to realise that if a scandal involving the assault of a junior boy, allegations of victimisation and accusations about gay teachers ever became public, the school was finished. Utterly and completely. And what made it worse was that he was powerless; events had to take their course.

Consequently, everyone was relieved when the evening of the twenty-second arrived. As Arthur remarked, 'By this time tomorrow, we'll know the worst.'

The occasion was a dinner party, given by Eileen as

her gesture of defiance. The guests were Arthur, Ian, Terry and Peter. Against all the odds, the evening was a roaring success, causing Ian to compare it with the ball the night before Waterloo. The repartee of the four guests, sharpened by many hours in the pub, was at its best. Bob and Eileen, initially the amused spectators, eventually joined in and more than held their own.

Arthur's remarks about the following day came during the second round of liqueurs and were greeted with a pained look from Eileen. 'I'm sorry,' he said. 'But I could see everybody going quiet. We're obviously thinking about it, so we might as well bring it out into the open.'

Eileen smiled wistfully. 'I suppose you're right.'

'Shall I tell you something?' asked Bob, slurring his words slightly. 'The worst thing is that you've all kept me in the dark. I know something's going to go wrong tomorrow but I don't know what.'

Anxious glances were exchanged round the table.

'What do you mean?' asked Arthur.

'You know perfectly well, you devious old bugger!' Bob replied, laughing.

'You're right, of course,' the old man replied, chuckling. 'But you're going to stay in the dark until tomorrow. There's no other way, I'm afraid.'

'Why? Don't you trust me?'

'It's precisely because we do trust you that it has to happen this way.'

Bob shook his head. 'I still don't understand.'

'You will, Bob,' said Ian. 'You will.'

A few miles away, another dinner party was also drawing to a close. In the private dining room of a small country hotel, a group of five men were laughing, having just finished a long and detailed discussion of the prospects for the next day.

'Gentlemen, I give you a toast!' said Martin Fisher. 'To Warton College – may tomorrow see its salvation!'

The others rose and drank. Lawrence inclined his head. 'Nicely put, Martin, very nicely put.'

'And I'll give you another toast.' said Ian Thomas's father. 'Martin Fisher – the man who brought us together.'

'I'll drink to that,' exclaimed Forbes-Smith.

'Hear, hear!' cried Ian Thomas.

Fisher glowed. 'Thank you, gentlemen. A most enjoyable evening, and, I hope, a successful day tomorrow. Now, if you'll excuse me, I'll go and put the first stage of our plan into operation.'

John Taylor sat and stared miserably into the fireplace. He could not see it all that clearly, and there were sometimes two of them, but it was better than going to bed. The room tended to spin if he lay down and he knew that any attempt at sleep would be futile.

The miracle was that nobody at school had noticed that Kate was gone. Whether that was a tribute to his ability to keep up appearances, or because of the preoccupation with the governors' meeting, he did not know. He suspected that it was the latter. But here he was, going in to work every day after two hours' sleep in a chair, hung over and increasingly haggard in appearance.

It was a good measure, he decided, of yet another failure: he was such a colourless figure that nobody took any notice of him. Well, if that was the way they wanted it, fine. He did not need a shoulder to cry on. Sod 'em!

That was all very fine and nice, but it did not cure the loneliness. It was true that everybody had been preoccupied with the meeting but Arthur would have helped, given the opportunity. But how could he tell Arthur? The man had been right to advise him against his marriage but how could John admit that now? And worse, admit why the marriage had failed, with all its implications?

John knew that Arthur was not, and never had been, a man to enjoy scoring points at other people's expense. Things could not go on like this and who better to seek help from?

'No,' he said out loud. 'I've got to work it out for myself.'

But how was he going to work it out? By drinking himself to death? By getting the sack? After all, failure to have sex with a woman was not the end of the world. And Kate walking out like that had made him the injured party. Maybe it was time that John admitted the truth. Peter had five years ago and with John's help. He seemed happy enough.

But I'm not like that! I was cured.

The Jordans' guests left very late amidst more laughter, which had to be hastily suppressed for fear of waking the whole school. The party split up quickly and Ian supported a somewhat unsteady Arthur back to his rooms. Terry and Peter strolled towards the car park.

'Are you coming home?' asked Terry.

'Not tonight. I don't think it would be very wise, do you?'

'Perhaps you're right. But try to get some sleep. Don't sit up all night worrying.'

'All right. I promise to go straight to bed.'

'Good.' They reached Terry's car. 'Get in a minute. I've got something I want to say, and this seems the best moment.'

Peter frowned, but did as he was asked.

Terry lit cigarettes for them both; he was trembling slightly, and there was a tentative quality to his voice. 'I've been thinking about this for days but somehow the time's never been right. Now it is, I think.' He turned to look at Peter and smiled slightly. 'The booze tonight has probably helped.'

'Is it good or bad?' asked Peter, trying to ease the tension.

Terry laughed. 'That, young Harvest, depends entirely on your point of view. But seriously, I want you to remember this – especially tomorrow when this bloody meeting's on. I love you, Peter Harvey, and whatever tomorrow brings, I think I always will. So don't give up on me ... ever, all right?'

After all that had been said over the previous few weeks about their relationship, Peter was taken aback. He also realised what it must have taken Terry to get those words out. A lump in his throat prevented him replying. He took a deep drag on his cigarette and eventually was able to speak. 'That goes for me too.' He took Terry's hand and smiled at him. 'And thanks – you couldn't have timed it better.'

Peter leant over and kissed him quickly then got out of the car. As Terry started up and drove off, Peter waved briefly and set off back towards his rooms, smiling to himself. The smile disappeared as he found a note pushed halfway under the door. He frowned as he picked it up and opened it.

Peter
No matter how late, would appreciate a word in person about matters of mutual concern. Very important and could be to your advantage.
Fisher.

His first reaction was to laugh; the language was straight out of a cheap thriller. Then he realised that this was probably the first stage of a plan for tomorrow's meeting and he became frightened. Finally, it occurred to him that they were probably going to try to blackmail him, and that thought made him very angry indeed.

He set off for Fisher's rooms.

'So those are your alternatives, Peter,' concluded Fisher.

'Just one question. Are you going to bring John's name into all this?'

Fisher thought for a moment and then shook his head. 'No, he won't be named – for the moment.'

'I see.' Peter tried to think rapidly but it was difficult having drunk so much during the evening. One thing was clear: they had not cottoned on to Terry. If they were going to use the gay thing against him, it would be based on something that had happened seven years earlier. In a way that made him angrier; an attempt to discredit him

The Stamp of Nature

over something that happened so long ago made the whole thing that much more contemptible. 'So,' he continued, 'I haven't got much choice, have I?'

Fisher smiled. He could hardly keep the excitement from his voice. 'I'm glad you see it that way.'

'No, of course. I've got no choice at all if I'm to keep my self-respect. I must tell the truth.'

'But of course! Nobody's asking you to tell anything but the truth, old chap. Simply admit your mistake, that's all.'

Peter's self-control finally broke. He grabbed Fisher by his lapels. 'Why, you snivelling little bastard, you're too thick to understand what I'm saying, aren't you? I'm saying no! Fuck off – *I'm calling your bluff*! Now the ball's in your court. Go on, tell the governors that I slept with another boy seven years ago and see what bloody good it does you! Do it – but you won't get rid of Bob Jordan!'

Peter flung Fisher across the room and walked out.

Chapter 30

'THANK you, Mr Fisher. Now, if you don't mind, I'm going to ask the other governors if they wish to clarify anything or ask any other relevant questions.'

The governors' meeting was a strange affair, Peter reflected, as Martin Fisher finished his opening statement. The boardroom was set out like a court-martial, with the governors seated at a long table, flanked by two small tables. At one of these sat the headmaster and his deputy, whilst at the other were Ian Thomas and his father. Directly in front of the governors, there was a chair for those giving witness statements, currently occupied by Fisher. Behind that a row of chairs had been positioned for the witnesses and observers. A watery November sun streamed in through the high Gothic windows, though the countryside beyond was obscured by a persistent mist.

After some early debate as to how the meeting should be handled, it had been decided that all the evidence would be heard first, followed by closing statements from each of the parties. Martin Fisher had opened the proceedings; Peter, Alan Kelly, Peter Baxter, Ian Thomas and finally Bob would follow him.

Lawrence asked the first question of Fisher. 'Can I clarify one point, Mr Fisher? You stated, did you not, that this incident was reported to you but that you took no further action?'

'That is correct.'

'Why not?'

'Because I didn't think the reports warranted any.'

'How so?' interrupted the chairman.

'The open warfare between Thomas and the rest of the sixth was common knowledge. I thought this was probably an attempt to discredit Ian in the eyes of a fairly green member of staff.'

'I can confirm the open warfare from my time as headmaster, Mr Chairman,' interjected Lawrence.

'I see,' said Jim Stewart, forgetting what he was going to ask next. Then he remembered and opened his mouth to speak but was beaten to it by Forbes-Smith. He was the quintessential retired military man. Now in his mid-sixties, with a florid complexion, he had bulging, bright-blue eyes, piercing and rather intimidating. Square-jawed, his salt-and-pepper hair was brushed back and cut in the traditional short back and sides style still favoured by the army.

'So you considered the report to be an exaggerated piece of tale-telling?'

'Precisely so,' said Fisher with a smile. 'And my conclusion was confirmed by the failure of the alleged victim himself to complain to me.'

There was a ripple of conversation throughout the room, as this was generally acknowledged to be a 'good point'.

'Thank you, Mr Fisher.'

'Mr Chairman.' It was Bob, unhappy with the way things were going; clearly Lawrence and Forbes-Smith were aiming to dominate the proceedings. 'Would it be in order for me to ask Mr Fisher some questions?'

Fisher paled slightly. Forbes-Smith and Lawrence exchanged anxious glances and a few quick whispers.

'I don't see why not.'

'Really, Mr Chairman!' Forbes-Smith said in his best parade-ground voice. 'I can't accept that we should prolong this meeting so as to allow all the witnesses to cross-examine each other.'

'I do feel that the headmaster holds a somewhat special position, major,' replied the chairman.

'I couldn't disagree more.' It was Lawrence this time. 'If such facilities were extended to Dr Jordan, I am sure that Mr Thomas would expect parity of treatment...'

'Certainly would,' came a bark from the Thomas table.

'...which, apart from delaying the proceedings unnecessarily, would probably lead to heated exchanges that are clearly undesirable when we are trying to decide this boy's future. Furtherm—'

'Very well.' interrupted the chairman resignedly. 'Dr Jordan, I feel that the answer must be no.'

Bob sat back in his chair, furious. It was, he muttered to Arthur, virtually all over.

'Could Mr Harvey come forward, please?'

Peter walked towards the chair, shaking. *Oh Christ, I'm not going to enjoy this.*

'Right, Mr Harvey. I think you've probably gathered how we intend to work. Could you begin by telling us your story, please?'

Peter ran through his statement, from the argument he'd overheard on the first day of the new half term, through noticing Perkins' injuries to the expulsion. He was surprised by his own eloquence and felt rather pleased as he drew to a close.

The chairman evidently agreed. 'Thank you very much, Mr Harvey, for such a comprehensive statement. Are there any questions?'

'Yes, Mr Chairman. Several, actually.' It was Forbes-Smith. 'I believe, Mr Harvey, that there was some dispute with Ian Thomas before the half-term holiday?'

'That depends what you mean by dispute.'

'I was referring,' continued the major testily, 'to the complaint that Mr Thomas made to the headmaster and subsequently to this Board, concerning the book *A Portrait of the Artist as a Young Man*.'

'Oh yes – that,' Peter replied nonchalantly.

'What was your reaction to that complaint?'

'Amazement, to be frank.'

'Why amazement, Mr Harvey?' interrupted Lawrence.

'That such exception should be taken to what is generally accepted to be a classic of modern English Literature and an accepted part of the A-level syllabus.'

'Mr Chairman, I must protest! It's unutterable rubbish!'

'Kindly keep your remarks to yourself, Mr Thomas!'

'I'm sorry, Mr Chairman, but really!'

'Pray continue, Dr Lawrence.'

It was Forbes-Smith who resumed, causing Arthur to mutter to Bob that it was like watching a comic double act like Morecambe and Wise.

'What was your reaction to the complaint to this Board?'

'The same – amazement.'

'Come, come, Mr Harvey. Were you not also angry?'

'Not at all. I was amazed, and not a little concerned, that a sixth-form student should demonstrate such blind prejudice and a total lack of comprehension.'

'Mr Harvey! Do you really expect us to believe that

a boy and his father attack your integrity as a teacher, particularly in your first appointment, and it doesn't make you angry?'

The chairman intervened. 'Major Forbes-Smith, this is not some courtroom drama for television viewers. Please do not badger the witness.'

'I'm sorry, Mr Chairman, but I would like Mr Harvey to answer the question.'

'He's already answered you twice, Major. Now, have you any other points to make?'

Forbes-Smith went even redder in the face. 'No, thank you, Mr Chairman.'

'Very well. Thank you, Mr Harvey.'

Peter's sigh of relief was almost audible – but then Lawrence intervened. 'I have no further questions at the moment, Mr Chairman, but would it be in order to ask Mr Harvey to hold himself ready to help us further at a later hour?'

'Would you mind, Mr Harvey?'

Peter swallowed hard. Bob shot Arthur a questioning look, which he answered with a shrug. Terry and Ian exchanged worried glances.

'Not at all, Mr Chairman. It was my intention to remain for the rest of the meeting anyway.'

'Thank you, Mr Kelly. An admirably precise statement.'

'Thank you, sir.'

'Any questions?'

'Yes, Mr Chairman.' It was Lawrence.

Jim Stewart looked at Bob and raised his eyes

heavenwards, whilst Peter shifted uneasily in his seat. Alan stared blankly ahead.

'Very well. Proceed.'

'Mr Kelly, you have been in the school for just over six years. Is that correct?'

'Yes, sir,' Alan replied, puzzled.

'And that puts you in the same year as Ian Thomas?'

'Yes, sir.'

'How would you say that you got on with each other over the years?'

'Not very well.'

'Would it be too strong to describe your relationship as one of dislike?'

'We've never been friends and we've had strong disagreements from time to time.'

'Now, I believe one of these – er – disagreements took place on the first morning of the new half. Is that correct?'

'Yes, sir.'

'During which Ian Thomas suggested that you owed your position as school captain to something other than merit?'

'I believe something of the sort was said. Yes.' Alan was worried now.

'Can you remember the allegation?'

'Not precisely, no.'

'Try, Mr Kelly, please.'

'Is this really relevant, Dr Lawrence?' asked the chairman.

'I think so, Mr Chairman. If Mr Thomas alleges in his letter that his son's expulsion was the result of a conspiracy by several people, each of whom had different reasons for wishing to see the boy expelled, I feel we are duty bound to explore those reasons.'

'Very well. Proceed.'

Bob looked at Arthur sharply. Arthur shook his head in resignation. Peter glanced at Terry, who whispered, 'Is he gay?' Peter nodded.

'Oh Christ. Poor devil.'

Eileen overheard, but still managed to smile reassuringly at her husband.

'Mr Kelly, shall I repeat the question?'

'There's no need, sir.' Alan was blushing furiously now and fighting to retain his self-control. 'Ian Thomas suggested that I owed my position to being a bum boy who serviced the staff.'

There was a gasp, followed by a long pause, whilst the meaning was explained to the less-worldly lady governors.

'What did you do when he said this?'

'I hit him.'

'Was there any truth in his allegation?'

'None whatever. I have never had a relationship of that kind with any member of the staff.'

Bob breathed a sigh of relief. Arthur relaxed his grip on the edge of the table. Fisher looked mildly disappointed at the denial but a small smile still registered his approval of the proceedings so far.

'Have you ever had that kind of relationship, as you put it, with anybody?'

Alan did not reply but looked appealingly at Bob.

'Mr Chairman,' interrupted Bob, 'I do not consider that question relevant to this hearing and I consider it outrageous for a boy to be subjected to this sort of character assassination when all he did was perform his prefectorial duties in an exemplary fashion.'

The Stamp of Nature

'The headmaster's statement remains to be proved, Mr Chairman,' countered Forbes-Smith, with a gleam of triumph in his eyes. 'Meanwhile, I think we can all interpret Kelly's silence correctly. I have no further questions.'

Alan left the chair and fled from the room. At a nod from her husband, Eileen followed. The questioning of Peter Baxter completed the morning's proceedings. By comparison, it was a fairly tame session; Fisher and Thomas had been unable to rake anything up from Baxter's past, so Forbes-Smith and Lawrence contented themselves with the suggestion that Baxter had taken part in the conspiracy out of misguided loyalty to his school captain.

Even so, lunch was a gloomy affair and the afternoon did not present a pleasant prospect.

'You deny that you beat Malcolm Perkins, then?'

'Yes, Mr Chairman.'

'Why did you confess to Dr Jordan?'

'He said that he had enough evidence to prove that I'd done it and that unless I admitted it and left the school within twenty-four hours, I'd get the same treatment.'

The room bubbled with amazement. Bob's self-control finally broke. 'Mr Chairman, that's absolute rubbish!'

'Rubbish or not,' countered Forbes-Smith, 'the boy knows what he's saying. He has as much right to be heard as you!'

'Kindly address your remarks to the chair, Major. Now, *please* may we have some order?'

'Ian, you say that Jordan had enough evidence to

prove that you committed the alleged offence...' this was Lawrence '...so why should these people lie about it?'

'Well, they all had their reasons for wanting to get rid of me.'

'What were they, Ian? Don't be afraid to tell the truth.'

Bob's face was now purple with anger. Arthur shut his eyes. Peter began to shiver and Terry shifted uneasily in his seat. Ian Palmer regretted not murdering the boy when he'd had the impulse, which had been frequent. Fisher gazed happily at the sunshine,

'We've already heard about two. Harvey—'

'*Who*?' said the chairman sharply.

'Sorry. *Mr* Harvey wanted me out because I complained about that disgusting book. And Kelly was worried because I knew about him being queer. Actually, those two spent a lot of time together, so I wondered about Mr Harvey as well...'

There was another communal gasp. Peter's eyes immediately sought Alan, who had insisted on returning after lunch, but he was looking straight ahead, his face scarlet again. Peter glanced at Arthur, who raised his eyebrows. This was answered in turn by a barely perceptible shake of the head, much to Arthur's relief. John Taylor, who had also come in after lunch, coughed. Eileen Jordan smiled sadly: she was steadily losing all her remaining faith in human nature.

'Stick to facts, please, boy,' said the chairman tersely.

'That's a laugh,' remarked Arthur, rather more audibly than he had intended.

'I think Perkins was probably blackmailed into saying it was me,' continued Thomas airily. 'And of course that suited the head, who knew I was leading the opposition to his reforms.'

There was a pause.

'Any more questions? Very well. You may return to your seat, Thomas. Now, Dr Jordan—'

Lawrence interrupted. 'Mr Chairman, may I now request that we ask Mr Harvey to answer a few more questions before we hear the headmaster?'

'Very well. Mr Harvey?'

Peter was blushing before he even sat down – it was as if all eyes in the room were drilling into him. Arthur was praying fervently, a rare event. John Taylor stared fixedly ahead, waiting for the blow to fall on him too. Terry was trying to match Arthur's fervour in prayer, whilst Ian Palmer was thinking up all the ways in which he could make Thomas's life hell when he was reinstated. Bob began to phrase his letter of resignation.

'Mr Harvey, what is your relationship with the school captain?' asked Forbes-Smith.

'I am his English master and assistant house master. I am friendly with him as a result of those two contacts.'

'Nothing more?'

'What do you mean, Major?'

Forbes-Smith smiled. 'You heard the allegation. I think we can all guess whether you are telling the truth or not, but I'll leave the matter there.'

Peter saw red. 'You bloody well will not. I'm sorry, Mr Chairman, but this – person has virtually accused me of committing a criminal offence. I will not tolerate such innuendo. I demand that he either substantiate his allegation or withdraw it.'

Peter's counter-attack took the meeting by surprise. The Forbes-Smith intervention had been unplanned; the expression on Lawrence's face made that obvious. Bob could have cheered, but it would have been premature.

'Well, Major?' asked the chairman.

Forbes-Smith smiled. 'Mr Harvey's anger does him credit, Mr Chairman, if not his way of expressing it. In reply, however, I must ask Mr Harvey whether he denies that he is homosexual.'

Peter's fear, momentarily banished by blinding anger, returned with new force. He had been expecting this ever since the meeting had been announced. John Taylor and Terry exchanged glances. Arthur cleared his throat disapprovingly, and Bob returned to phrasing his resignation letter.

'With respect, Mr Chairman,' Peter said eventually, 'that is not the point at issue.'

'No,' agreed Lawrence. 'But I'm sure that the governors would be interested to hear your answer.'

Peter was shaking from head to foot, but refused to budge. 'I repeat, Mr Chairman, that Major Forbes-Smith has suggested that I have had a homosexual relationship with a pupil of this school. Were that to be true, I would be guilty of a criminal offence not to mention an unforgivable breach of trust. Now, is he going to withdraw that accusation or do I leave this room now and institute proceedings for slander?'

'I withdraw the accusation unreservedly.'

'Thank you, Major,' said the chairman, with a sigh of relief. 'Now are there any more questions for Mr Harvey?'

'As I recall, Mr Chairman,' said Lawrence doggedly, 'Mr Harvey has yet to answer the last question. Is he or is he not homosexual?'

Bob tried to intervene. 'Mr Chairman, I really don't see

the relevance—'

'With respect, Mr Chairman,' Forbes-Smith interrupted, 'it is for the governors to decide the relevance or otherwise of the evidence we hear today. Now, can we please have an answer to Dr Lawrence's question?'

'The answer, Mr Chairman, is yes. I am not, like others have done today, prepared to sit in this chair and tell lies. Nor am I prepared to apologise to this meeting, or to anybody else, for something that is my private business and totally irrelevant to the matter under consideration.'

'On the contrary, Mr Chairman,' retorted Lawrence. 'I consider it extremely relevant that a boy due to take his A-levels in seven or eight months' time should have his career jeopardised on the evidence of two self-confessed sexual perverts who had separate, but equally compelling, reasons for wishing the boy out of this school.'

'I've heard enough, Mr Chairman.' Forbes-Smith spoke on cue. 'I propose that question now be put.'

'Seconded.' This came from Mrs Stamford, one of the lady governors. Her backing of the move to curtail the proceedings spelt disaster.

'Mr Chairman, I will be heard! As headmaster of this school, I demand that the governors hear me before making a decision!' Bob shouted.

'I am afraid that the headmaster is out of order, Mr Chairman,' Lawrence responded, keeping his tone reasonable. 'There is a motion on the table.'

'I am well aware of the fact,' the chairman snapped. 'However, I feel that the headmaster—'

'Order!' Forbes-Smith interjected. 'You have no alternative but to put the motion. Now please do so!'

'Major Forbes-Smith, I will *not* be shouted at! Kindly

restrain yourself and allow me to finish! I was about to say that I feel that the headmaster should be allowed to have his say in order that the governors may have the benefit of his guidance.'

'With respect, Mr Chairman,' said Mrs Stamford, 'if the governors require that guidance, they will defeat the major's motion and allow the meeting to continue.'

Jim Stewart sighed. 'Very well. The motion is that the question now be put. Can I see those in favour? Against? I declare the motion carried by four votes to two. I shall adjourn for ten minutes, after which the governors will reconvene in camera to consider their findings.'

Chapter 31

'SO now you know,' Arthur said with a sigh.

Bob nodded but said nothing,

'I'm sorry, Bob,' Peter added. 'Perhaps we should have warned you, after all.'

'I can't deny that it's been a shock and that I would have preferred it to have been broken gently, in stages. But I also understand why you've done it this way.'

The conversation was interrupted by Eileen bringing in cups of tea. It was a grim gathering, she reflected. Alan Kelly look ghastly, slumped in a chair in the corner. Terry, Ian and Peter sat on the sofa, silently staring at their feet. Arthur was perched on the edge of an armchair, leaving it occasionally to pace up and down. Her husband stood by the fireplace, leaning on the mantelpiece and staring grimly at the glowing embers.

'Tea up!' she said brightly. The tea was welcome but the response was half-hearted.

'Peter, for my own peace of mind, is there anything between you and Alan?'

Peter looked offended by Bob's question and did not have time to reply before Alan stepped in. 'No there isn't,' he snapped. 'We were telling the truth.'

'There is between Peter and me, though,' added Terry.

Bob looked up sharply. 'I don't want to know that,

Terry. It's none of my business.'

'But...'

'But nothing. What you do in your private life, off these premises, is your own affair. No doubt our esteemed governing body would disagree but I'm not about to give them the opportunity. That will remain true as long as I'm headmaster here.' He paused, then added sadly, 'The trouble is, how long will that be?'

Arthur grunted. 'As long as you want.'

Bob shook his head and was about to speak when there was a knock on the door. 'Come in.'

It was a fourth-form boy, carrying a large, sealed envelope. 'Jolly Ro— I mean Dr Lawrence told me to give you this, sir.'

'Thank you, Phillips. Where is Dr Lawrence now?'

'He's left, sir, and so have the others, I think.'

Bob frowned. 'Oh well... thank you, Phillips, you may go.'

'Yes, sir.' The boy left quickly, eager to relate his part in the drama to his mates.

There was silence as Bob tore open the envelope. Inside were two sheets of school notepaper. He read aloud:

'*THE GOVERNORS OF WARTON COLLEGE, at their meeting on 23 November 1973, felt that the events which took place during the early part of the meeting rendered it desirable that they should leave the school without seeing any of the parties again, and consequently that their findings, recommendations and observations should be communicated in writing.*

'*IT IS RESOLVED:*

'*FIRST, that on the specific issue of the Thomas expulsion, there exists sufficient doubt to render the case not proven.*

'SECOND, that the boy should be given the benefit of that doubt, and will therefore be reinstated with immediate effect.

'THIRD, that in view of the various facts and suspicions which came to light during the meeting, the school no longer requires the services of Mr Peter Harvey, His employment will, therefore, be terminated at the close of the Autumn Term.

'FOURTH, that, in view of the various facts and suspicions which came to light during the meeting, the headmaster should invite the School Captain to resign the position, ensure that the boy seeks medical help, and warn him that (a) any public expression of any views, or (b) any behaviour, which might be interpreted as sympathetic towards homosexuals or homosexuality, will result in his immediate expulsion, without right of appeal to this governing body.

'FIFTH, that in view of the various facts and suspicions which came to light during the meeting, the headmaster and his staff should be required to increase their vigilance in watching for and stamping out any signs of homosexual activity within the school.

'SIXTH, that the Governors should meet again to review progress in this direction, and other related matters, before the end of term. A second emergency meeting will, therefore, take place on 18 December 1973.

'TWO MEMBERS of the Board of Governors, Mr R S J Stewart (Chairman) and Miss Y L Armitage, LCC, wish to make it clear that they totally disassociate themselves from the above recommendations and observations.

'THE GOVERNORS OF WARTON COLLEGE wish to state that, whilst they recognise that this resolution may lead the headmaster to reconsider his position, it is their unanimous and fervent hope that he decides to remain.'

Book Three, Chapter 31

Bob flung the sheets on the table. 'Pompous, melodramatic, bloody rubbish!'

'I quite agree,' said Jim Stewart, the chairman, standing in the doorway.

'Jim!' exclaimed Bob. 'I thought you'd left.'

'As one of the dissenting voices, I didn't see why I should stand by that bit either. Besides, I wanted to apologise to you all for that disgraceful exhibition. I've never seen anything like it in my life.'

'Thanks, Jim, that's much appreciated,' replied Bob. 'We know it wasn't your fault – but thanks for coming back.'

'What are you going to do now?'

'Resign. What else can I do?'

Jim Stewart grunted. 'That's another reason why I came back. I thought you might say that.' He regarded Bob with a steady gaze. 'If you resign, I'll never speak to you again.'

'Oh, come off it, Jim! What alternative is there? The governors overrule me on an expulsion on the flimsy pretext of smear campaigns against Peter and Alan, coupled with a tissue of lies. I can't take that!'

Ian Palmer spoke for the first time since the adjournment. 'You must, Bob. Look, you know as well as I do that this was a put-up job to force you out.'

'Yes, and a bloody good job they've done, too.'

'But that's the whole point,' Ian retorted. 'They haven't done a good job at all. Think about it. The Fisher gang tried to say that it was all a conspiracy to get rid of Thomas. Well, they failed. All this resolution says is that there is some doubt. They haven't overturned the new rules. They couldn't accuse you of covering up for Alan and Peter, because you didn't know they were gay. Neither of them teach here because of your decision: Alan was Jolly Roger's choice for school captain, and Peter was engaged before you arrived. Peter's dismissal without any evidence is clearly illegal and they'll have to back down on that. All you've got to put up with is Thomas's return – and he'll put his foot in it again PDQ, don't you worry!'

'But it's the principle of the thing!'

'Oh sod the principle!' interrupted Arthur, red in the face. 'Bob, I thought I knew you better than that. Don't you believe in what you're trying to do with this school?'

'Of course I do.'

'So are you really going to give up?'

'I've got no choice.'

'Of course you've got a choice! You're putting your own bruised ego before anything else.'

'I suppose that's one point of view, but—'

'There are no buts, Bob,' Terry interrupted. 'That campaign of lies and half-truths today was aimed primarily at you. In the end, as Ian says, they failed to nail you. Admittedly they've done a pretty good job on Peter and Alan, but it's you they were after. Now they'll be expecting you to go. That's why they didn't call for your resignation – they didn't think they'd need to. But you don't *have* to do the decent thing. Why shouldn't you play as dirty as they did?'

Ian Palmer resumed. 'You were right just now, when you said that you'd no choice. You haven't – you must stay!'

Then Eileen chipped in. 'He's right, you know, Bob.'

Bob held up his hands in surrender. 'All right, you win. I'll stay. But what do we do next?'

Chapter 32

DURING one of the less traumatic moments of the governors' meeting, one thing struck Arthur with some force: John Taylor's appearance. His clothes looked as if he had slept in them, and his face was haggard. As always with John, his eyes were the real clue. As before, they were flitting nervously from one thing to another and blinking constantly. There was definitely something wrong. Acting on this, Arthur collared him immediately after the adjournment and arranged to see him at six o'clock.

John was taken by surprise and found himself alternating between being glad of the chance to talk and determined not to keep the appointment. He realised that once Arthur had spotted something wrong, he would not let go until he found out what it was.

'Ah, John. Come in and sit down.'

'Thanks.'

'That was quite a day, wasn't it?'

'You're not kidding. Is Pet— I mean everyone all right?'

'*As well as can be expected* is the correct phrase, I think.'

'Good. What about the head? He's not resigning, is he?'

'No, thank the Lord. It was a near thing, though. It took five of us to talk him round.'

'Phew. That's a relief, anyway. I was a bit worried about that.'

'Were you?'

'Yes of course! What do you mean?'

'I thought that, judging by the look of you, you had something else on your mind.'

'Me? No, no. Everything's fine.'

'Look, John, it's no good trying that line with me,' Arthur responded, with what he hoped was an encouraging smile. 'We may not have seen much of each other this term but I still know you better than that. Besides, you and I have had this conversation before, when Peter left to go up to Oxford. Remember?'

John nodded.

'Right. So what's up?'

There was no reply for a moment while John studied his feet very carefully. Part of him wanted to keep Kate's absence quiet and was putting up one last struggle, but to no avail. He looked up eventually and blinked. To Arthur, he looked seventeen again, a frightened boy.

'Kate left me a fortnight ago. I...' The rest of the sentence was inaudible as he broke down and cried for the first time since she had left. It was as if telling somebody else made it real, instead of a very bad dream.

Arthur went to the drinks cupboard and poured two large scotches. He placed them on the coffee table then perched on the arm of John's chair and patted his shoulder.

'I'm sorry,' John said, sniffing loudly.

'Don't be daft, lad. Now have a drink. It's better to cry than keep it all bottled up inside. Why on earth didn't you come to see me before?'

'I don't know really. You were all worried about the meeting and I didn't want to make it worse. Besides, I...'

'Didn't want to admit it?'

John nodded. 'You advised me against the marriage and I couldn't face admitting I was wrong.'

Arthur grunted. 'Perhaps I should have kept my mouth shut. But in September I thought that everything was okay.'

'We must have been putting on a good show, then.'

'Oh?'

'It was no good from the start.'

'Why?'

John opened his mouth to speak then hesitated. He drank some more whisky and stared out of the window.

Arthur broke the silence. 'No matter how hard I try, I can't make this any easier for you.'

'You know the answer. I don't know why I can't say it,' John replied.

Arthur remained silent. John got up and walked towards the window. Staring across the fields, he found the words. 'I couldn't make love to her.' He turned to face the older man. 'I succeeded once, on our wedding night, when I was so pissed that I couldn't remember it the next morning. But that was it.' There was another pause. 'I tried – God, how I tried! – right up until the night she left, but it was no good.'

'Maybe she wasn't right for you.'

'Oh, I thought of that but it won't wash. I'm just not attracted – quite the opposite, in fact.'

'So?'

'So,' echoed John. To his surprise, he had already taken the next logical step, so the words came easily. 'We've come full circle. Here I am, face to face with something I've been running away from for five years. I'm gay.'

'I'm sorry, John. Very sorry.'

The Stamp of Nature

'Oh, don't be! After all, Peter's happy enough, isn't he?'

'He was until this afternoon. But I didn't mean it in that sense – I'm only sorry that it's taken so long and cost so much for you to come to terms with it.'

John looked up. 'I just feel so *angry*. Those people in the hospital convinced me that I could be cured. They told me it was what I needed to be able to forgive myself for my parents' accident. What a load of rubbish! They were projecting their false morality and their fear of being *different* onto me! So they fuck up my life, ruin Peter's happiness and—' He shrugged. 'Yeah, well. I suppose it's Kate I really feel sorry for. I was so selfish to marry her in the first place.'

'Yes, but she's young enough to make something of the future.'

'We both are – I hope.'

'Peter, are you awake?'

'Mm,' he said sleepily, turning over.

'Come on then. I've got us something to eat. I was lying here and suddenly realised that we've had nothing since lunchtime.' Terry smiled. 'Besides, your amorous demands have made me hungry.'

Peter sat up and grinned, pushing the tousled hair away from his eyes. 'What time is it?'

'About eight, I think. Now come on or you'll have these cold.'

'Oh, bacon butties – great!' They both ate hungrily without speaking. 'That was just what I needed. Cigarette?'

'Please.'

Suddenly Peter's face grew serious. 'Terry – thanks.'

Terry laughed. 'What for?'

'Being alive. Being there this afternoon. Bringing me back here. Making love. Anything – you name it – but thanks.'

'I always thought you were more than halfway round the bend. Now I'm convinced.'

'Definitely – and decadent with it,' Peter replied. 'Going to bed at six in the evening.'

'But waking up for bacon butties at eight.'

'Yes, that was the best bit. Hey! You know that would make a good book title? *Bacon Butties at Eight* by Friar Degg.'

Terry choked on his coffee. 'All right,' he said, recovering. 'How about *Bread Buttered on Both Sides* by Ivor Knife?'

'Not bad. Not bad at all.'

'Or the famous *Marooned* by I C Noships?' This was a parting shot as Terry took the tray back to the kitchen. When he returned to the bedroom, the smile had left Peter's face and he was staring blankly at the wall. Terry got back into bed and took him in his arms. 'Don't think about it, Peter. It's over.'

'I can't help it.'

Terry was silent.

Pictures of the afternoon flashed through Peter's mind, principally Bob reading the words of the resolution. '*The school no longer requires the services of Mr Peter Harvey. His employment will therefore be terminated...*' He shivered. It was all very well talking about victories and defeats, resignation and principles, but it was him they'd sacked.

And for what? Because he was gay. Simple as that. No matter that he had refused to sleep with the school captain, that he was no more interested in casual sex with fourteen year olds than a straight teacher in a girls' school. Why, then? Because he didn't conform; he was so different that he had to be classed as a monster, not fit to teach at Warton, or anywhere else for that matter. And how had they found out? Because some bastard, who couldn't teach a cat to catch a mouse, had tried to blackmail him and hadn't been bluffing.

The school no longer requires the services of Mr Peter Harvey ... should have his future jeopardised by two self-confessed sexual perverts... Are you homosexual? Have you ever had a relationship of that kind, as you put it, with anybody?

He moved violently away from Terry, trying to shake away the memories, but they remained: *...should have his career jeopardised...*

'Hey,' said Terry gently.

'I'm sorry. I can't stop thinking about it. Words keep going round and round in my head.' Terry raised himself on one elbow and looked at him. Tears welled up in Peter's eyes. 'They sacked me, Terry. The bastards *sacked* me.'

'But Bob'll get your job back. Don't worry. I thought you were bloody marvellous this afternoon. So did everybody.'

'I was frightened to death.'

'Well, it didn't show. The way you rounded on Forbes-Smith – I shall chuckle about that long after the rest of it is forgotten.'

'Yes, I enjoyed that bit.' Peter smiled briefly, but then sighed. 'Poor old Alan, though.'

'Yes, he had a bad time.'

'He's worse off being on his own. At least I've got you.'

'Yes, but everyone will rally round.'

'It's not the same.'

'I know, but he'll survive – he's got a tough hide, that one.'

Peter began to cry. Terry held him again but said nothing: some sort of reaction had been inevitable. Terry recalled the hatred that Forbes-Smith had managed to pour into the word 'homosexual'. It made him angry: how dare they use people's private lives as a weapon? Were their own lives so bloody perfect? Who the hell were they to judge and condemn? What sort of fucking bastards were they?

After a few minutes, all was still again. He glanced down and saw that Peter had drifted off to sleep. He smiled; perhaps the world wasn't so bad after all.

'Yes?'

'Can I come in for a minute, Martin?'

Fisher was surprised, and not a little disturbed, by his visitor; he could not recall having received a social call from John Taylor before. 'I suppose so,' he said truculently.

'Thanks.'

'What can I do for you?'

'It's about today's meeting.'

Now Fisher really was worried. 'What about it?'

'I'd just like to know why, that's all.'

'Why what?'

'Why you put together that fabric of lies and half-truths to try to destroy everybody.'

'Why worry? Your name wasn't mentioned.'

'No, no, that's true. I should be grateful for that, I

The Stamp of Nature

suppose. But I'd still like to know why.'

'To save the school.'

John laughed. 'Save the school? From what?'

'From destruction by trendy, left-wing reforms.'

'Oh, I see. That explains it all. Thank you very much,' John replied with a smile.

Fisher also smiled, but with relief as they moved towards the door. Suddenly, John turned round, hit him twice and sent him sprawling across the floor. 'But you're still a bastard,' he said. 'And a stupid one at that.' And he walked out.

'Cocoa, young man?'

Alan smiled and nodded. He had been looked after continuously since the meeting and had had no time to think about what happened. In one sense, that was fine; it was easier to shut out the memory than to face it. But face it he must, and Arthur was the best person to help him do it.

They reached Arthur's rooms and sat down. 'I have a feeling that scotch might be more appropriate than cocoa, don't you?'

Alan grinned. 'I'm certainly not going to argue.'

Arthur busied himself with the drinks. 'I suppose,' he said with a smile, 'the bastards would sack me as well if they saw this.'

'Probably, but I'd say it was ginger ale.'

'I should think so! Here you are – don't drink it all at once. How do you feel?'

'God knows. I certainly don't.' Arthur remained

silent. 'I suppose,' Alan continued, 'that losing the school captain's job will hurt...'

'*If* you lose it.'

'If?'

'The head hasn't asked for your resignation, has he?'

'No.'

'And I shall be very surprised if he does.'

'Oh. That's the only thing that would really hurt. The rest of it doesn't mean much. When you spend so long throwing the same insults at yourself and coming to terms with them, it doesn't matter if other people repeat them.'

'That's a very phlegmatic attitude, I must say. I'm impressed.'

'It's the only way; I decided that a long time ago. The funny thing is, though, that it all happened as Peter said it would.'

Alan smiled sardonically, realising he had trapped himself into a confession. 'How do you mean?'

'Before half term, I told Peter that I was in love with him.'

'You did *what*?'

'I told Peter that I was in love with him and wanted to go to bed with him.'

'You don't mince your words, do you?'

Alan laughed. 'That's what he said.'

'And what else did he say?'

'In a word, no. He said it would be wrong and the risk was too great. It wasn't worth it.'

'And?'

'I got annoyed and we had a row. He said that there was more to life than sex and the rest of his life was more important. I called him a coward. But the silly thing is that it didn't matter in the end. You don't have to do anything wrong – just say the word "gay" and bang! You're out. That makes me so bloody mad, especially when the people who profit by preaching this false morality are lying, cheating bastards like Thomas and Fisher.'

'I couldn't have put it better myself,' replied Arthur. 'But they've got history on their side, I'm afraid. Little boys must be protected, etcetera.'

Alan laughed. 'And I don't need protection. They can put me in the stocks and throw names and abuse at me and sod the consequences. I don't matter, because I'm an outcast already. *"If they prick me, do I not bleed?"'*

'I'm afraid that's spot on, Alan. Depressing, isn't it?'

'So what if you'd taken the same attitude as Fisher and the rest? I could have gone out and drowned myself tonight. What then? I suppose they'd say that I couldn't stand the guilt.'

'Something like that. Or that you were already off the rails, being queer and all.'

'Bloody marvellous, isn't it? And we call ourselves a Christian civilisation.'

'Yes, but things *are* changing, Alan.'

'Are they? After this afternoon you could have fooled me.'

'I can understand that, but even that lot will be forced to think it through in the end. At least they no longer send people to prison for it.'

'They could have sent Peter, if he'd accepted my offer. Besides, there are more ways of punishing people than sending them to prison, as we saw today.'

'Yes, but you've got to hope, Alan. Especially at your age.'

'I agree but sometimes it's bloody difficult. You can never really forget that you're different. Walking along the street, seeing a boy and girl holding hands. Parents and friends joking about girlfriends. Mates swapping stories about adventures during the vacation, and so on. You get used to it eventually, but it's there all the time.'

'Yes, but remember that so-called "straight" people can be equally unhappy.'

'Oh, I know, but you always have the feeling that they've started at least a lap in front. Don't get me wrong. I'm not one of those who thinks that you can't he happy if you're gay. You can be – but only if you accept your fate and stop feeling guilty about it.'

'I'm glad you've got that far, anyway.'

'Yes, but not without a struggle. And you learn all the time. For example, Peter taught me that you can only go so far. There are constraints and you've got to strike a balance somewhere. The bloody sad thing about today is that Peter thought he'd struck his, but he still lost.'

'True. I only hope your philosophy stands the test of time.'

Alan grinned. 'Oh, it will – if only because you can always adapt your philosophy to changing circumstances. It's arriving at one in the first place that's so hard.'

Arthur laughed. 'There are times, young Kelly, when you're too precocious even for me.'

'Don't you agree then?'

'Oh, yes. But it took me far longer than eighteen years to get there.'

The Stamp of Nature

As he drove home, John could not work out why he had even gone to see Fisher, still less hit him. 'Release, I suppose,' he said to himself. 'All the tension since Kate left finding an outlet – first with Arthur and then clouting Fisher.' He smiled; whatever the reason, he felt better for it – which was more than Fisher could say.

On a sudden impulse, he did not turn towards home but decided to walk by the sea. Parking his car on the deserted promenade he set off, talking to himself and feeling happier than he had for a very long time.

'Poor old Martin! Fancy hitting him like that. He really believes he's done the right thing. I suppose that makes it all the more sad, really. He's lived with an illusion and can't stand seeing it collapse in front of his face. Well, I know how that feels. Of course, he'll lose in the end – bound to. Bob'll find a way to hit back and then everything will settle down again. Ah, the gents. I could do with a pee.'

Vandals had smashed the lights inside the toilets. In the half-light from the blue street lamps, the place was eerie with deep black shadows. John had the feeling that he was being watched. After a few moments, a young, slim figure moved into a patch of light. John swallowed hard and shut his eyes. After a moment, the figure moved closer and reached out to stroke him.

Something within John shouted at him to leave, to run away; instead, he found himself responding, reaching for the stranger.

'I have a flat – would you like to go there?'

John was unable to speak.

The boy took this as assent. He smiled slightly. 'Come, it is this way.'

✥

Book Three, Chapter 32

The road was straight and wide, shimmering in the heat of summer. The air was heavy with the aromas of melting tar and newly mown grass. Peter strolled along happily, whistling to himself. After a while the school became visible. At first the view was hazy, like a mirage, but gradually the outline became firmer. He smiled; it was like coming home after all those years as a boy and now being a master.

As he drew closer, though, subtle changes became apparent. The walls were higher, topped with broken glass, and sentries patrolled the gates. Blue coated, with white cross straps, they carried muskets.

Peter was amused — Warton's own tin soldiers! What on earth was going on? An end-of-term prank, perhaps, especially with those bright-red cheeks and button noses.

His laughter died as they stepped forward and barred his way, crossing their muskets. 'All right, chaps,' he said. 'Move over. I've got a class in ten minutes.'

They did not move. He drew closer, then spoke again. 'Come on, can't hold up the workers...' The words froze on his lips as the two figures became recognisable. Despite their absurd get-up, one was clearly Jolly Roger and the other Forbes-Smith. Their eyes were cold, their movements those of automatons, but their features were unmistakeable. Then they spoke in unison. 'We are the Guardians of Warton College. The school no longer requires the services of Mr Peter Harvey. His employment is therefore terminated.'

Peter's response was derisive. 'But this is absurd!'

'You are dismissed,' they continued. 'You may not pass.'

'But what shall I do? Where shall I go?'

'That is not our concern. The school no longer requires

The Stamp of Nature

the services of Mr Peter Harvey. You must take your chance, on The Road.'

They raised their muskets to point back along the road, and Peter saw his chance. He made a dash for it and passed them, but the gates were locked against him. He tried to climb them but the soldiers flung him to the ground. 'We are the Guardians of Warton College,' they repeated. 'The school no longer requires the services of Mr Peter Harvey. His employment is therefore terminated.'

Peter picked himself up, feeling bruised and dishevelled. He started to walk away. The soldiers began to laugh, shrill, echoing laughter, mocking and insulting him. He turned again, angrily. The soldiers stopped laughing and took aim with their muskets. Undeterred, he kept walking towards them.

They fired.

'Peter, Peter! Wake up. You've been dreaming again,' said Terry.

Chapter 33

PETER looked up and glared round the room. The fourth form was in a particularly trying mood this afternoon and he did not feel up to it. 'If you lot can't keep quiet and do as you're told, somebody will be visiting the headmaster. Clear?'

Two weeks had passed since the governors' meeting and, with one week to go, preparations were well-advanced for the next one. Fortunately, precise details of what had happened in the meeting had not leaked out but Thomas's reappearance had given the whole school a pretty good clue.

In a stormy interview the morning after the meeting, Bob had made it perfectly clear to Thomas that any discussion of what had taken place would land the boy in serious trouble. Somewhat to Bob's surprise, the message had got through. Even so, the atmosphere in the staff room when Martin Fisher appeared was very difficult, and sixth-form English lessons had become a nightmare for Peter. A separate timetable for Thomas was clearly out of the question but concentration, with him in the class to act as a constant reminder, was virtually impossible.

Peter's mood did not help either. Despite repeated assurances that his reinstatement was central to Bob's plans for a counter-attack, he was convinced that there would have to be a compromise and that he would be the victim. The message of his dream, which had recurred several times, seemed clear: he was out and that was that. It left him depressed and irritable.

It was the relationship with Terry that kept him going. Now confident of the depth and sincerity of Terry's love, he trusted and relied on him. Whatever his fears about the future, he was sure that Terry would always be there. The problem was that leaving Warton would also mean leaving Terry – and that was only three weeks away.

The bell rang signalling the end of school for the day. Peter breathed a sigh of relief – but then remembered that it meant that his departure was another day nearer.

'I'm worried, Arthur.'

Arthur looked up from his beer in surprise. 'You? Worried? Terry, I don't believe it.'

Terry smiled. 'There are things I don't believe about myself after this term. But there we are.'

'Go on, then. What's up?'

'It's Peter. I can't get him to understand that Bob will look after him next week. He's convinced that there'll be a compromise and his dismissal will stand.'

'But that's bloody ridiculous!'

'I know. I try to get him to talk about it, but he says he wants to forget about it when we're on our own. I can understand that, but what can I do if he won't talk? It makes me feel so bloody inadequate, that's the trouble.'

'Well it shouldn't,' replied Arthur sharply. 'You're doing more than any of us could by simply being around.

God knows what would happen if Peter didn't have you.'

'Yes, I suppose you're right.'

'In any case, it's only a week till the meeting. He'll know for sure then.'

'Yes, but...'

'But what?'

'Oh, nothing. You're right – it'll soon pass.'

Martin Fisher sighed and looked at his watch. He hated this eight-till-ten duty; it was difficult to settle to anything between patrols and ruined the evening completely. His mood was not improved by the realisation that the victory at the governors' meeting had been a hollow one.

When he had read the resolution, he had been dismayed to find that the advantage he had gained had not been fully pressed home. However, an optimistic Dr Lawrence had assured him that they could not have gone further and won so large a majority and that, in any case, Jordan's resignation was inevitable.

As the days had gone by, however, it was apparent that there was nothing inevitable about it at all. Strong rumours started to circulate that a counter-attack was being planned for the next meeting. The fact that Kelly remained entrenched as school captain seemed to confirm this.

Fisher stood up and paced the room in frustration. Using his mother's tactics wouldn't help him now – he had no weapons left. Besides, his own position after the disciplinary interview was weak and he could not afford any more personal gestures.

His thoughts were interrupted by the sound of running footsteps. He frowned. They stopped outside his door and someone knocked urgently. He answered immediately.

'Quick, sir, please, sir. There's trouble, sir, a fight.'

Fisher's heart sank as he was led to the sixth-form corridor. The door to Thomas's room was open and three pairs of scuffling feet were protruding into the corridor. Kelly and Baxter were trying to restrain Thomas whilst Perkins, the earlier first-form victim, cowered in a corner trying unsuccessfully to staunch the flow of blood from a cut over one eye.

The struggling stopped as Fisher appeared in the doorway. There was silence for a moment and then Alan Kelly spoke breathlessly. 'You believed it this time, then ... *sir?*'

Fisher winced at Kelly's tone. He could only nod in reply. Then he looked at Thomas. 'Oh, you bastard,' he said. 'You stupid, fucking bastard.'

'Thanks. See you again sometime.'

'Sure,' John responded with a smile. He shut the front door on the retreating figure, returned to the lounge to pour himself a drink, then went into the bedroom. He grimaced at the disordered bed and quickly set it to rights.

He felt none of the guilt he had experienced the first time with the foreign waiter – what was his name? Mario, that was it. John laughed now as he remembered the walk back from Mario's flat. His sensations of guilt had been explosive and he had sworn at himself volubly, using his entire vocabulary of homosexual abuse. He had vowed that it would never happen again.

But it had, the very next night. Sitting alone in the bungalow, watching television, he recalled the previous evening. Excitement had spread in the pit of his stomach; it was irresistible.

The pick-up had been simplicity itself. Afterwards the guilt had returned, and once more he vowed never to go back. He had stayed away for more than a week and felt smugly virtuous. But gradually the depression reappeared and the impulse had been welcome then. The mechanics of getting ready and going out took his mind off things. Sexually, the encounter had been disappointing but in the aftermath his guilt had been reduced to a mere flicker. And now, tonight, surely the best yet.

He smiled again. What had he been missing for the last five years? Sex was great – and the more the better. Of course, there were dangers and pick-ups in toilets were a bit sordid but what was the alternative? How did you meet people? True, there were pubs and clubs but they were in London; there was nothing like that in this part of the world, was there? In any case, he could not afford to be seen in that sort of dive, especially after the governors' meeting.

It was a pity that none of the people he had met so far seemed interested in another meeting, but he had to give it time. And there was no reason why that time should not be passed pleasantly.

'We seem to make a habit of late-night drinks in a crisis,' remarked Bob with a smile.

'Yes,' replied Arthur, smiling. 'Although I can't pretend that this one is unwelcome. Apart from young Perkins, of course. How is he?'

'Matron thought the cut might need some stitches, so she whisked him off to the infirmary.'

Arthur let out a low whistle. 'That bad, eh? What have you done about Thomas? Sent him packing again?'

Bob nodded. 'I told him that he'd be on the nine o'clock train from Carnforth in the morning. You know, I'm rather looking forward to telling the governors. I shall enjoy watching their faces.'

Arthur chuckled. 'Yes, I'm sure you will.'

They were silent for a moment.

'The funny thing is,' Bob said eventually, 'I felt rather sorry for Fisher tonight, having to come and report it.'

'I wouldn't have.'

'Don't worry, my sympathy didn't last long, believe me!' Bob responded.

'Did he apologise?'

'Not then. But he came back to see me later, to apologise – and to resign.'

'*What* did you say? Do you mean that you've let me sit here for twenty minutes without telling me?'

'Yes ... well, I thought I'd save the good news till last.'

'Rotten sod. What did he say, then?'

'He came back just after Matron set off for the hospital. He said that he felt he couldn't stay after what had happened, and could he leave at the end of term? I said that I quite understood and yes, he could certainly leave at the end of term. He's ... er ... off sick until then. Oh, and I got it in writing before he could change his mind.'

Arthur laughed. 'I don't blame you! That's marvellous

news. I feel as if somebody's lifted a ton weight from my shoulders.'

Chapter 34

PETER smiled as he put the letter down. It was typical of Mark, a poor correspondent at the best of times, to end a three-month silence with a five-line note.

Dear Peter
Sorry to have been so long writing, but have been v. busy with a play (yes, a job at last!). We open on the 12th – how about coming down this weekend to see the play and have a natter?
Yours ever, Mark.

Still, the invitation was welcome. A break from Warton would do him good and it would be nice to see Mark again; he might even be able to offer some advice about a job, now that Peter was about to get the sack. The only snag was what Terry would say, but he was not the jealous type and he could come too. Yes, that would be great; they could get down in time to see Mark's play on Friday night, then go to a concert on Saturday. Terry and Mark would get on like a house on fire.

Peter was full of enthusiasm and broached the subject with Terry as soon as he could, catching him in the quad at the end of the first period. 'Do you fancy a weekend in London?'

'Eh? What?'

'I've had a letter from Mark. You remember the actor I

told you about? He's opening in a new play and wants an audience. I thought we could both go down.'

'Oh.'

'Don't you want to go, then?'

Terry was taken aback by Peter's sudden change of mood and not best pleased about the cause of it. 'Not particularly,' he responded.

'Why ever not?'

'I'll think about it. We'll talk tonight.'

'I wanted to let him know today,' replied Peter, crestfallen.

'Well you go. You two won't want me there while you talk about old times.'

'Don't be daft.'

'I'm not going, Peter, and that's that. Now, I've got a class. I'll see you later.'

Peter opened his eyes wide in realisation and let out a short laugh. 'Terry, you're jealous!'

Terry glanced at him coldly. 'Don't be so bloody stupid,' he said, and stalked off.

'What was the matter with you this morning?' asked Peter later.

'Nothing,' replied Terry sharply.

'Oh, come off it!'

'All right, then. If you must know, I was bloody annoyed with you. One minute you're moping around as if the end of the world's come, then you get a letter from this bloke and you're full of the joys of spring and bouncing off to London. It hardly puts me in a good light, does it?'

The Stamp of Nature

'You *are* jealous. My God.'

'Peter, what did you expect?'

'I thought we said at the start ... I mean...'

'It was different then. Surely you understand that?'

'Yes, but it only makes it worse.'

'How do you work that one out?'

'You know how I feel about you, so why don't you trust me?'

'You're determined not to understand, aren't you?'

'I'm trying, believe me, but you aren't explaining yourself very well.'

'If you can't understand what I'm saying, I'm certainly not going to spell it out – I'm too tired. Now goodnight.' Terry switched off the lamp and moved as far away from Peter as he could. Peter lay still for a moment then got out of bed and started to dress.

'Where the hell are you going?' Terry demanded.

'Back to school.'

'Fair enough. See you tomorrow.'

Terry's cold tone was new to Peter and it hurt and baffled him. But there was no point in staying now; if he said any more, they were likely to have a blazing row. He left the house cursing, but still determined to go to London.

Peter left Mark at the stage door. He had seen the play, in which Mark played second lead, the previous night. He had thoroughly enjoyed it but seeing it two nights running was a bit much and, in any case, there were no seats left.

'What time did you say?' he asked.

'About eleven should see me clear – and Peter?'

'Yes?'

'Cheer up, man, for God's sake!'

Peter managed a smile, which seemed to satisfy Mark as he disappeared towards his dressing room.

Peter turned to face the glitter of London's West End. The morass of taxis, buses and people moved at a uniformly slow pace, all seeming to lack direction or purpose. More by instinct than design, he made his way to a nearby gay pub. He eventually managed to get a drink and settled down to assess the talent.

'Bloody rubbish,' John said to himself, turning the television off. 'Call it Saturday night entertainment – it's not worth the bloody licence fee!'

He sighed, and turned the radio on. 'And now on Radio Three, we have the first broadcast performance of...'

No, thank you. Then he smiled, feeling the familiar grip tighten on his stomach muscles. Only one answer, really. He went into the hall and fetched his coat.

Peter decided that he could not spend all evening in the pub. It was pleasant to be amongst his own kind again and a reminder of how many gay people there were in London. That had been a surprise when he'd first moved to the capital five years earlier; now, he found it comforting. The place was already busy and he knew from experience that it would get worse. It was also too full of memories.

It was easy to remember what it was like to be on your own, something he felt keenly tonight because he was here without Terry. The desperation that crept up if the evening wore on without meeting anybody 'suitable'; the agony of screwing up the courage to speak to somebody, only to be brushed off; the trying-to-be-casual 'give me a ring sometime' to somebody you liked, knowing damned well that they would not. He shivered. Never again.

He finished his drink and left, heading away from the West End, which seemed much noisier and more tawdry than he remembered. Walking towards the river, he wondered whether the trip had been a mistake. Terry's reaction had not changed during the week; the subject had been avoided when they were together and that had inevitably made for a strained atmosphere.

On the other hand, it was doing him good to be away from Warton for a couple of days and it was good to see Mark again. He had changed and seemed much more militant about being gay than before. Two or three years earlier, Mark had had the knack of adapting to the realities of gay life and building a satisfying existence within them. Peter had learned to do the same, hence the teaching and the return to Warton. Now, when he needed some reinforcement, Mark had turned away and was engaged in a struggle that, to Peter, seemed at best futile and at worst counter-productive.

John was frozen. It was a cold night and the wind was blowing straight through the entrance to the toilets. It was quiet, too; he had been out nearly an hour, but nobody was about. This was a waste of time.

He returned to the car but, once there, could not face

Book Three, Chapter 34

the thought of going home alone.

'Give it another half hour,' he said to himself.

Peter walked down Northumberland Avenue and reached the Embankment, mounting the steps to Hungerford Bridge. This was one of his favourite spots in the capital; it restored his faith in the grandeur and nobility of the city. Fine buildings from four centuries surrounded him: St Paul's from the seventeenth; Somerset House from the eighteenth; the Houses of Parliament, visible across the railway, from the nineteenth, and the South Bank complex from the twentieth.

He crossed the bridge and descended to the promenade in front of the Festival Hall, passing a lone busker playing jazz on a saxophone. He leant on the parapet and stared into the black water below. It was surprisingly quiet; the traffic noise was a distant growl, the wind rustled in the trees, and above all this came the plaintive note of the saxophone. The only disturbance was the occasional rumble of a train crossing the river into Charing Cross.

John looked up and saw a figure approaching along the promenade. He was young, judging by the clothes, anyway. Perhaps this might be it.

The boy glanced quickly at John's car, then turned and went into the toilets. John got out of the car and followed him.

What had been really disturbing, reflected Peter, was Mark's view of recent events at Warton. He had said that it was a typical case of anti-gay oppression, something that Peter could not argue with. Then he had suggested that the case should be used in the gay press to illustrate the point. 'Why not?' he had asked. 'You've got nothing to lose.'

'No, Mark.'

'Give me one good reason.'

'Because it's not that sort of fight. I've been used as a pawn in a battle over how to run a school. The fact that I was gay was a useful weapon, but that's all.'

'What's the difference? They shouldn't have been able to use that argument against *anybody*!'

'I agree, but that's not the point.'

'But it is! Don't you see? You're branded as gay and because of that, somehow you're worthless. It's precisely the sort of thing we have got to fight against!'

'Look, Mark. Two years ago, you told me to build a life based on something other than being gay. I took your advice and built that life. Now I've been lucky enough to meet Terry as well.'

'And your life is being destroyed by people who can't accept you as you are.'

'Yes, but the framework is still there – friends, allies and now maybe a partner – and they're far more important. What do you think would happen to all my friends – and to the school – if the story was plastered across the front pages? How many newspapers would be sympathetic? It would ruin the school, finish Bob and make that little bastard Thomas's case for him!'

'Possibly. But if a few people can be convinced, surely it's worth it? Not only to you but to other gays as well.

Book Three, Chapter 34

We've got to stick together. It's the only way to beat the establishment.'

'But I don't want to beat the establishment, I want to be part of it! Look, here I am, Peter John Harvey. One individual among thousands of millions on this earth. God or Fate or Nature or whatever decreed that I should like men rather than women. There's not much I can do about that, but it's only a small part of me. I still have ideas, perhaps even a contribution to make to the world. All I'm asking is to be allowed to get on with my life in the same way as other people, and for those other people to mind their own damned business about who I sleep with. Now you want me to go round broadcasting the fact that I'm gay even if it harms my friends and damages my other beliefs. Well, I'm sorry but I won't!'

Mark recognised defeat. 'You did listen well two years ago, didn't you?' He smiled and ruffled Peter's hair.

The blast of a hooter on the Thames brought Peter back to the present. The arguments were all very well but they would not pay his salary after Christmas. The governors would never agree to his reinstatement, regardless of what anybody said.

Then he smiled to himself. There was always Terry. Despite the problems this weekend, there was always Terry.

The chimes of Big Ben rang out the half hour. Time to head back.

They had been standing there for a few minutes. John looked across and met the boy's eyes. They moved towards each other and reached out. The boy sighed quietly and happily under John's touch. 'My place?' he whispered.

Suddenly, there was a bang. The door behind them burst open and two figures rushed in. 'Okay, you two! That's enough. You're under arrest.'

Chapter 35

IT was late when Peter got back from London on the Sunday night and, although he woke at the usual time on the Monday morning, it was difficult to raise enough enthusiasm to get up. He heard the rain lashing at the window and turned over.

When he awoke again, it was after nine. He leapt out of bed and rushed round his rooms, washing, shaving and dressing in record time. He did not notice the envelope that had been pushed under his door until he was about to leave. Recognising Terry's handwriting, he forgot his lateness, tore open the envelope and started to read.

Dear Peter
This isn't an easy letter to write, but I've done a lot of thinking over the weekend, and write it I must.
First of all, I owe you an apology. I have allowed our relationship to develop into something far more serious than I ever intended. It was wrong of me because I should have known what would happen in the end.
The row last week was the start of the process, and I've decided that I'm not going to allow things to get any worse. So, I'm afraid it must be over between us.

Peter felt his head swim. He stopped reading and slumped onto a chair. He was shaking, so he rested the letter on the chair arm.

You see, if we can't talk about things when we disagree,

there's no hope. You won't protect love like that, you'll kill it.
I suppose I could go on writing all night without making you understand properly.
I know this couldn't come at a worse time for you, but it's better than drifting, making ourselves even more unhappy. Once the governors' meeting is over this week and you've got your job back, you'll be able to cope.
Please accept this as final. I won't change my mind. If I did, it would only make matters worse in the long run,
Please try to understand,
Terry

Peter got up from the chair and looked out of the window. He tried to understand, to come to terms with what was surely the final blow. There was no hope, now; the new life he had built was smashed to pieces.

The view blurred as his eyes filled with tears. He blundered back to his bedroom and lay down on the bed, sobbing his heart out. After a while, he fell asleep again.

Arthur strode across the quadrangle. He was not pleased. 'I don't know what the hell the place is coming to.' he muttered to himself. 'First John Taylor rings in sick and now Peter doesn't turn up for his class.'

He had managed to cover the lessons and was on his way to find out what had happened to Peter. He could see that his bedroom curtains were still drawn.

'Overslept after gallivanting off to London for the weekend, I suppose. Not bloody good enough.'

He reached the door and knocked. No reply. The door was unlocked, so he opened it and went in. Through the bedroom door he saw that Peter was indeed asleep but fully clothed. Arthur frowned. Then his eye fell on the letter. Without thinking, he picked it up and read it.

'Damn and blast.'

John shut the front door and leant against it, eyes shut, breathing deeply. After a moment he recovered and went into the lounge. He poured himself a drink, sat down and closed his eyes once more.

He saw it all again. In the police car, then in the station, emptying his pockets; in the cell, staring at the whitewashed brickwork; the officers, back in uniform, talking gently, seeking co-operation and a statement. 'Ever been in trouble before?' 'Any other offences you want to talk us about?'

Yes, against Peter, Mum and Dad, Kate – but not against the law.

Then, this morning in the court. The policeman giving evidence. How revolting it all sounded.

'Is there anything you wish to say before sentence is passed?'

'No, thank you.'

The whispered consultation on the bench then, 'A serious offence, especially for somebody in your profession. Fined £100. Very serious view taken if either defendant appears before this Court again. How do you propose to pay?'

John shook his head. It was over and he had to stop thinking about it, concentrate on the future. But what if it was in the newspaper? What future would there be then? '*Teacher on Toilets Charge*' – Christ! A back court, they'd

The Stamp of Nature

said. No reporters, usually. But who was that bloke taking shorthand notes, then?

Please, not that!

When Peter awoke, he was surprised to find that it was early afternoon. The room felt stuffy and he had an appalling headache. He tried to remember whether he should be teaching, and then saw a note on his desk.

Have covered your timetable. Come and see me when you feel up to it. Arthur.

He decided to go for a walk to try and clear his head. The school was decked with Christmas decorations but they meant nothing to him. He was tempted for a moment to tear them down or set fire to them but he smiled at the impulse: vandalism would achieve nothing.

In the hall, he found the dramatic society having a dress rehearsal for the pantomime. It was good to see the tradition revived, a chance for everybody to enjoy themselves and a rest from the tedium of ham-acted Shakespearian tragedies.

It was never the comedies, he reflected; perhaps it was thought rude to laugh at Shakespeare in school. No, *Cinderella* was a good idea – good, clean fun. Except of course that the boy playing Cinderella might enjoy dressing up as a girl a little too much and the Prince may make a bit of a meal of the kiss in the final scene... But that sort of thing meant nothing; it was traditional, after all. It was only when you actually loved another boy that it was to be sneered at and used to blackmail you.

He left the hall, and walked through the quadrangle into

the chapel. The choir were rehearsing for the carol service. Peter never failed to be moved by Christmas music, and it worked its magic once again. Young Edmonds' clear voice in the solo first verse of *Once in Royal David's City* was a delight; it was a pity that the boy was such a little sod in class.

Then came his favourite hymn, always sung on the last day of term.

Saviour, again to Thy dear name we raise
With one accord our parting hymn of praise.

Suddenly, he was a student at Oxford again, visiting Warton for the day to take John out, seeing Arthur for cocoa and confessing his love... His voice joined the choir and tears ran down his face.

Guard Thou the lips from sin, the heart from shame
That in this house have called upon Thy name.
Grant us Thy peace, Lord, through the coming night
Turn Thou for us its darkness into light
From harm and danger keep Thy children free
For dark and light are both alike to thee.

The dismissal hymn started. Peter got up to leave.
Lord, dismiss us with Thy blessing...

'Ah, Terry, come in.' Arthur looked grim, and his voice was different.

Terry shrugged, supposing it was the strain of this never-ending term.

'I'd have had a word with you earlier, but I was too busy covering Peter's timetable.'

'Oh? Isn't he well?'

'No, he isn't. And frankly, I'm not surprised.' Arthur

paused and removed a letter from his inside pocket. 'Not after receiving this.'

Terry recognised it immediately and rose to leave. 'I'm not prepared to discuss—'

'*Sit down!*' Arthur roared.

Shocked, Terry obeyed.

'Why, Terry? Less than a week ago, you sat with me in the pub going on about being worried about Peter and his depression – and then you send him this!'

'I don't see what business it is of yours.'

'Balls! I thought I was your friend. If friendship means anything, it's the ability to be frank with each other.'

'I would have thought it also means knowing when not to interfere.'

'Indeed. But this isn't one of those occasions. And I owe it to Peter, even if I do lose your friendship as a result.'

'Peter's old enough to fight his own battles, without using you as a messenger.'

'Peter doesn't know I've seen this letter, so you can forget that line.'

'How did you get hold of it, anyway?'

Arthur sighed. 'It doesn't really matter, but if you must know I looked into his rooms earlier to find out what was wrong. He was asleep and I saw the letter on the floor. Terry, how could you send this, today of all days, with the governors' meeting tonight?'

'I decided – and it *is* my decision, after all – that it was for the best.'

'But why?'

'I failed him. I couldn't shake him out of his depression but that bloody letter from London did. So if Mark Foster is more important to him than I am, fair enough. I'm not going to compete – I've had enough of that in the past.'

'You don't really believe that, do you?'

'What else can I believe? This always happens, Arthur. I get so jealous that in the end I drive people away. Last night I decided that I'd be the one to make the break for a change. It'll be better for Peter in the long run.'

'You bloody fool.'

'What's that supposed to mean?'

'Do you love him?'

'Yes – too much.'

'There's no such thing as too much.'

'I happen to think there is but I'm not going to argue.'

'Does he love you?'

'You seem to think so.'

'Well, then...'

Terry laughed bitterly. 'I wish it were that simple.'

'You've yet to convince me that it isn't.'

'I get too involved, Arthur. I lose control and that frightens me. So I say and do stupid things and everything falls apart. I thought it would be different this time but this last week has proved me wrong.'

'In other words, you're frightened.'

'Yes.'

'And feel guilty.'

Terry frowned. 'About what, for heaven's sake?'

'Loving a man.'

'Bloody nonsense!'

'Subconsciously, I think you do. Oh, on the surface – intellectually – you've accepted that you're gay but something inside you still tells you that it's wrong, that you don't deserve to be happy. So you run away.'

Terry laughed and shook his head. 'My God! I've heard

some half-baked theories in my time but that takes the biscuit! Where did you dig that up from?'

'A close observation of people over the last two and a half decades. You can laugh if you like, Terry, but you go away and think about it.' There was a pause, then Arthur spoke again. 'Tell me, did you actually ask Peter why he wanted to go to London?'

'No.'

'Why not?'

'I didn't need to. It was obvious.'

'Terry!' Arthur snorted. 'I thought better of you.'

'What's that supposed to mean?'

'I think that he simply wanted to get away from what had happened – to switch off for a couple of days. Surely you can understand that?'

Terry's face showed his confusion and slight panic, which he deflected into anger. 'Oh, for God's sake! You get me up here and browbeat me, telling me how to run my life. Who the hell do you think you are? I've had enough!' With that, he stormed out of the room, slamming the door.

Arthur felt that he had made his point.

Chapter 36

JIM Stewart used his gavel to call the meeting to order and then started to speak. 'Ladies and gentlemen, this emergency meeting of the governors of Warton College has been called in accordance with the resolution adopted at the last meeting on the twenty-third of November. We are here to receive the headmaster's report on the implementation of that resolution. Dr Jordan.'

'Thank you, Mr Chairman. Ladies and gentlemen, I propose to present my report tonight in the same format as the resolution of the twenty-third.' Bob looked up and glanced round the room. It was clear from their expressions that Forbes-Smith and Lawrence had no idea what was coming; Fisher had evidently not been in touch with them since his resignation. Bob smiled to himself. He was going to enjoy this even more.

'The first two items deal with the specific issue before the last meeting of the Thomas expulsion. I must say straight away that I considered your decision to be hasty and ill-judged, based largely on a scurrilous campaign – not without support from some governors – to discredit two members of the school.'

'Mr Chairman, I must protest!' exclaimed Forbes-Smith.

'Kindly reserve your comments until the end of the

The Stamp of Nature

report, Major,' snapped the chairman.

'But—'

'Order! Please continue, Dr Jordan.'

'Thank you, Mr Chairman. As I was saying, a hasty and ill-judged decision, especially in the light of subsequent events...'

Lawrence and Forbes-Smith exchanged anxious glances.

'...for I must now inform you that Ian Thomas has been apprehended for a similar offence. This assault, on the same boy, took place last Monday and was reported to me by Mr Fisher. The victim required three stitches in a cut over his right eye. As a result of the incident, Thomas has again been expelled.'

Peter finished his marking and sighed. It was probably the last set of books he would have to correct at Warton. He noticed with an ironic smile that the final essay was from Alan Kelly. He re-read it and upped the grade; Kelly would need all the encouragement he could get. Putting the book back on the pile, Peter glanced round his rooms.

He ought to start packing but he could not face it. His stuff had been going to Terry's but now it would have to go to his parents' house. His mind veered away from any thoughts of Terry but the room held persistent memories: the settee, where they had first embraced; things they had bought together – silly things, like a new ashtray, a couple of records, some posters... Near to tears again, he decided to go out.

Book Three, Chapter 36

When John woke, he felt remarkably bright. That was a surprise, considering he had drunk nearly half a bottle of whisky on his return from the court. Perhaps he was not in as hopeless a mess as he had thought earlier. If the case was not reported in the press, he did not need to tell anybody about it. Knowing his luck, though, that was a pretty big 'if'.

He went into the kitchen and switched on the kettle. He was putting some instant coffee in the cup when a thought struck him: the local paper was due out the next day. At least there wouldn't be long to wait. He returned to the sitting room. He needed to know now, though – but how?

'I could ring up and ask, I suppose,' he said to himself and then laughed. What could he say? 'Excuse me, I was done for gross indecency today. Could you tell me if it's in your paper tomorrow?' Hardly.

Then he had another thought. If the paper was on sale in the morning, it would be printed and distributed the night before. He knew that already, of course – one of the estate agents had told him when he was looking for somewhere to live back in September. 'Try to get the paper the night before,' he had said. 'You'll find all the properties gone by the morning.'

He ran into the hall and fetched his coat.

'The third paragraph of the resolution, Mr Chairman, concerned Mr Peter Harvey – an Old Wartonian, former school captain, captain of cricket and now a member of the teaching staff, whom the governors decided to dismiss.

'There are two points I want to make here. Firstly, your

actions were totally unconstitutional. Dismissal in such a peremptory manner is a clear breach of the agreement on disciplinary procedures reached last year with the staff representatives. Those representatives have wasted no time in pointing this fact out to me. You should therefore be in no doubt that redress will be sought if that decision stands tonight.

'Secondly, from my point of view, I feel that your action was grossly unfair. Mr Harvey has a distinguished record with this school, as both a pupil and a teacher. The fact that he is homosexual has never interfered with the performance of his duties. It is totally irrelevant to his employment, and none of the governors' business.'

Bob paused again. Most faces registered surprise.

'I can see from your faces,' he continued, 'that you are surprised by this point of view but I urge you to consider it seriously. I know that two of the ladies present tonight are also governors of girls' schools in the area. I'm sure that they have never considered dismissing a master there because he happened to be heterosexual.'

Terry Fowler peered at Ian over his glass: it was his fourth large whisky and he had just finished an account of his row with Arthur.

'Arthur's right, old son,' said Ian.

Terry shook his head. 'I'm sorry. You don't know me as well as I do.'

'That's as may be, but I do know this: I've never seen a man change as much as you have this term. I've known you for more than four years now and when you first told me you were gay, I felt sorry for you—'

'Oh, thanks.'

'Shut up, Terry, and listen. Not because of what you were but because of your approach to it. The world had dealt you a blow, so you were going to get your own back by being the most cynical bastard alive. Love and emotion were so much crap, you said, and gay love couldn't work. I believed you and felt sorry for you because I'd been in love and knew how bloody marvellous it could be. If being gay meant missing out on emotions like that, you certainly deserved sympathy.'

Terry opened his south to speak again, but Ian forestalled him. 'Hear me out. Then Peter arrived and it was obvious that you were smitten. The wit, the nickname, the constant invitations to join us here ... you scored, didn't you? And then the change began. You both stopped coming in here so much; your cynical remarks became less barbed and you were more buoyant than I'd ever seen you. I recognised the symptoms quickly enough because I was going through the same thing with Liz. And now look what's happened: I'm getting married but you're running away.'

Terry remained silent, wishing fervently that he had kept his mouth shut about Peter.

'My advice to you is to stop running. The mask has slipped, mate – you're no more a cynic than old Arthur. The only person you're deceiving is yourself and there's nothing to be gained from that, as anybody who's gay should know. Now, I'm going to back to school. Eileen wants some company while the meeting's on. Are you coming?'

Terry shook his head. 'No, I'm going home. I want to think – and get thoroughly plastered.'

Ian shrugged. 'Okay, but just make sure there's more thinking than drinking.'

'To turn to the fourth paragraph, Mr Chairman. I have not asked for the school captain's resignation and I do not intend to do so. Exactly the same arguments apply here as in Mr Harvey's case: Kelly was appointed – by you, Dr Lawrence – because he was the right person for the job. You made a good appointment, and he still has all the qualities that you were looking for.'

There was less surprise round the table this time; they had obviously been expecting it after his remarks about Peter.

'The fifth item was a general paragraph on the question of homosexual activity within the school. No instructions have been issued to put this into effect, nor will they be. A distinction must be drawn between what has always been accepted as normal adolescent behaviour and other, more acute, problems of sexual orientation. Both matters require handling on an individual basis with tact and understanding. The use of disciplinary sanctions is not appropriate and could do more harm than good.

'However, I will give you this assurance: I will deal with such problems personally, and I will exercise the judgement for which you pay me.' He paused, noting more surprise but at the tone rather than the content of his words, he suspected.

He prepared to finish his submission. 'That, Mr Chairman, ladies and gentlemen, concludes my report on the matters relating to your resolution of the twenty-third of November. I should add that following, and indeed in view of, the second assault by Ian Thomas, I have received and accepted Mr Fisher's immediate resignation.'

Peter drove towards Heysham. For some reason, he thought he might find salvation there as he had done in September. It was still only mid-evening when he arrived and the pubs in the village were busy, the music and laughter spilling out into the quiet street.

He walked into the churchyard, up to the chapel ruins, and sat down on a rock. It was a clear, frosty evening, with a strong north-westerly wind. He was shivering despite his warm overcoat but he ignored the cold, concentrating instead on the view and the sound of the sea. At least those were still here, as they had always been.

He sat back and closed his eyes then he saw the road. Well-remembered from his dreams, it stretched endlessly ahead, stark and unwavering. He felt himself attracted to it but sensed that, at some level, it was a fatal attraction.

The immediate reaction to Bob's report was confused. Several people tried to speak at once and it was some time before Jim Stewart restored order. Lawrence promptly requested an adjournment but that had been foreseen.

'I'm sorry, Dr Lawrence, but there are several other matters to discuss tonight and I am anxious to avoid a late finish. Now, ladies and gentlemen, are there any comments or questions on Dr Jordan's report?'

Predictably, Forbes-Smith was first into the fray. 'I must say, Mr Chairman, that Dr Jordan's open defiance of the governors' clear instructions is astonishing. What makes it worse is the obvious relish with which he displays such defiance.'

Bob waited for more but there was none. They were clearly nonplussed.

'Miss Armitage?'

'Mr Chairman, I find myself in a bit of a quandary. I agree with Major Forbes-Smith when he says the Dr Jordan has defied the instructions given to him three weeks ago. That is something that would disturb any governing body. On the other hand, as one who voted against the resolution, I cannot find it in me to blame him. The question we must decide is whether such defiance was justified. In view of what happened with this boy Thomas, I feel that Dr Jordan has his justification.'

'Mr Chairman,' said Lawrence in his usual measured tones. 'On the specific question of the Thomas expulsion, Dr Jordan's report demonstrates that we were in error three weeks ago. However, I must disagree with Miss Armitage; the crucial question is whether the latter parts of the motion are directly relevant to the expulsion. In other words, would the governors have taken the actions against Harvey, Kelly and homosexual activity in general, if they had come to our notice in another context? It is my submission that, notwithstanding Dr Jordan's eloquence this evening, the answer must be in the affirmative...'

Bob was amused; this was precisely what he had expected, which was why he had prepared the next stage of the offensive so carefully. Meanwhile, Lawrence continued, making a brave attempt to recapture the initiative.

Book Three, Chapter 36

'...I must, therefore, with some regret, propose that Dr Jordan's report be "not received".'

'Mr Chairman,' intervened Bob, forestalling Forbes-Smith's attempt to second the motion. 'Perhaps I could assist the governors further in their deliberations...'

John turned the corner full of hope but this newsagent was also shut. Surely one must be open somewhere. Armed with the Yellow Pages and a street map, he had visited ten newsagents so far, only to find each one closed.

Having consoled himself that all could be well if there were no report in the paper, he was obsessed with the need to check. He had to know tonight.

Teacher on Toilets Charge

His imaginary headline kept returning to haunt him. It was bound to be in the paper. But he had to know. Tonight.

Terry stayed in the pub for a few minutes after Ian had left, then finished his drink and returned to school to fetch his car. He felt miserable. The letter to Peter had not been an easy one to write but he had been sure of his ground, convinced that the whole business about going to London showed that Peter's feelings were not as strong as his own.

Now, though, doubts were starting to creep in. He remembered his own petulant behaviour a week earlier; perhaps if he had explained to Peter why he resented the visit... No; if Peter had wanted to understand, he would have done so. And then today ... if Peter felt that bad, why hadn't he sought him out? But if what Arthur said was true and Peter hadn't been fit to? Surely that meant... No, Peter couldn't have taken it *that* badly.

Suddenly, the memories returned: of Peter in his arms the night of the first governors' meeting, eating bacon sandwiches; then, earlier, Peter's first week at school and the row with Stanley Sharpe; sitting in the pub, catching Peter looking at him; the night of John's dinner party, in Peter's rooms, listening to his story, putting an arm round his shoulders, kissing him...

Tears were stinging the back of his eyes. They started to move down his face.

'Mr Chairman, I received this weekend, from my former colleagues in the Department of Education at the University of Westmoreland, an advance copy of a report which they intend to publish shortly entitled *Private Education: Help or Hindrance?*

'The report contains much that will please those of us who believe strongly in the benefits of private education. However, it is not totally uncritical; indeed, it makes some astringent comments. Perhaps the most controversial section of the report is the school-by-school assessment, in which schools are rated out of ten for different aspects of their work. Warton scores twenty-eight out of seventy, which makes it the second lowest in survey of thirty schools.

'I will quote from the conclusion:

"This school is a bastion of the old guard, maintaining rigid rules of conduct and the institution of "fagging", whereby

Book Three, Chapter 36

younger boys are forced to undertake menial tasks for the older ones. Its facilities to teach all but the most basic and general of science subjects are virtually non-existent, and the sixth-form curriculum is severely limited. There is a grave inability to offer a sound, broad education, or to allow specialisation when it is needed. Overall verdict: poor.'"

Bob looked up from his papers and glanced round the room. The reactions varied: Lawrence went very pale; Forbes-Smith, perhaps predictably, went red in the face. A couple of mouths dropped open in astonishment but the chairman wore a discreet smile.

Bob continued. 'The authors of the report accept that there have been numerous changes since they completed their research and I was appointed headmaster. They have, therefore, agreed to postpone publication and visit the school again in the new year for a further assessment...' he paused and waited for relief to register on their faces '...provided that I remain headmaster. And you will understand, ladies and gentlemen, that my continued presence is entirely dependent upon you accepting and endorsing my report tonight.'

Forbes-Smith could contain himself no longer. 'Damn it, man! That's blackmail.'

'Your word, not mine, Major. No doubt that is something your friend Mr Fisher told you about, having tried to blackmail Mr Harvey into lying to the governors at their last meeting.'

Peter gradually grew used to the presence of the road. As he did so, the vision changed. He was running along it now and the sides were marked with posts. As he passed each one it became a figure, reaching out to stop him. He recognised John, then Alan, his mother, father, Chris Simon, Arthur, Bob, Eileen, Ian, Mark…

He ignored them all and kept running. There was only one figure who could stop him, and that face did not appear. The road began to climb, gently at first but then more steeply. He was exhausted but moved on. He reached the summit, saw a blinding light and … nothing.

'Hello, Terry,' Eileen said. 'Come in and have a drink.'

'No, thanks. Just popped in to see if there was any news yet?'

'No, I'm afraid not, love. Still, they shouldn't be long now.'

'Good. The suspense must be killing you.' He paused; surely he had waited long enough before asking. 'Is Peter here?'

'No. I haven't seen him all day. Arthur said he wasn't well.'

'I know. But I wanted to see him rather urgently and thought he might be here.'

'I told Arthur to tell him not to come if he didn't feel like it. Why don't you pop along to his rooms?'

'Okay. Thanks, Eileen – and don't worry. Bob'll win.'

Terry left and Eileen returned to the lounge.

'Who was that?' asked Arthur.

'Terry. He was looking for Peter.'

Arthur and Ian exchanged glances and grinned.

Miss Armitage broke the silence. 'Mr Chairman, I think we should ask Dr Jordan to withdraw for a few minutes. It would be fairer to discuss his report on our own, I think.'

'Thank you, Miss Armitage. I was about to suggest that myself.'

Bob nodded and rose to leave. The Chairman winked impartially.

John sighed heavily. He had never realised how many news-agents there were in the area – and every single bloody one of them was shut. He was now driving to the last one on his list.

If only... But no. It was impossible. Apart from anything else, it was getting on for nine o'clock. In summer he might have stood a chance, with all the visitors about, but not in December. He would have to wait until the morning. The prospect of going home filled him with horror. The waiting would drive him mad. He had to know *tonight.*

As he turned the corner, he saw a light in the shop. His spirits rose but only until he realised that it was a light left on at the back; the place was not open. Even so, he got out of the car to have a closer look. The shop was indeed closed but there was a figure at the counter, marking up some papers for the morning. Heart pounding, John knocked on the door. The figure looked up and reluctantly moved to open it.

'I'm sorry to trouble you and I know you're closed, but I'm after a copy of tomorrow's local paper. It's very important – I'm looking for somewhere to live.'

The man in the shop was a friendly soul, getting on in years. He smiled. 'I'm not supposed to sell them before morning, you know.'

John felt a surge of hope. The man's tone was understanding. 'Yes, I understand, but it really is important. My wife's expecting, you see, and our landlord's chucking us out tomorrow.'

'Well, I don't think it'll do much harm just this once.' The newsagent moved towards the counter. 'There you are, lad. And good luck.'

John took a pound note from his wallet and pressed it into the man's hand. 'Keep the change and buy yourself a drink – I can't thank you enough.'

'There's no need for that.'

'No, please.'

John could hardly stop himself from looking at the paper there and then but he managed it. He left the shop and returned to his car.

When there was no reply from Peter's rooms, Terry began to worry. He went back to the car park and saw that Peter's car was not there. That was even more disturbing. Where the hell could he be? At his parents, perhaps? Better ring them. But no – what could he say if Peter wasn't there? Had he gone to the pub, then? He wouldn't have taken the car.

Suddenly, his mind swept back to September and meeting Peter here in the car park late one night ... *the night* ... and being invited up for a nightcap. Peter had been somewhere on his own that night too.

Terry smiled, then ran to his own car. He drove away from the school grounds at high speed.

Peter opened his eyes. The meaning of his dream all was clear: there was no solution, so he had to escape. The pattern of the past was too strong to allow hope for the future. Whatever happened beyond this life could not be worse. How, though? He smiled. The road would show him.

Then he began to be frightened, as the enormity of his decision became clear. 'Is it really that bad?' he asked himself.

'Yes,' came the reply.

'What – no hope at all?'

'None. You could have survived at Warton without Terry. You could have survived with Terry away from Warton. But without either? No chance.'

'Could somebody ask the headmaster to return, please?'

Miss Armitage got up and left the room. She returned a few moments later with a very nervous headmaster, who had spent an unpleasant half hour wondering whether his bluff would be called.

'Dr Jordan,' said the chairman. 'I must advise you that the governors have voted, by five votes to one, to receive and accept your report in full.' Bob's eyebrows shot up. That meant that one of the original plotters had backed down. 'Accordingly, your expulsion of Ian Thomas is ratified, Mr Harvey is reinstated, Kelly's position as school captain is confirmed, and your assurances regarding problems of sexual orientation accepted. I should add that two governors have tendered their resignation.'

'Thank you, Mr Chairman,' replied Bob, with a

solemnity that he certainly did not feel. 'May I say how sorry I am that such a situation had to arise and that it has led to the loss of two of our governors.'

'And may I say, Chairman,' interjected Forbes-Smith, 'how glad I am to depart from a body which endorses sexual perversion and submits to blackmail. Good night.' He stormed out.

Lawrence spoke. He was shaking with emotion; never had the nickname 'Jolly Roger' been more ironic. 'Mr Chairman, before I depart I wish to apologise to the governors – and particularly to you, Dr Jordan. It was my ambition during my time as headmaster to see this school respected among my colleagues as a place where the old-fashioned virtues of honour and good manners still prevailed. From what I heard tonight in the University of Westmoreland report, I realised that I failed.

'I fought you, Dr Jordan, because I could see all that I had worked for being thrown away. I now realise that I was wrong to fight. Worse, in doing so I disregarded honour and good manners to an extent of which I am greatly ashamed.'

Terry drove down the hill into Heysham Village. He spotted Peter's car and breathed a sigh of relief. He parked and ran down the street into the churchyard. He picked his way up the crumbling steps and saw a figure sitting on a rock.

'Hello, Peter.'

Book Three, Chapter 36

John got up from his chair and put on a record. He turned the volume up and poured himself a drink. As the opening chords of the 'Emperor' concerto blasted out, he sang along loudly.

After all, celebration was certainly in order. He had been through every news item in that paper three times. The court case had not been reported.

Epilogue: later that night

BOB walked the chairman to his car.

'So, you can relax and get on with the job now, Bob.'

'Yes, thank God. I'll let the staff know in the morning.'

'Forget it for now and go and celebrate. I'll give you a ring soon – you and Eileen must come over for a drink at Christmas.'

'Yes, that would be lovely. And thanks for all your help, Jim.'

'A pleasure. No more than a chairman's duty. Goodnight.'

Bob sighed happily as Jim Stewart's car disappeared up the drive. Looking up at the sky, he shivered. It was clouding over and there was a lot of snow up there. He turned into the house where Eileen, Arthur and Ian were waiting to hear the news.

He told them about the meeting over a celebratory drink. Eileen hugged him enthusiastically, whilst Ian and Arthur, more sedately but with no less pleasure, shook him by the hand.

'How does it feel to have won, then, love?' Eileen asked.

'Bloody marvellous! The best bit was Jolly Roger's apology. That must have cost him a lot.'

Epilogue

'He must be mellowing in his old age,' Arthur replied, with a grim smile.

'I doubt it,' said Ian. 'He was probably without his wife for the day. Her absence would be enough to cheer anybody up.'

They laughed.

'We'd better make some arrangements to tell the rest of the staff, Arthur,' Bob said.

Arthur noticed with amusement Bob's sudden reversion to business-like headmaster. 'I tell you what, extend morning chapel by ten minutes. I can cope – possibly with your help, Ian – while you hold a quick staff meeting, Bob.'

'Okay, that's fine. Now, you've all get empty glasses. Come on, hand 'em over!'

'I'm sorry about the letter, Peter. I shouldn't have sent it.'

Peter smiled.

'Why the smile?'

'Hmm? Oh, it's just that I remember somebody else saying that to me – a few centuries ago.'

'John?'

'Yes. The funny thing was, he wrote to ask me whether I was sure I was gay. Bloody rich, considering what happened afterwards.'

'Yes, that's true. I wonder...'

'Enough! Don't let's talk about John now.' Peter looked up and grinned. 'Now, you were in the middle of a grovelling apology. Do carry on.'

'Oh well, if that's your attitude! No, seriously. I *am* sorry. I always was a selfish bastard but that took the biscuit.'

'I'm not going to disagree. I'd like to know why, that's all.'

Terry paused to light cigarettes for them both. The interval was enough to allow him to order his thoughts. 'It was because Mark's letter cheered you up so much – that was the real trouble. I wasn't bothered that you might sleep with him, but it seemed that he could cheer you up when I couldn't. I felt that I'd failed. I decided that your feelings weren't as strong as mine and I wanted out. I couldn't stand the thought of all the jealousy and rows that would follow. I've been through it all before and couldn't face it again.'

Peter sighed. 'It was my fault, I suppose. It wasn't that I didn't want to discuss how I felt – it didn't seem to matter when we were together. Other things were more important. I could switch off, you see.'

Terry nodded. 'And going to London was another means of switching off?'

'Exactly. Why did you change your mind tonight?'

'I got told off, first by Arthur and then by Ian. I had a row with Arthur, actually, then I went down to the pub and told Ian, expecting some sympathy, but he started on me as well! All about how I'd changed and could never play the cynical bastard again.'

'And?'

'And I went back to school to fetch the car. I stood in the car park and started to remember things. I'd avoided thinking about you all weekend by concentrating on abstract things like love and jealousy that couldn't answer back. But when I started to think about you – meeting, talking, making love, I...' He broke off, tears welling up in his eyes.

'I've got your number now.' Peter laughed gently. 'You're

Epilogue

just as sentimental as the rest of us. Come here.'

Terry nodded and relaxed into Peter's embrace. 'My place?' he asked after what might have been for ever or only minutes.

Peter tightened his arms round him briefly in reply. Then, standing up he extended his hand.

They drove back in separate cars, playing around by overtaking each other, passing, dropping back, flashing headlights and taking turns to be in the lead. Fortunately, they had the road largely to themselves. Once they were settled at Terry's, they calmed down and their playfulness quietened. Then, the phone rang.

'Oh, bloody hell. Who's that?'

'Don't answer it,' Peter suggested.

Terry started to smile. 'I think I'd better – I've just realised who it night be.' He disappeared into the hall, returning a few minutes later, attempting to suppress a broad grin. 'It's Arthur. He's a bit the worse for wear but he'd like a word with you.'

John lay in bed. For the first time for many months, he could relax. Of course, life now had almost as many uncertainties as before but he knew that he was more able to deal with them.

His court case had brought him up sharp. Though he had previously accepted that he was gay, he realised now that he had been shying away from it, trying to keep it in a water-tight compartment separate from the rest of his life. That was no good at all. You could not spend your life isolated from gay people in case somebody spotted you and gossiped about it. If you did, all that was left was picking

The Stamp of Nature

up people in toilets and, almost inevitably, getting caught.

What a waste of time the last few years had been. Why? Fate, he supposed. It was fate that had killed his parents and led him to blame himself for their deaths. It was fate that had made him marry Kate, poor girl. When you came down to it, it was fate that decided if you were gay.

He smiled. At least he had survived. Now surely, fate would allow him a few years of calm – perhaps even happiness. Yes, he had a feeling it would.

Still smiling, he fell asleep.

'I must get cracking with the fundraising for the new teaching block.'

Eileen laughed. 'Bob, you're much too drunk to think about that now. For goodness' sake, come to bed.'

The headmaster of Warton College tottered unsteadily towards the bed. Once there, he snuggled up close to his wife and kissed her. 'None of it really matters,' he said, 'so long as you're around.'

Still smiling, he fell asleep.

Arthur Benson was in bed. Even at the age of sixty-four, life could have its marvellous moments and that phone conversation with Peter would always be amongst the best. He just hoped that he wasn't so drunk that he wouldn't remember it in the morning.

Still smiling, he fell asleep.

Epilogue

The road was straight and wide, shimmering in the heat of summer. The air was heavy with the smell of melting tar and newly mown grass. In the distance there was a house, a beautiful white detached house that stood on a slight rise overlooking the surrounding countryside. The garden was well-kept, with large rhododendron bushes in full flower, bordered by a neat privet hedge.

Peter stopped to survey the scene and smiled. Home again. As he started towards the house, a figure emerged and came down the path to meet him. Peter's smile broadened, his step quickened. 'Hello, Terry,' he said. 'Everything okay?'

Terry, still awake, looked down at his dreaming lover and smiled. 'Yes, Peter. Everything's fine.'

Then, still smiling, he fell asleep too.